A
THEME PARK
FOR THE
DEPRAVED

A
THEME PARK
FOR THE
DEPRAVED

J.E. Mershon

Published by J.E. Mershon

ISBN 979-8-9859186-0-1 (Paperback)

Epigraph used by permission from Annie Dillard,
Holy the Firm (Harper & Row Perennial Library edition, 1988), 42.

Cover Design by Louis Pescevic
Yourmemoriesrenewed.com

Interior Book Design by Iram Allam
on LinkedIn and Facebook as Irissa Book Design

For my niece, Laura—
beloved of God; a survivor

The joke of the world is less like a banana peel than a rake, the old rake in the grass, the one you step on, foot to forehead.

—ANNIE DILLARD, HOLY THE FIRM

Prologue

Trixie's was busy for a Tuesday. Construction workers who got rained out were still there from the day shift, and the suits started coming in after six; by nine the house was full. There were three stages and twenty-seven dancers, which meant about four sets per dancer during the night. With this in mind, Cat picked longer numbers for her main stage act. When business was slow, she picked short songs to dance to, but it was busy tonight and she was leaving early anyway.

She moved slowly around the stage, looking for the men who held out money, allowing them to slip the bills into a black leather garter she wore for the purpose, squatting down, crawling over to them like a sensuous jungle animal, doing a little more when the tip was a twenty. The smoke machine kept the stage in a haze, Sara Jay's whispery voice sang "Dissolved Girl." Cat picked this song because it was soothing to dance to, and also because the song transported her outside the club with its hungry-eyed men. In her imagination, she was dancing for Chloe. Her friend, her lover, the woman she wanted to be with more than anybody, only she would not give herself to a full-time relationship, just a tryst once a week on Tuesday nights. She would leave work early and spend three hours at Chloe's, then go home to her daughter, her sweet Sylvie. She would not allow anybody to enter their life, and Sylvie didn't know anything about Chloe. She returned home in the early hours on Wednesday mornings as if she was coming in from work, never later than three am.

Cat was tall, and muscular from doing pole tricks. She wore black. Black eye makeup, black lipstick on her full lips, black hair cut very short, a black leather dog collar with spikes, full-sleeve tattoos in an intricate black flower design, and a thin black velvet ribbon laced around her slender torso, held in place with steel corset ring piercings. Black nail enamel, and bare feet on stage. She wore a short, clingy, tattered black shift which she would shed during the second song, Massive Attack's "Angel." Then she'd be down to her corset ribbon and lacy black G-string panties, which she would allow the men to stuff full of money when her garter was too full to hold any more bills.

She sometimes wondered what they would think if they knew that she liked girls—that she couldn't tell customers one from another half the time—they all looked the same to her. The exception was the occasional regular who was a big spender, and these men got special attention. Sometimes she would even smile at one of them. There was another exception, men who stood out for creepiness. One man in particular made her shudder because he never tipped, stayed back from the stage and yet was there, for every set she did when he was in the club, standing back in the shadows, following her from stage to stage, his wet mouth slightly open, mean little eyes devouring her person. He was in the club tonight, and she would try to ignore him. Just this one last set and she was out of here.

She loved the city streets on a rainy night—the shiny reflection of neon, traffic signals, colored lights off the wet pavement. Rain always made her feel safe, like a subliminal reminder of the womb. Her heart was purring with anticipation, and the satisfaction of having made a couple hundred dollars in just three hours at work. It had been a good night, and it was going to get better. Chloe was her one indulgence; the rest of her life was devoted to her daughter, Sylvie, but her devotion didn't feel like a sacrifice, her daughter was her primary joy.

She turned into the big apartment complex and found a space in guest parking. She grabbed her dance bag which contained a bottle of good wine, got out of the car then hit the button to lock it as she began to walk across the lot to the part of the complex where Chloe lived. When she approached the enclosure where the dumpsters were, a man stepped into her path. It was the creepy guy from the club, only this time his eyes were glittering with sadistic pleasure because he had bagged his prize. She knew it, too. She had a canister of pepper spray attached to her keychain, but he was holding a taser. As he zapped her with the gun her last anguished thought was for Sylvie, then the darkness.

Wednesday

1

New Orleans, July 2017

Adrian carried his bowl of cereal into the living room, set it down on the table, and used the remote to turn on the TV. It was time for *Legends of Chima*. He could hear his mommy in the bathroom, getting ready for work. He was looking forward to daycare because Wednesdays they had art afternoon, his favorite activity of the week.

He heard the screen open and somebody rang the bell. It was too early for anybody to come over. He put down his spoon, crossed to the window, and looked out. An old white man stood in the shadows of the screened in porch. He wore a plaid shirt and light pants, the kind with big pockets on the legs. He had a backpack on. Adrian wasn't supposed to answer the door, but his mommy was in the shower and the guy looked harmless. He crossed over to the door and opened it up a crack.

"Is your mother home?" the old guy asked, smiling.

"She's getting ready for work. She'll be out in a few minutes."

The man shoved the door open fast, hitting Adrian in the face and knocking him down, then pulled a gun from the pocket on his pant leg. "Don't scream," the man said, evil darkening his face like he'd ripped off a mask. He kicked the door closed, bent down and grabbed the boy by the arm, jerked him to his feet and marched him down the hall to the bathroom, where they could hear the shower running. He opened the door and spoke loud to the silhouette behind the curtain. "I have a gun to your son's head. Any noise and I'll shoot him first. Get out of the shower."

Thursday

2

Sylvie worked the front desk at the Magnolia Courts. The motel was located on Airline Drive, a stretch of road in the New Orleans suburb of Metairie which was treeless, trashy and punctuated with used car lots, seedy motels and bars. She took the bus from the French Quarter where she lived. The trip wasn't too bad, except for the block-and-a-half between the bus stop and the motel. Women pedestrians were targets everywhere but this stretch of Airline Drive was known as a ho-stroll.

As she stepped down from the bus she scanned the street, looking for predators. "Dirty Deeds, Done Dirt Cheap" was blasting from the Friendly Lounge, where an old red-faced mullet head stood in the doorway giving her a hard-eyed appraisal. Sylvie hurried past, reaching in her pocket for the pepper spray, wondering if she could run while dragging her roll bag. She dug her cell out of her purse as she turned into the motel parking lot—it was twenty to eight, there was time to smoke a cigarette before her shift.

May looked up and smiled a greeting from behind the counter, which was partitioned off from the rest of the lobby with bulletproof glass. "How was it last night?" Sylvie asked as she entered their work area.

"Quiet," May said. "And slow. No problems, but no business either."

"Yeah, hopefully things'll stay quiet today." Sylvie went back to the storage room to put her water in the fridge. She looked for the bag of food that Bernice Davis always sent when she paid her rent Wednesday nights, but there was nothing in the refrigerator but a can of soda and a couple of bottles of Corona. "Hey, didn't Miss Bernice send us a bag?"

"I don't know what's wrong. Bill knocked on her door and nobody answered. If she doesn't call the office today, he'll probably have to go in her room."

Bernice was never late with the rent, and she always sent May and Sylvie each a bag of food when she paid. "I'd go check on her, but she hates to be bothered. You know how she is," May said.

"I could try calling her, couldn't I?" Sylvie was worried about her friend who, though reclusive, was dependable as the rising sun.

"She keeps her phone off. This hasn't happened in five years and last time she had somebody else come in and pay."

Sylvie went in the bathroom and used the toilet. She was thinking about Bernice—something wasn't right. She and Sylvie were pen pals, and had been writing back and forth from the time Sylvie started working at the motel—almost three years. Sylvie didn't have any close friends, and the relationship meant a lot to her. She went back out front and looked at the monitor, checking the area where her friend stayed. "Hey, would you mind staying over a few minutes while I go check on her? Old people fall sometimes. If she doesn't answer the door I'm going in and see if she's okay."

"Yeah, go on, I know you two are close. Take your time, I'll wait."

The motel was laid out in a capital T, with two floors of regular rooms going to the back of the property, then a cross section of nicer rooms with sitting areas, kitchenettes and sliding glass doors on the bottom floor which opened onto a small garden area and a fenced in swimming pool. Bernice Davis lived in the back section. She had lived at the Magnolia for eight years, and only opened her door for the owner, Bill, to collect the rent Wednesday evenings, and to allow a maid in to clean. Though reclusive she was a kindly woman and gave Bill two bags of food for Sylvie and May every week along with a check for the rent. Sometimes the bags also contained little gifts—hair jewelry or a beanie baby, something small. At Christmas she gave everybody in the motel, including the regulars who lived there, something, like a coffee cup filled with candy and a card. She gave the gifts to Bill to distribute. These small gifts meant a lot to Sylvie, who sometimes gave Bill a little something for Miss Bernice, some lotion or a box of pralines that she could consume because Sylvie imagined she didn't have much space to accumulate stuff.

That's how they became pen pals, because Sylvie wrote a thank you note and slipped it under Bernice's door. The next week she found a letter in her bag of food, mostly asking her about herself, how she liked working at the motel, and about her life. Their friendship grew as they exchanged letters once a week, Sylvie slipping her letter under Bernice's door, but Bernice never opened the door and it was understood she didn't want to go that far. Sylvie had given her cell phone number, but Bernice didn't call. She wrote that she didn't talk on the phone, and didn't own a cell.

Bernice did have a woman visitor who Sylvie and May saw going there with groceries and other bags. The visitor dressed well, drove a Prius, and sometimes carried a briefcase. Sylvie thought she might be an attorney. It was rumored that Miss Bernice was rich, though why she'd want to live at the Magnolia was anybody's guess. The people who lived at this motel were poor, often addicted, and worked the streets, hustling and begging and sometimes coming up short on rent. Bill usually gave long-time tenants a grace period of a couple of days to get caught up when they'd had bad luck with money.

Recently Sylvie had asked her in one of the letters why she lived at the Magnolia, and she was thinking about what Bernice told her with growing trepidation as she walked back to her room, smoking a cigarette. Bernice had told Sylvie she was hiding from her son, because he had killed her husband and tried to kill her. She said the police wouldn't believe her story because he was a schoolteacher, maintained a nice guy persona, and had never been in trouble with the law. Sylvie believed Bernice's story. She knew all about how some people pretended to be nice but were secretly evil. She'd learned this living in homes after her mother disappeared, leaving for work one night and never coming back.

Sylvie reached her friend's room and put her ear to the door. She could hear the TV, one of those morning talk shows. She knocked loud, calling out "Miss Bernice, its Sylvie. Are you okay?" When there was no answer after repeated knocking, she put the master key in the slot and opened the door. She scanned the room in a glance. It was sparsely furnished and neat, with a couple of plants by the glass door. A set of silky blue pajamas and a pair of underwear were laid out on the bed, the covers turned down. Her gaze fell on a picture in a light wood frame, sitting on a shelf of books. The couple in the picture were standing on a beach in bathing suits with the ocean in the background, the woman beautiful, young, with dark curly hair blowing back in the wind, her eyes snapping with laughter as she faced the camera, while her tall blonde partner was looking down at her as if she were the entire universe and then some.

There was nobody in the room and it was beginning to smell. Sylvie had never smelled death before but she'd read about it in crime novels. She felt her stomach lurch, didn't want to open the bathroom door. She had never seen Bernice alive and did not want to see and remember her friend as a decayed corpse. Still, what if she was alive in the bathroom? What if the smell was from her body waste because she might be hurt and unable to move for days in there? She forced herself to open the bathroom door and look in, then turned away and vomited.

Sylvie wore her cell in a holster when she was on the job. She took it out and speed dialed the office. May answered after what seemed like twenty rings. "May, this is Sylvie. Call Bill and call the police. Bernice is dead. I think she's been dead for a while. I'm staying by the room. I'm scared. I need help."

"Go sit outside, I'll be right there." May hung up.

Sylvie read crime stories all the time and knew, even in the state she was in, not to touch anything else and to get out of the room. She had to flee the horrible image of Bernice lying in the bathtub naked and dead—her eyes frozen wide in terror—and the smell. She had left the door open and she closed it behind her and headed around back to the garden.

3

Detective Camille Hebert was not liking this. The deceased woman had apparently fallen backwards, naked, and hit her head on the faucet of the bathtub. Though there were no visible wounds she looked terrified and, Camille guessed, may have been in coronary arrest. She was preparing to take a bath at the time of death. Her bathrobe hung on a hook on the door, slippers placed neatly on the bathmat. Part of the shower curtain was pulled down, as if she'd grabbed onto it in her fall. But her eyes told a different story. Also, what was she doing in a dry tub, facing away from the faucet? People turn on the water and adjust the temperature before getting in the bathtub, which requires facing the faucet. She looked as if she'd stepped into the tub to hide from an intruder, perhaps grabbing the shower curtain to shield her nakedness, then had been so scared she'd lost her balance and fell, hitting her head. Or, had a heart attack and fell.

Camille knew that unless she found some hard evidence, this one was going down as death due to natural causes. She'd be expected to sign off on it because people who live at this motel were low priority—many of them were addicts who made their living in shady ways. She couldn't figure out what an elderly woman with independent means was doing living here. Bottom line, if they could ignore this one, they would want to. But Camille had investigated cases off the clock before, if she felt that the situation warranted it.

Camille talked to the woman who had found the body first, Sylvie Compton. She didn't look like the kind of person who could kill, but then neither did a lot of them. She was young and pretty, maybe too pretty to be working at this motel, a natural blonde with brown eyes. She was calm, her answers thoughtful, though it was evident she was in shock. Camille guessed she had seen more than her share of the dark side of life. She asked her exactly what happened when she found the body and what, if anything, she had handled. Then she asked about her relationship to the victim. When Sylvie told her about the letters and what Bernice had written about her son, Camille told her to gather the letters together for the police to look at and not to leave town. She let her go after CSI took her prints.

Next Camille talked to the owner of the motel, Bill Champlain. The man was sixtyish, rail thin with gaunt features, shaggy salt and pepper hair and a distance in his pale blue eyes that told Camille he'd seen a lot. It was obvious he hadn't had time to shave this morning. She asked him what happened when he went by her room to collect the rent the previous night.

"Somebody was in there, is what happened. Miss Bernice paid her rent like clockwork, seven- thirty Wednesday night for eight years. I went by to get the rent check and she didn't answer. So I tried opening the door and the chain was on. After I called out to her and nobody answered, I just figured she was busy and I'd get it today. The woman didn't have visitors, just her lawyer, Andrea Sharp. The lawyer would come by regular with supplies, and what all. She's the only person I know of Bernice would see. She told me if anything happens to call this woman, and I did. She's on her way here now."

"Do you know of any reason somebody would want her dead?" Camille asked. "Or if not dead, just to threaten or scare her?"

"No way. I don't know what she's doing here, but sometimes people stay at motels because they're hiding. Tell you who would know, Andrea Sharp."

Bill told Camille that the maids were the only people besides the lawyer Bernice allowed in her room, and they each had a master key for all the rooms and access to most areas of the motel. The front desk employees had access to the master key, and all areas of the motel. Camille asked him to give her the surveillance tapes, and to find out who had been the last maid to clean the room while Bernice Davis was alive. She wanted a list of employees' personal info, a list of all guests going back a month, and copies of their IDs. Bill told her he had it all on a database, with information going back a couple of decades. He'd have a copy of the past month ready for her by noon. Camille had a bad feeling about this one, and it got worse the more information she gathered.

A silver Prius pulled in, drove straight back and parked. Camille guessed this must be the lawyer. The woman who got out was dressed in a navy suit and a white shirt. Creole, medium height and build and looked to be in her forties. Her penetrating amber eyes scanned the premises and took in everything. A small crowd had gathered at the periphery of the crime scene and the woman moved through the crowd like a knife through warm butter—people instinctively got out of her way. Camille approached her and held out a hand. "Detective Camille Hebert."

"Andy Sharp. I'm Ms. Davis's attorney. What happened?"

"We don't know much yet. She fell in the bathtub, possibly during coronary arrest."

"But you're a homicide detective, so apparently there's more to it."

"This is just part of the routine, gathering evidence to eliminate any possibility of foul play. Ms. Davis lived alone, and this isn't the safest area. Do you know of anybody who might want her dead?"

"Okay, she fell in the bathtub and maybe had a heart attack. That's not unusual for a woman her age. She's eighty-four years old. How does it add up to murder?"

Camille considered how much she should tell this woman. The woman was there to get information, not to share it. And she was a lawyer, so she knew she didn't have to give out anything. Camille's instinct told her that this woman was on the vic's side, and had more to gain from a live client than a dead one. They walked back out to the Prius so they could talk. She told her about the crime scene, that things didn't quite fit. "Did she suffer from dementia? Would hiding in a bathtub be normal behavior for her?"

"She was sharp as a tack. I've never known a woman her age in better mental shape. And she didn't scare easy. She kept a gun in the room and knew how to use it. She didn't receive visitors, ever. Did somebody break in?"

"We haven't found signs of forced entry. And there was no gun in her room. At least not by the time we found her. What kind of gun did she have? Have you seen the gun?"

"Yes, she showed me. It was an old .38 special revolver. Smith & Wesson. She said it belonged to her husband."

"Well, the gun's missing. Can you look at some pictures of

her? I want you to see what she looked like at the time of death. Then maybe you can tell me if you know of anybody who might want to harm her. The medical examiner's with her..."

"That's a no brainer," Andy snapped. "She's been hiding from her own son for a decade. He's already tried to kill her, and she believes he murdered her husband, though she can't prove it."

"What did he do?"

"It was right after their forty-fifth wedding anniversary. She was supposed to be with her husband that day—they were going to check out a Winnebago, maybe buy it. They wanted to do some traveling. But she wasn't feeling good, and she changed her mind and stayed home. Her son had been house-sitting for them while they were in Mexico City, and this happened the day after they got back in town. She said her son tried hard to get her to go with her husband, but she was tired from her trip and insisted on resting. Her husband went alone. His brakes and steering failed and he crashed into a truck in the oncoming lane of traffic. There were three other vehicles involved, with four people injured and two fatalities, one of them a three-year-old girl. Bernice moved away after the funeral, and she's been hiding ever since. She was certain her son tampered with their car."

"I want you to see what she looked like at the time of death," Camille said, taking her cell out of her shirt pocket. She showed Andy the pictures she'd taken of Bernice's corpse. Bernice's hands were still clutching the shower curtain, which was bunched up on top of her and covered most of her body. Her mouth was a frozen rictus of horror, eyes wide open.

Andy gasped. "She looks like she was scared to death!" she said. "What do you think happened?"

"I'll have to talk to the medical examiner to be sure, but it looks like she had a heart attack. She cracked her head pretty bad on the faucet so there's a serious contusion, but that wouldn't have been the cause of death. She died almost instantly. It's why her eyes look shocked."

"Can you estimate the time of death?" Andy asked.

"Not precisely, but judging the condition of the body and the temperature of the room, she's been dead around twelve hours, maybe longer. They'll have to do an autopsy to narrow things down."

Andy's eyes radiated cold anger. "This wasn't an accident. I want it investigated thoroughly, and money is no object. She's worth millions."

There's the motive, Camille thought.

Andy swiped away a tear. "I want whoever did this punished."

"I promise I'll do everything I can," Camille said. "I'll need you to answer some more questions, okay?"

"Whatever I can do to help."

"Who stood to gain the most from her death? The son?"

"No. She disinherited her son. There's a young woman who works here, Sylvie Compton? Bernice set up a trust, and she named Ms. Compton as a beneficiary. She's going to be paid a generous stipend if she agrees to the arrangement. But all this was going to happen soon, and it wasn't contingent on Bernice's death. She wanted to give the money away ever since she inherited, and she hoped Ms. Compton would help her do it."

Camille stood there thoughtfully, watching as the ambulance drivers emerged from the room carrying a stretcher with the corpse in a body bag and loaded it into the back of the van. "Okay," she said. "Does Sylvie Compton know any of this?"

"Not that I'm aware of. Why would she still be working here if she did? Bernice wanted to tell her about it a week from now on her birthday, July twenty-first. This girl would have no reason to want Bernice dead, even if she did know about it. It was supposed to happen while Bernice was alive. She planned a surprise party. Well, sort of a party. The only people attending would be the three of us. Listen, I emailed Bernice at five-thirty yesterday. You can check her computer and see if she read it. If she opened it, she was still alive at that time. She had an invitation ready to give Sylvie Compton. Ms. Compton would have gotten it this morning when she came to work."

"What about now?" Camille asked. "Will Sylvie still have all this now that Bernice Davis is dead?"

"If she wants it, it's a done deal. I've spent the past year investigating Ms. Compton, and I have the document ready for her to sign."

"Well, we can't check Bernice's computer because it's gone. Do you have a copy of the email you sent her?"

"She's my client, so I save copies of all our communications. Listen, we need to talk. It's complicated."

"Okay. Where can I reach you?"

Andy withdrew a steel card case from her jacket and handed Camille a business card. "I'll be available any time, or get back to you as soon as I can. Right now, I'm going to have to contact Ms. Compton and give her the news."

"Could you hold off on that until I talk to you?"

"Whoever did this might have Sylvie in their sights next. If it's the son, he may think with both of them out of the way the money would revert back to him. It won't. Bernice made sure of that."

"If you can get somebody to watch her, it would help. Just hold off on telling her for now. We can't eliminate her completely at this point."

"Okay, talk to you soon. But try to expedite it. I don't think the girl had anything to do with all this. I've already had her investigated."

"Can you get somebody to guard her now?"

"I'm on it."

"Great. See you later."

4

Twilight was fading to darkness as Camille pulled up at the shotgun house where Amanda Butler lived. Amanda was the maid who had let herself in to Bernice Davis's room the previous evening, right before the time of Bernice's death. She had called in to work that morning, said that her son Adrian had the flu. The surveillance video showed her letting herself into Bernice's room. The problem was she didn't look like she was entering the room because she wanted to. She was shaking so bad she could hardly get the key card to unlock the door, looking around furtively to see who was watching.

Amanda's old blue Caprice was parked in the drive, but the house was dark and it looked like nobody was home. Camille decided to forgo knocking on the front door and went around back, thinking maybe they were in the kitchen. The back was just as dark and quiet as the front. A scooter leaned up against the house by the concrete steps and a child's plastic bucket and shovel lay in a narrow flower bed. Her intuition told her that something wasn't right here, and she considered calling for backup. But this was New Orleans, and Jefferson Parish cops didn't work well with the NOPD. She walked up the back steps, opened the screen and banged on the door. There was no movement in the house. She peered in the window on the door; the kitchen was neat, no signs of anything unusual. She got out her cell and called the number Bill had given her for Amanda Butler, but didn't expect an answer. The answer was in this house, she could feel it, and it wasn't going to be pretty. As she walked back around to the front, she sensed the stillness of death. She hoped she was wrong, but when she opened the trunk of her car to get her lock picks and a flashlight, she also got out a pair of crime scene gloves and some shoe covers.

She could have skipped the picks and used a credit card to get in—the deadbolt wasn't engaged, just the handle lock, like somebody who didn't have a key had locked the door upon exiting. The smell of blood and body waste hit her as soon as she opened the door. She shined a flashlight beam around the room. There were two bodies in the area to the right, one of whom she recognized from the motel surveillance video as Amanda Butler, the other a small boy. She walked over and shone the light down on them. The woman was seated on the floor facing the boy, body collapsed against the sofa, head sideways in a splatter of gore, right hand resting near a .38 revolver which Camille guessed was the gun missing from Bernice Davis's room. The boy had plastic wrap wound around his head so tight that his features were distorted; his limbs had been hogtied behind his back with duct tape; his small body was still. Camille raised her gun and started back through the dark house, clearing it room by room. It was empty. She dialed Andy Sharp's number.

"Detective Hebert. What's going on?"

"It's not good. I just found the body of a maid who entered Bernice's room last night. It looks like she killed her child, and then shot herself. But I don't believe it. I think it was staged. You need to protect Sylvie Compton. Tell your bodyguard she's in immediate danger. Oh, and you can tell her about the money now. I don't think she had anything to do with any of this."

"Don't worry about Sylvie. I rented the apartment below hers today for her bodyguard, so he's there right now."

"Just be careful, this is bad. The boy was tortured. I'll call later, bye."

Camille hung up without waiting for an answer and switched on the light. Then she walked over to the two bodies. The boy was propped up against the sofa facing his mother. His face was smashed up against the tight wrapping, eyes closed, mouth open like he'd been sucking for air, and there was moisture condensed on the plastic from his tears. He was wearing a pajama short set printed with cartoon cars. There were what looked like multiple cigarette burns on his feet and legs.

His mother was seated on the floor about three feet away, facing him. She was unbound, her knees up with her whole body sagged against the sofa. There was a bloody hole in her right ear and the skin was torn and burned in a way that indicated the gun was stuck into her ear. A skull fragment was lying a few inches away from where her head rested, mouth open and eyes staring wide in what looked like a startled expression of surprise. Women suicides didn't usually shoot themselves in the face, so for her to stick the gun in her ear made some sense, but the fact that her eyes were open and looked surprised did not make sense, because most people who shot themselves shut their eyes first.

Camille was sickened and scared and she wanted to get out of the house. But she needed to get all the information she could because she didn't trust the New Orleans police and thought they might write this off as a murder suicide, just as the killer wanted them to.

She looked around the room. It looked like what a single mother who worked as a maid could afford. A card table stood in a corner, covered with a plastic flowered tablecloth. A laptop computer sat on the table, and an open pack of Salem 100s with a red disposable lighter, but there was no ashtray. The ashtray was over on the floor by the child's body; there were a few cigarette butts in it and Camille took one and put it in a baggie. A plastic stackable chair was pulled out in front of the laptop like somebody had been sitting there using the computer. On the wall opposite the sofa there was an entertainment center which held a big screen TV and DVD player. A couple of Netflix DVDs sat on a shelf in their red envelopes. Camille went over and checked them out: Antz and Animal Odd Couples, both children's movies, nothing violent or weird. She went back through the house shining the flashlight.

Adrian's bedroom was directly behind the front room. It was painted light blue with red trim, the bedspread and curtains in the Cars motif. There were animal posters, books in a shelf, and plenty of toys. Amanda took good care of her son. Camille went through the drawers and closet and found normal kid stuff, the kind of clothes you got at Target. She went down the hall to Amanda's room. It looked like a monk's cell in its simplicity, like whoever lived here was too busy to care about decorating. There was a computer desk and laptop. So, the one in the front room was Bernice's. She went through the closet and drawers. The clothes were as functional as the furnishings. There wasn't anything to suggest a party lifestyle. Amanda was an honors student and a mom, apparently a good one, who worked full time. At least she had been, Camille thought, sadness and anger overwhelming her for a moment. She wouldn't have had time for much else. Camille checked out the bathroom and kitchen, but found no psychotropic meds or drug paraphernalia, no booze, nothing that would remotely explain or account for the events of the past couple of days or the horrific scene in the living room. She took out her phone and speed-dialed Andy.

Andy answered on the first ring. "Hi Camille."

"Andy, I'm still at the crime scene. It's gonna take a while to get out of here, but we need to talk. Can you meet me for a drink later on?"

"Why don't you come to my office? I keep a full bar for clients and I'm right downtown."

"I don't know how long this is going to take. It may be late. How late can it be?"

"I don't care if it's four in the morning. I'm going to go see Sylvie Compton. After that, there's a sleeper sofa in the office so I could nap."

"Thanks. You're fantastic."

"Well, I want the bastard caught. See you in a bit."

"Sure. Just make sure Sylvie Compton knows to be careful."

Camille called her ex-husband Allen next. He was her friend, and also a vice cop with the New Orleans police. She told him about Bernice Davis, and about the crime scene at Amanda Butler's house.

"Jesus. Are you okay?" he said.

"No. Listen, I have to call NOPD now, and I don't want any shit for letting myself in over here. Can you help out?"

"Oh, man, you know how they get. Let me call homicide and see what I can do and I'll be right over."

"Thanks. Do you think you can get them to cut me loose quick? I have somebody to talk to who might have information on a suspect. But this is just between us."

"I'll do what I can. You know what it's like working with these clowns. They could hold you for questioning if they want."

"And I could return the favor in my jurisdiction. I wish they'd work together with us. We'd solve more crimes."

"Sometimes I think it isn't about solving crime with these guys. I'll do my best."

"Thanks. By the way, I'll need inside information from forensics. I have a bad feeling our psycho has another vic in his sights. Can you swing that?"

"Yeah, probably. Anything else, queenie?"

"Get off my ass. I'm going to personally nail whoever did this to a wall."

After Camille hung up the phone she walked through the house and took pictures of everything with her digital camera, then went out to her car to wait for New Orleans' finest, dreading the encounter with what she viewed as a gang of thugs who were sometimes worse than the criminals they were supposed to be trying to catch. But, like all groups, the NOPD was a mixed bag; there were a few good cops on that force.

5

Sylvie sat at her desk playing mahjong and drinking beer until she felt numbed. She kept seeing Bernice lying dead in the bathtub, her face frozen in a mask of horror. What if her son had gotten to her? He'd still be around. What would he do next? Though she didn't want to think about it she couldn't help wondering what kind of evil monster could make his mother hide out in fear of her life. As always, Sylvie felt indignation at people who weren't grateful to have good parents. Bernice Davis had been a good person. Sylvie had known enough messed-up people to recognize goodness when she found it. She realized she was scared, and very much wanted that detective to find out what happened.

She wanted a smoke, but didn't want to go out the bedroom window and sit on the roof like she usually did. She did not feel like meeting her new neighbor. The narrow rooftop outside the bedroom window of her attic apartment had a square opening in it with iron fire escape steps going down to the balcony of the apartment below. That apartment had been vacant since she'd moved in, but this afternoon when she'd gone down to get supplies from the store on the corner, she saw the door cracked open, and a couple of boxes stacked in the entry. She found her cigarettes and lighter and went in the bathroom. She opened the window, lit a cigarette, blew smoke out towards charcoal rooftops silhouetted against the night sky. She looked across at the lighted gallery of the slave quarters at the back of the courtyard, wondering why she rarely saw other tenants. Somebody let out a drunken party hoot and she could hear laughter and shouting above the sounds of street traffic. She realized a reason the evening seemed peaceful was the beggar who stationed himself across from her building on Saint Peter and sang the same old spiritual over and over again wasn't there today. Though she was grateful for the respite she wondered what had happened. It was Thursday, tourists were in for an early weekend and he hadn't missed a weekend night since he'd started singing across the street almost a year ago.

She reached for the ashtray she kept on a shelf, stubbed out the cigarette, and lit a stick of Nag Champa. The combination of nicotine and beer had her sedated, and she felt ready to do a couple of things before bed. She was looking through her linens for something to nail up over the bedroom window when her cell rang. Sylvie rarely received phone calls and had to wonder who'd be calling this late. Was it the detective? She dug the phone out of her purse. "Hello?"

"Hello, is this Sylvie Compton?"

"Yes, who's this?"

"Andrea Sharp. I'm Bernice Davis's lawyer. Ms. Davis mentioned you in her will and we need to talk. I don't want to explain on the phone, it's too complicated. Can you meet with me tonight?"

"I have to get up early for work. Can we meet tomorrow afternoon? I get off at four."

"Tonight would be better. It's urgent. I've already got your address; I could be there in a few minutes."

31

"Okay fine. Just ring the bell for apartment seven and I'll buzz you in the gate. You walk through the entry and there are stairs to your right. I'm at the top, three flights. I hope you're wearing walking shoes. Or I could come down and we could go around the corner for a drink."

"I'll come up. We need to talk in private. I'll be right over. Bye."

Sylvie felt funny about this. How did the woman get her address? And why the rush? Did Miss Bernice leave her something in her will? It was rumored she had more money than her teacher's pension. What if the son had something to do with his mother's death? Wouldn't he come after her next if his mother left her the money he felt entitled to? These thoughts were racing through Sylvie's mind when the buzzer rang. She pushed the button to buzz her in, then went out onto the landing to wait. The lawyer's footsteps echoed off the brick walls, her shadow preceding her up the stairway. She watched as the woman ascended the last curving flight. She was dressed in a loose white cotton dress with embroidery around the yoke, leather flip-flops, and she carried a big cloth bag. She looked sweaty and a bit winded from climbing the stairs in the muggy heat, but her lively, piercing gold eyes were alert and friendly. Sylvie got good energy from this woman and her anxiety eased up.

The lawyer huffed as she stepped onto the landing, then smiled and held out her hand. "Hello, Sylvie. You can call me Andy. This is an interesting place you have here."

"Thanks." Sylvie grasped the hand. "You can call me Sylvie. Not many people would climb those stairs to see me."

"And isn't that convenient?" Andy's eyes were sparkling.

"Very." Sylvie waved her in then followed, shutting the

door and engaging the deadbolt. "Can I get you a beer? I have a couple of Heinekens in the fridge."

"That would be fantastic. It's been a long day." Andy looked around the apartment with appreciation. "This is a cute place. I didn't know they could do such great makeovers with attics."

"Thank you, I was lucky to find it. Please sit down."

Andy took a seat at the table. A big purple candle in a brushed steel holder cast flickering shadows on the walls. The room seemed spacious, the high ceiling slanting up to a peak—the rooftop of this historic building, cross beams painted the same cream color as the bare walls, with one wall left as exposed brick. It was sparsely furnished with a futon, recliner, small computer desk, and a glass and steel bistro table with chairs upholstered in different colors—magenta, royal blue, turquoise, and black.

Sylvie called out from the small kitchen, "Did you want a glass?"

"No, bottle's fine."

She brought the beers along with a couple of coasters, set them down and took a seat across from Andy at the table. Andy guessed that Sylvie could receive shocking news very well, so she started right in with what she'd come to talk about. "Sylvie, I said Bernice mentioned you in her will to give you a little time to think, and to soften the news. It wasn't really a will. In other words, the document she mentioned you in wasn't dependent on her dying first." Sylvie winced at the reference to Bernice's death. "She set up a trust. Do you know anything about trusts?"

"All I know is it's something for rich people, right?"

"Mostly. That's the area of law I practice in, estates and

trusts. I represented Bernice in this matter pro bono, in other words, free."

"Why would you do that?"

"Good question. Lawyers do pro bono work for charity, and Bernice set up a trust with her inheritance to benefit kids. She wanted to help orphans, and kids in trouble. Bernice was from a wealthy family. Have you heard of the clothing line, Blackwell & Sanders?"

"Everybody's heard of them. But I've never been in one of their stores—they're too expensive."

"Yes, they're very expensive. Bernice was a Sanders—her family owns the chain. They started with a cotton plantation and expanded their business to include a textile mill, then a clothing factory. They became very rich, very fast. One of the reasons for this was they kept manufacturing costs down. Essentially the family used orphaned children as slave labor which was perfectly legal back then, and there were plenty of orphans after the Civil War. They replaced their slaves with a cheaper work force. Cheaper because they didn't actually own the people they used as labor, so they didn't have an investment to protect. They used them up fast."

"What do you mean?"

"I mean that they were not nice to their workers. When Bernice found out how her family got their money, she was ashamed. After she finished college she went away, married another school teacher, and lived her own life."

"But how did they get away with that?" Sylvie exclaimed. "I mean the family."

"They didn't have laws protecting workers in the nineteenth century. Child labor was legal. A lot of bad things went on. They didn't have to pay the orphans a nickel, and even boasted they were doing the kids a service. People believed them because it was easier to believe the kids were taken care of."

"Kind of like it is now," Sylvie said, her eyes clouded with knowing.

"Maybe, only much worse." Andy took a swig of Heineken, watching Sylvie's features in the flickering light. She could see that Sylvie's attention had wandered, that her thoughts were in a dark place. "I know you're wondering where you fit into this." She was gratified to see Sylvie's attention return to the present. "Bernice's father died and left her part of the family fortune, which she never spent. She wanted to give the money back to the kids. She was planning to donate it to organizations that help kids. But she didn't want the money spread thin. It was her dream to help individual kids by making sure they have what they need, stability and a good education." Andy saw she had Sylvie's full attention. "Then you came along, an orphan. Bernice took your friendship as a godsend. For one thing, you might understand kids in bad situations—what could help them heal and thrive."

Sylvie reached up and blotted her eye with the back of her hand. "How much money is it?"

"Seventy-two million."

Sylvie blanched. She reached for her beer with a shaky hand, took a long swig.

"Are you okay?"

"I don't know. This is a lot to take in. I don't know how to help anybody."

"Well, you don't have to do anything tonight. Just think about it. Listen, there's a reason I wanted to see you right away."

Sylvie closed her eyes momentarily, overwhelmed. "What?"

"Bernice told you she had a son, right?"

"Yeah. She said she was hiding from him. He got to her, didn't he?"

"We don't know yet. But the detective you met thinks so. She asked me to protect you until we find out."

"I got the feeling she thinks I'm a suspect."

"Maybe she did at first, but not now."

"What changed her mind?"

Andy did not want to leave Sylvie knowing about the deaths of the motel maid and her son. "I can't say. But she thinks the son's involved, she doesn't know how yet. If he is, you may be in danger."

"He's coming after me?"

"It's a possibility. I'm meeting with her tonight to give her what I have on him. In the meantime, I wanted to warn you. It's why I insisted on seeing you right away."

"I don't understand about the money. Did she leave me something that he wants?"

"She didn't leave you anything. It's a job. If you accept, you'll start out at sixty thousand a year. It's a decent amount of money but maybe not for this kind of responsibility. Bernice wanted you to take the job to help kids, not because of the money. The trust is already set up. It wasn't dependent on Bernice dying first. But the way it's set up, you can only spend it helping kids in trouble. She was planning to offer you the job on your birthday, next week."

"Could I help their parents, too? Like, if a family needed help to stay together or get back together?"

"Yes, because that would be helping the kids. But I'd have the final say on what projects you use the money for. If you didn't want the job, it would be up to me to use the money to benefit kids, and I'd pay myself a salary, only I can't do it full-time. I make more money practicing law and I have my own kids to take care of."

"Why would her son want to kill me if he won't get the money anyway?"

"Who knows? People are at their worst when there's money involved. I've already taken steps to protect you that you need to know about. I've hired a bodyguard and rented the apartment downstairs for him. He doesn't look tough, but he's highly trained. He can use lethal force if necessary. I want you to know he's there and why. But you still have to use common sense and be careful. If you go out, give him a call. Here's his number." Andy handed her one of her business cards with the name Trey and a phone number on the back. "He won't escort you, but he'll be around watching. Please work with us on this. It's temporary, until we find out what exactly happened to Bernice. Are you okay with all this?"

"Well, I've been a little scared. I don't like the way Bernice looked when she died, and she did say her son tried to kill her. I guess I'm relieved to have some protection."

"Okay. We have to keep you safe. When do you go to work tomorrow?"

"I have to be there at eight, so I usually leave before seven."

"Call me when you're ready to go. I'll be by to pick you up, okay?"

"Okay."

"You don't have to decide about the job right away. We should talk more about that. The important thing is that you be safe, and careful. It's the reason I came by tonight."

"Well, thanks."

"I see you have a futon. Are you going to be okay tonight? I could ask Trey to come up here and sleep if you're scared. He's your bodyguard for now."

"No, I'll be fine."

"You have my number in your phone, right?"

"Yeah, I can save it."

"Good. I better leave and let you get some rest. I'll be downtown at my office for a while. Call if anything else comes up tonight."

"Alright. I have to buzz you out the gate." Sylvie followed Andy out so she could listen for her to get down the stairs. "Goodnight, Andy."

"I'll see you in the morning. Just be careful." Andy turned and started down the stairs. She liked the girl, and saw why Bernice picked her for the job. Hopefully they'd do some good work together. Andy wished the day was over, but there was one more thing to do. She'd already compiled a file of everything she had on Jim Davis. It contained pictures, a brief history, everything Bernice had told her about him, and Bernice had made a video in case something happened to her. Hopefully the detective would call and they could finish up soon. It was eleven-thirty and she was wiped out.

6

Lionel loaded his pipe with a big piece of glass. It was good taking a night off from the street, but that white dude sure was creepy. Lionel's first thought was to double cross him, keeping the up-front pay without doing his end of the deal, but his survival instinct warned him not to do it. His instinct told him not to do business with this man at all, but he was quick to see that he didn't have a choice—if he didn't want to play, he'd be the one to pay. So, he quieted that voice inside him screaming danger with meth and a bottle of Skyy. No cheapass booze tonight. No cheese-speed tonight either. He gazed at the pipe as he rolled the stem slowly between his fingers over the flame of a disposable lighter, mesmerized by the long, beautiful legs which were forming on the sides of the bowl. He was holed up at the Alexandra, a motel that featured cheap rooms in a closed space where you had to walk past the front desk and show some ID to get in.

The dude had approached him in the evening, when he was just getting ready to catch the crowd coming back out after the rain. He had just set his tip bucket on the sidewalk, and this old square-looking jackass came walking up and asked him if he was having a nice day.

"Yeah, man. It's a fine fucking day to be homeless. What about you? You got any spare change?"

"Well, that depends. Take a walk with me." The man was smiling, but with the eyes of a shark.

"Man, I'd love to take a walk with yo ass, but I got a job to do here."

The smile was gone. "It wasn't a request. Come on." The man put an arm around his waist, and he felt the point of a knife poking into his back. "This way," the man directed, turning him towards the river. "I'm parked right over there, in that parking lot across Decatur. Take a ride with me. I have a business proposal for you. It's easy work."

"Man, I ain't up for no homo shit."

"Listen to me," the man turned and crowded him against a brick wall. "If I wanted a queer to suck my dick I'd find somebody clean. I just need you to do something easy, no questions asked, and I can pay more than you make in a year on the street. What do you say?"

Lionel tried to shrink away from the creep, but his back was against the wall. He swallowed. "Man, I can't do nothing illegal. One more felony and I'm down for the count."

"It's not illegal. It's easy. Come on, let's take a ride. We can't be seen talking out here."

As they walked across the square towards Decatur the man turned and looked after the white woman who lived across the street from Lionel's spot. She was crossing the square towards St. Peter. After a moment he said, "Did you see that woman who just walked past? Young blonde?"

"You mean the white bitch with the brown eyes?"

"That's the one. Do you know her?"

"I know she's a pain in my ass. She came downstairs one night and told me to go somewhere else and do my gig. She say my singing keeping her up at night. She say she have to go to work. Man, it must be nice, having a place to sleep and a job to go to. I told her I can't move. That's a money-making spot over there. Then she asked if I could sing something else for a while. I told her the song I sing is the only song I know makes money. I don't pick the song, the tourists do. Then she told me she's gon' talk to the cop over at Rouse's about me. And I told her that she could talk all she wants. I got a license to be a street performer and if she don't like the noise she need to move. She can find a place anywhere, but I can't sing anywhere. I got to go where the money is."

They'd crossed Decatur and walked down past the Jackson Brewery tourist mall. "Man, before we go any further you got to tell me what you want me to do," Lionel said, hoping for a way to back down.

The guy kept walking; turned into the parking lot next to the mall. "Get in the car." He pulled a gun out of the pocket of his cargo pants and was holding it down, waving it towards a gray Civic. Just the kind of car this Mr. Square, psychopath would drive. He pulled out the keys and the car lights flashed as it unlocked. Lionel got in warily, looking around the interior for signs of anything weird. There was a backpack on the back seat, nothing else. The car looked freshly cleaned—it was spotless. The creep got in, started the car, and pulled out of the lot. "Where do you stay?"

"I don't got a place. I'm homeless."

"I already know that. I asked you where you stay."

"What you wanna know that for?" Lionel's voice betrayed anger and fear.

The man slammed on the brakes and turned to face him, cars honking behind on the busy street. "Listen, you stupid fuck" he said, smiling, "I don't give a shit about you. And neither do the cops. I'm offering you an opportunity to make some money here. I just need to know where I can find you when you're not making noise and bothering people who work. Now." He started driving forward again. "Let's start over. Where do you stay?"

Lionel told him he sometimes slept in an abandoned house on the corner of St. Anthony and Burgundy. "Sometimes I get a room for the night so I can take a bath."

"I can tell that hasn't happened lately. Jesus, you stink."

"Listen, I didn't ask to be in your funky-assed car. This is summer. There ain't a lot of money here in the summer. And it's hot as hell out. So, if you don't like the way I smell why don't you quit asking questions and let's get down with the business so I can get the hell out a here."

"You know that woman I pointed out. I need you to watch her. I'm going to give you a cell phone, and I want to know when she comes and when she goes."

"Man, what you want with her? She leave your ass or something?"

"She's my daughter. I need to make sure she's okay. I may need to talk to her, see if she'll let me help her out. I don't like her living in the city by herself. All I need you to do is watch her come and go, and call me when she leaves. You don't have to be obvious about it. You can go somewhere and use the bathroom to call, can't you?"

"Not if I don't have any money I can't go nowhere and use the bathroom. I need money to buy me a drink or something to eat to use the bathroom in the Quarter. Most folks don't give a shit about you if you on the street."

"I'm going to give you enough money to take care of that. Oh, and take the night off. Go somewhere and get a bath.

Here, there's a number in this phone in the contacts, under B. My name is Bob. What's yours?"

"Lionel. Shit. Why you had to pull a knife and stick me and all that other shit? Don't you know how to talk to folks?"

"I needed you to shut up and listen. I needed you to quit being a smart-ass, and I needed to talk in private, where we wouldn't be seen together."

Lionel knew bullshit when he heard it, and this dude was full of it. When he smiled, he was even creepier—something about his eyes. But he needed the creep to let him out of the car without shooting him so he played along. "Okay man. How much money are we talking here?"

"I can give you three hundred a day. Here's for today and half for tomorrow." Bob or whatever his name was took out some bills he had folded in his shirt pocket. Lionel opened the folded bills—four hundreds and a fifty. Lionel folded them back up and put them in his front pocket.

"I'll give you the other half for tomorrow on Saturday, when we meet. I want a full report. But you can take tonight off and go get a bath. Just consider the first three your sign-up fee."

"Okay, man. Are we finished?" They had crossed Canal Street and were driving down Magazine.

"No, there's one more thing." Bob continued up towards the warehouse district. "Do not fuck with me." He turned and looked at Lionel with pale, icy eyes that mirrored a soul with no bottom. "I'll know if you're out there doing your job." He pulled over to the curb and used his control panel to unlock Lionel's door. Lionel exited the car in a cold sweat, watched the dude drive off, and used the phone to call his connect.

He'd been holed up in the room for hours, thinking about how to deal with this trouble. He decided to save his last piece of ice for later—it was time to try and get some rest. The room didn't have a window, just a bed, nightstand, TV, and bathroom. Even though the Alexandra was a closed access place, Lionel was listening for noise from the hall. He took a swig of vodka. Jesus, this was spooky. He'd dealt with plenty of hoods in his time, but this guy creeped him out worse than all the others. Because he looked straight, like a camouflage, and his eyes were bad. Lionel had seen eyes like this dude's, but usually the person was tatted out, dressed in gangsta' clothes, a prison guard or cop uniform, something.

Friday

7

Andy stepped aside as Camille entered her office suite, her eyes clouding with concern. "Please sit down. How are you?"

"I just came from the worst crime scene ever. I need a drink. What kind of protection did you arrange for Sylvie?" Camille crossed the room and took a seat in a big, soft chair. The office was spacious—furnished with big, plush contemporary pieces that you could sink into and a scattering of antiques, with two full walls of legal tomes surrounding a big desk.

"What are you drinking?"

"Double scotch, water back."

Andy told her about Trey as she poured four fingers of Glenfiddich into a tall glass and took bottled water from the mini-fridge in the wet bar alcove. "Trey's good. He doesn't look like a bodyguard. Security's his side work. He's a glass-blower by trade, works at a shop in the Tremé. Nobody expects trouble from him because he's little so he has the advantage of surprise. He disarmed a robber without using a weapon when he worked at a bar in the Faubourg. Took his gun away and held him while they called the cops. His body is his weapon but he can use other things if necessary. I've been using him for years but I don't need him very often. Things can get ugly when families are fighting over money."

Andy handed Camille her drinks, went back and got a bottle of water, and took a seat across from her on the sofa.

"Tell him about the crime scene. He needs to know what this perp is capable of," Camille said. She took a big gulp of whiskey and chased it with water. Then she recounted the details of finding Amanda and Adrian. "It was staged to look like she tortured and killed her son, then shot herself. But there was no gunshot residue on her hands. I suspect whoever did this has killed before, but not with a gun. They haven't found any trace evidence—hairs, fibers, footprints, nothing. So, the killer knows to bring gloves, hair and shoe coverings; the same equipment crime scene techs use when they process a scene. That means experience and planning. But he overlooked an important detail. With all the other precautions he took, leaving something out that important tells me a couple of things about him. The lack of trace evidence means that the killer may be experienced in using forensic countermeasures, but not in using guns. I'm thinking guns might be too quick for this asshole. He's a sadist; he uses a gun to gain control, then he switches to torture. I need to know everything you have on Bernice Davis's son. Do you think he's capable of this?"

Andy went to her desk and took a file folder, handed it to Camille, then sat back down. "I put this together after you called. There are pictures. Bernice wanted me to locate him because she was scared, but he went off the grid around the same time she did."

"What do you mean?"

"I mean he disappeared off the records. My investigator is very good at finding computer records, like addresses, bank and credit card trails. He couldn't find any records dating back further than a couple of months after Bernice went into hiding. Bernice gave him three million dollars when she inherited, around fifteen years ago, and he doesn't have the kind of habits that would account for spending that much money. He was married when he was younger but only for a few years. He took early retirement from teaching so he has that money, too. He's going under fake ID, has to be, and it isn't hard to get if you have a little money."

Camille was going through the file as Andy talked. She held up a picture of a middle-aged man sitting at a patio table that was shaded by a big umbrella. He looked nondescript with regular features, wire glasses, a short-sleeved button-down shirt. His smile did not extend to his eyes. His brown hair was graying, cut short but not too short. This was a person who would blend into ordinary settings. The kind of guy you wouldn't be able to remember seeing if you passed him on the street.

"How long ago was this one taken?" Camille asked.

"Around ten years ago, right before Bernice's husband was killed and she went into hiding."

"Do you mind if I keep it? Have copies made?"

"The file is yours. Do whatever you need to do."

"Did Bernice tell you what he did to lead her to believe he was dangerous? I mean, besides messing with their car."

"Bernice never liked her son. She said he always acted like everything she and her husband Jack did for him wasn't enough—like they owed it to him and more. He had entitlement problems. The younger brother, David, was killed by a car. Bernice suspected Jim had something to do with it. He asked if he could take his little brother to the store that afternoon, and Davy supposedly ran out into the street. The driver said she didn't see the boy, that she'd looked away for a moment, and the next thing she knew she'd hit him. She was turning, so it was close enough to the curb that he could have been pushed. When Jim asked if he could take Davy, Bernice assumed they were going to the corner store at the end of the block but they were on a main thoroughfare several blocks away when Davy was killed. Bernice told me that even though Jim cried a lot and pretended he was sorry, she had a bad feeling about it and didn't believe him. Davy was always crying to go with his big brother, you know how little siblings are. And Bernice told me that Jim had always seemed more than annoyed by Davy. He was cold towards his little brother, not in an obvious way but it was there."

"How old was Jim?"

"Nine." Andy saw that whatever sedative effects the whiskey had on Camille were gone. She was sitting up in her chair, face grim, tapping the file folder with her short-clipped nails. "So," Andy continued, "he got his brother out of the way."

The file contained pictures of Jim going back through the years, from the most recent to a couple of pictures of him as a small child. What was it that creeped Camille out about this guy? She sat holding a picture of him as a teen with his father at Galveston Beach. The date on the photo read July 4, 1972. He was standing next to his dad in front of a concession stand. There were people in the background, a few sitting at a café table, a couple walking past. Jim stood in stark contrast to the other beachgoers who looked like they were alive, more or less, most of them having fun. His look was plain—blue swim trunks, gray T-shirt; hair cut short, thin smile, dead eyes. It was what was absent that was disturbing. This person wanted to remain invisible and didn't like having his picture taken. He looked bored and angry. The file contained a list of every address Jim had lived with his family and as an adult, and every job he had held in his life, dating from 1972 when he got his first job at Mc Donald's, a teen living with his family in Dallas, to 2007 when he disappeared.

"This file is thorough. Whose idea was it to compile all this information?"

"Bernice thought the time might come when her son was being investigated. She half-expected him to find her and felt sure he'd try to kill her. She suspected him of other murders. She wanted police to have everything she had on him. She wanted unsolveds investigated around where he's lived."

"What's this?" Camille held up a CD in a plain sleeve.

"That's a film of Bernice talking about her son. After her husband's death, she reported her suspicions to the Dallas police, but they wouldn't listen. They were going by the fact that Jim Davis had no criminal record and he was a school-teacher. So, she wanted to get it on record that she was afraid of her son, in case he got to her."

"She sounds like a smart woman."

"She was smart, and one of the sanest people I've known. She loved children and for her to dislike her own son would be evidence enough for anyone who knew her."

Camille sat and sipped her scotch, wondering what suspicions could have played through a mother's mind over the years, and the regrets she must have had that she hadn't done anything about them. And what could she have done? He had likely killed the rest of her family—her husband and little Davy. Nobody would listen to her anyway. "Do you mind if I smoke?" she asked.

"No, go ahead. I keep Sherman's for clients. You want one?"

"Thanks, but I smoke desert dogs, like my dad." Camille removed a pack of Camel no-filters from her purse, and Andy found her a small ashtray, it looked like cut crystal. The furniture grouping they sat in stood by a tinted glass wall facing St. Charles Avenue, the night beyond it black, with a few lights shining from across the street. Camille drew on her cigarette and looked out into the dark, wondering where the killer was at. "How did you meet Bernice?" she asked.

"She contacted our office a few years ago. When I found out she wanted to set up a trust to benefit kids, I talked to the partners and we agreed to represent her pro bono. Quite frankly I've never met or heard of a client who wants to give away an entire fortune. Most of our clients are fighting over money, and we saw this as an opportunity to be part of something good. When our clients leave charitable bequests, we usually do that work pro bono but Bernice Davis is the first strictly pro bono client I've had. Most of our clients use donations as tax shelters."

Andy could see that Camille's mind was wandering and she looked tired. "Is there anything else I can help you with tonight?" she asked. "We both need to get some rest."

"This is the reality of the situation," Camille said. "We could be absolutely certain Jim Davis is behind all this. But unless we can prove it he walks. The D.A. won't charge him without proof. And something tells me he's been getting away with murder for a long time." She lit another dog and took a sip of scotch, then continued. "If he's going after Sylvie Compton—then we can't stop him unless we put him in jail. I mean, how long do you think you can protect her? Because I can tell you, if he's the kind of monster the evidence says he is, he won't give up. It's all about power and control with these guys and if Sylvie is getting the money he thinks belongs to him, he's going after her. I even thought about using her for bait. But that's risky and we can't do it without telling her and getting her willing participation. He might go after you too, if he blames you for helping his mother disinherit him. Look, I can go on for hours about possible outcomes because we don't know what he'll do next. Just be careful. Right now, I don't have anybody else with a motive and I'm pretty sure he's our guy. The problem is what's missing. There was no trace evidence at the crime scene, which is why I think he's killed before. That and he didn't have a problem with torturing a four-year-old boy. Everything you've told me confirms this. Just looking at his pictures you can see something's wrong." Camille finished her whiskey and set the glass down hard. "I can promise you one way or another, if he did this, he's going down for it. This file and what you've told me is extremely helpful. We need to stay in touch, okay?"

"God yes. Let me know if there's anything I can do. You know you can crash here if you want. You look exhausted, and I need to get home." Andy glanced at her watch and saw it was almost two a.m.

Camille thought about it for a moment. "That sounds great. Sure it's okay?"

"No problem. Honestly, with this bastard on the loose he might find a way to break in here next. And we do have good security, but it doesn't hurt to have more. I'll tell our night guard you're staying in case you need to leave before I get back."

"Okay. I need to be gone early. But I'll be in touch and let you know if we find anything new."

Andy went in the bathroom, pulled a couple of pillows out of a closet, and began to take the cushions off the small sofa. "This is already made up and there's a coffeepot behind the bar. And some snack food in the fridge. Please make yourself at home."

"Thanks, I'm beat. Do you have a DVD player in case I want to watch the film?"

"Yes, use the TV." Andy opened a tall cabinet which contained an entertainment center. "Bernice wanted to show that she's a sane person with a normal appearance so we filmed the interview." Andy pulled the bed out, then got the TV remote and placed it on the table next to the sleeper sofa. She went back in the bathroom and came out with a cotton nightshirt. "I stay here sometimes when I'm working late. This is more comfortable than street clothes. Okay, I'm going."

"See you later," Camille said. "Be careful. He could be anywhere now."

"Well, I always pack a gun, and I'm calling security to let her know I'm coming down. Don't worry about me."

"A gun didn't help Bernice. Stay alert."

"Stop worrying and get some rest. If you stay up worrying you won't be worth a damn tomorrow."

"Okay, goodnight."

"Night."

Camille thought about watching the video after Andy left, and decided to wait. She was too tired to think any more. She went in the bathroom and changed into the nightshirt, then smoked another desert dog and crawled under the covers on the sleeper sofa. When she closed her eyes, she saw little Adrian Butler's face squashed against the plastic wrap, the condensation of moisture from his tears. She got up and went to the bar, found the bottle of scotch, and sat up drinking and chain smoking until she could pass out.

8

Sylvie sat on the roof outside her bedroom window. Though it was after three, it was still hot and muggy and four stories below the street was alive. She could hear the tipsy chatter of a group of girls going by towards the square and down the street a car honked and somebody screamed, "Fuck yeah!" A couple of young guys walked past, drunk and talking loud.

"Come—hic, come on. Let's go back to the room."

"I wanna go check out them chicks at Sugar Daddy's. It's almost closing time."

"Aw man. Those broads don't give a shit about you—hic, less you're stuffin'—hic their panties with money…"

The voices faded out down the block, and then there was another holler and a tinkle of broken glass. Sylvie wondered what it would be like to be young and so carefree that you could go on a weekend party in another town. She'd never felt young, at least not that she remembered. It was always survival, first in foster care after her mother disappeared, then as an under-aged stripper when she ran away. And then there'd been her ex. That was a hard lesson she was still recovering from, emotionally and financially.

She was stunned by the events of the day—overwhelmed with the prospect of having control over such a huge sum of money, and that Bernice had assumed that she'd know how to help kids. The sixty grand a year wasn't all that much—she'd made more stripping when she did it full-time. But the responsibility of helping kids in trouble—it was a lot to contemplate. She thought about it, about how angry the whole foster deal had made her and how she just wanted to run as far away from that life as she could.

Did she mention to Bernice that she wished she could help those other kids? Of course she did, but she didn't say she knew how. And everybody's situation was different, but if she had to name one problem that put kids in homes it would be poverty. That and single mothers, because it was usually the mothers, being alone in the world with kids and poor. The kids who wound up in homes didn't have other family willing to take them in when something went wrong. Seventy-two million wasn't going to save the world. But it could sure make a difference for some people.

Sylvie finished her beer and decided to try to get some sleep. Of course she'd take the job, who wouldn't in her situation? She didn't have anything better to do. But she felt a premonition that it wasn't going to be easy, especially with a sadistic monster out to get her, and she was afraid that Bernice's son was one of those. Maybe like the same kind of thing that happened to her mother. Sylvie had never allowed herself to dwell on what exactly had happened to her mom, but she knew it was bad and that likely her mom had died a hard death. There was no way she'd just run off, no matter what those asinine cops in Dallas had wanted to believe about strippers.

9

Camille sipped black coffee and waited for the Advil to kick in. Her headache was starting to ease up. She checked the time—it was just after seven a.m. She had a lot to do and first on her list was watching the recording Bernice Davis had made. She switched on the TV and DVD player, inserted the disc, turned up the volume and sat back down.

Bernice looked a lot different than she'd looked lying dead in the bathtub. She sat in the easy chair in her motel room, wearing a light blue blouse and black slacks. She was an attractive woman, with a dignity about her person that seemed both trustworthy and likeable. Her shoulder length gray hair was thick with a natural wave, her blue eyes calm and clear, and she wore a touch of pink lipstick which added color to the pallor of her skin from staying indoors. She looked calm, poised, and sane. "Hello," she said, looking evenly into the camera. "My name is Bernice Davis and if you're watching this film, chances are that I'm dead. I want to thank you in advance for everything you're doing to find out what happened to me. The reason I'm making this recording is that I believe my son, Jim Davis, is responsible for the death of my husband, and I believe that he plans to kill me, too." Here Bernice ventured a thin smile and added, "That is if he can find me, and I've been in hiding for eight years now.

Before you draw any conclusions regarding my sanity, please consider that I have inherited a very large sum of money, and my son feels entitled to this inheritance. At the time I received the money, when my father died, I gave Jim three million dollars of it, and I have always planned to leave the rest to charity…"

Bernice went on to talk about the circumstances of her husband's death and about Jim's odd behavior over the years. She spoke of her other son David and of her suspicions about Jim's role in his death. She said that when she taught school in Dallas in 1971, there was a tragedy involving a student, a kindergartner in her class who was killed along with his mother and sister in a home invasion. She said at the time she suspected that her son was responsible but couldn't say why, aside from the fact that he had met the boy and his mother shortly before they were killed. She said she'd checked out his story that he was working the late shift at McDonalds on the night they were killed and it was a lie. "I believe my son is a sadistic psychopath," Bernice said, her eyes and demeanor showing a dogged determination to be thorough and convincing. Her voice remained calm, describing the things about her son that seemed abnormal. "He's never shown any real affection for anybody. He gets enraged when people don't give him his way. Things have happened, more than once, to people who have had contact with him. I've always suspected the worse." Bernice paused, took a drink of water, and continued. "We gave up trying to keep a family pet. They all disappeared—dogs, cats. Nobody caught Jim abusing the animals, I just knew. They annoyed him; he didn't like anything or anybody, really. You should check out any unsolved murders in areas where Jim lived, with our family and since

59

he moved out on his own. Check out unsolved crimes in the early years. There you may find evidence tying my son to one or more tragedies. I am making this recording because nobody in law enforcement has listened to my warnings about Jim, but the circumstances of my death might cause you to take another look at my son. I've instructed my attorney to turn this over to investigators if I should die under suspicious circumstances. I believe my son is a killer. I hope you can stop him. Thank you for your time."

The video made Camille's stomach churn. A creepy feeling came over her, like the one she'd had at last night's crime scene. She believed that Bernice Davis was sane and that she knew exactly what she was talking about with her son. Her description of him was chilling in that she described an absence, something she couldn't name that made her sense her son was lacking in normal human affection. Who would know better than a mother? Camille thought back through her years as a homicide detective. In every single case she'd investigated—gang members, addicts, cold-blooded and calculating killers, she had never met or heard of a mother that didn't believe her child was innocent, or that they were basically good no matter what they'd done.

Camille finished her coffee, made up the sleeper, and gathered her things to leave. She had a ten o'clock meeting with Mason Delaroux, the New Orleans detective assigned to the Butler case. He wanted to meet at a diner on Canal Street, which was a little irregular, but Delaroux had a rep: he was a maverick who got the job done when nobody else could, so they let him alone to do it his way. She needed to go home and shower, then check in at the station. She wanted to talk to the M.E. Steve Morgan about the autopsy results before meeting with Delaroux. Amanda's and Adrian's deaths were classified as homicides, not as the murder-suicide she'd feared they would be. Now she needed Bernice's death classified as a homicide so she'd have authorization to investigate.

10

Gloom was thicker than the humidity at the motel, and the atmosphere was charged with anger and fear. Crime-scene tape was still up around Bernice Davis's room, and a seal was taped to the door. A few guests were hanging out in the back parking lot talking in low voices, looking anxiously around at the grounds and the street beyond as if the killer was out there watching them, targeting the next victim. The house-keeping staff was terrified after hearing about Amanda's and Adrian's deaths. One of the maids called in, so there were only two out of four to handle the day's work, which meant that they would have to clean the rooms alone rather than in two-woman teams like they usually did.

Sylvie went about her duties in a daze. Andy had told her about Amanda and Adrian on the way to work and she was sad, scared, and having a hard time focusing on her job. Checkout time was eleven o'clock; still an hour away but people who had watched the morning news were calling the office. A couple of longtime guests called to say they were checking out, and could they get a refund on the rent they'd paid in advance. Sylvie had already made two mistakes on the computer database and was trying to make up for being overwhelmed by working slow and careful. Still, she was glad she'd come in. They were shorthanded, and Sylvie felt she owed Bill some loyalty—he'd given her a job when she needed a way out of stripping full-time, and most people don't hire strippers. He was coming in early today and Sylvie needed to talk to him, though she hated to do it on a day like this. She'd wait until later in the afternoon, after he'd had time to deal with the crisis created by the early morning news broadcast.

She looked up from her paperwork and saw Brittney Peters enter the lobby. Of all the guests and employees, Brittney alone did not appear fazed by the events of the past twenty-four hours. But Brittney had plenty of trouble of her own to worry about. She was a day behind on her rent, and with three kids she could not afford to be out on the street. Sylvie had seen her around town for years and knew all about her from the small community that made up the strippers, bouncers, club owners and regulars of those French Quarter nightclubs that featured nude dancers. Every time Sylvie saw her she felt sad, like the feeling you get when you see a stray dog roaming the street dirty and starved. Brittney had been stripping since she was thirteen years old, starting at Sugar Daddy's and, as the years used her up, winding up at the off-Bourbon clubs that featured back rooms. Booze and drugs had taken their toll on her looks so that though she was only thirty-one and not the oldest dancer by far, she looked gaunt, tired, and old beyond her years. Her long blonde hair needed a cut and hung in thin, dry hanks, probably from the dehydration of whiskey and meth. Her features, which at one time must have shown a delicate beauty, were set in hard lines, and a front tooth was beginning to go bad. But it was her eyes, pale blue and ringed with smudged makeup from the night before, that looked worst of all—haunted but also hard, like she was backed in a corner and determined not to show fear. Sylvie usually didn't see Brittney much on the eight to four, but today she was behind on rent.

"Morning, Brittney."

"Hey," Brittney said, her hoarse voice sounding fatigued. "I have somebody coming over in a couple of hours to pay my rent. Things are slow right now at the club. That okay?"

"Sure, I'll let Bill know. Is there anything else?"

"Yeah, you can give me a wake-up call for two. I'll be in by four with the rent. Thanks."

"Sure thing, Brittney."

As she watched Brittney leave Sylvie tried to envision this young-old woman in a healthier persona than the beaten-down state she was in. Life had not been kind, and hers was exactly the type of situation where help was called for—a lot of help. Brittney and the kids had been at the motel for over a month, ever since she'd left her live-in after he beat her up. From what Sylvie heard through the strip-club grapevine, she'd come home early and found him in bed with another woman.

But some people, Sylvie knew, didn't want help and so could not be helped. Brittney had a boy, fourteen and two girls, eleven and seven. Things were complicated by her addiction to booze and meth, and Sylvie realized that most addicts do not recover. Still, Sylvie wondered if she would want to recover if given a chance at a better life for herself and her kids—a life where she could have a decent-paying job earning enough money to take care of her family, and with some dignity and respect. Strippers, Sylvie knew, did not get promotions and raises with years on the job. Sylvie suspected that for Brittney, such a life had never been an option and she did not allow herself to have such dreams because it would only make her situation more unbearable. The drug use was probably the only relief she had from the hopelessness she lived in, along with the knowledge that things would most likely get progressively worse as she aged out of the clubs.

Sylvie tried to envision Brittney off the drugs, bright eyed, with a little weight on her. What would it take to effect such a change? For one thing, it would take Brittney wanting to change and wanting it bad enough to do the work. And there would be plenty of work and a difficult path, but not an impossible one. The first step on the path would have to be sobriety—no more meth, no more booze. This would probably require rehab, and for her to feel free to go to rehab, she'd want to know that her children were safe. Did they have rehab for mothers with children? Could she do outpatient if she had the resources?

Miss Bernice trusted me to use her money to help kids, and here's a family in trouble right in front of me. I know Bernice would approve if the money could give Brittney's family a hopeful future. I'm going to talk to Andy about this tonight. And what if Andy okays it? How do you approach somebody with an opportunity like this? With so many questions, Sylvie decided the best way to proceed would be one step at a time, and not to count on anything coming of this idea, because helping Brittney and her kids was so exciting and fabulous that it was scary. It would be a huge disappointment if things didn't work out. And so many things could go wrong, not the least of which would be for Brittney to be insulted by an offer of help and turn it down cold.

Sylvie had never been comfortable meddling in other people's business, even with good intentions. Still, she had a family in trouble right in front of her, and what harm could it do to help out? With seventy-two million she could get Brittney cleaned up and trained for a good paying job, and keep a roof over their heads so they were secure during this metamorphosis.

Sylvie snapped back to the present with the ringing of the phone. "Front desk," she answered, seeing room 128 on the switchboard.

"Hey, can you tell that bitch next door to turn her music down? I'm trying to sleep. I gotta work tonight."

"What room are you talking about?"

"That crazy woman in 127. She's probably already drunk. This is every fucking day, the same shit. Next they'll be screaming at each other. I wish you'd move me to another room, but not right now. I need to sleep a few hours. Just get her to shut up, okay?"

"I'll see what I can do. Thanks for calling."

"You're welcome. Listen, I need to talk to Bill when I get up. How long's he gonna be here today?"

"He usually stays 'til five or six. Will you be up by then? I can give him a message. What do you need?"

"I need to sleep! If you don't move either me or those assholes next door, I got to move somewhere else. I'm gonna lose my job. I work security in the Quarter and I can't be beating up tourists just cause I'm tired."

"I'll let Bill know. I'm going over there now and ask them to be quiet. If the noise doesn't stop, call us back. Okay?"

"Yeah, man. Okay. I been complaining about this for a week and nobody's done jack about it."

"I'm going over there now."

The guest hung up the phone, and Sylvie grabbed the

keys to the lobby. Just then Beau from 112 came in. Beau was behind on his rent after spending a few days in jail. He was carrying the big sign he used for begging: VIETNAM VETERAN! WILL WORK FOR FOOD. Beau could not have served in Vietnam—he was too young, though he did look crazy enough to have been over there. He was wild-eyed and his long tangled brown hair, facial included, looked like it hadn't seen scissors or a razor in years. He had a pronounced limp, wore wrinkled, dirty camouflage pants and a tattered T-shirt that looked like it was tie-dyed by somebody who'd had too many magic mushrooms.

Beau set his sign down by the door, limped across the lobby to the front desk counter, reached in his pocket and came out with a handful of bills. "I got thirty-eight dollars in change. Can you take that now? Then I can go get the rest. I don't want to leave it in my room cause the last time the maids stole it."

"You can just give me the money or you'll have to wait a minute. I have to go handle a problem right now." Beau usually paid in dollars and coins and he'd want to count first, then wait while Sylvie counted it.

"I'll wait, but hurry up. I need to go back out so somebody doesn't get my spot."

"Okay, but I need you to step outside the lobby so I can lock up."

"I can stay in here and watch things for you."

"Bill doesn't allow that. Come on, I have to go."

Sylvie unlocked the door to the office, locked it after her, and turned to exit the lobby. Just then a car pulled into the drive and Beau hobbled outside and started waving his sign. Sylvie was amazed at how fast he could move despite his

limp. She followed him out, putting up the Back in Five Minutes sign and locking the glass lobby door while she yelled
over her shoulder, "Beau! You can't beg here!" Beau ignored
her so she took off towards the back.

11

Camille pulled into the parking lot of the Canal Pancake House. The diner was a rectangular red brick building with big windows and green wooden shutters that could be closed for hurricanes. The lot was packed, which meant good food in New Orleans.

She was fifteen minutes early for her appointment with Mason Delaroux, the lead detective on the Butler case. Everybody in local law enforcement knew about Mace, the maverick NOPD homicide detective who'd closed the Pearl River Slayer case, rescuing the ten-year-old girl the Slayer kidnapped and bringing him in alive to face the needle at Angola. Camille had met him briefly the night before, and had been shocked because he did not look anything like what she'd expected. It was like how she felt when she first saw a picture of Sylvester Stallone, that he was a short guy. According to Mace's rep, he worked alone, but Camille was determined he would not shut her out of this case. She had the goods on the only viable suspect; if he wanted information, he'd have to let her in.

She'd just come from the meeting with Steve Morgan. He told her that Bernice Davis died from stress cardiomyopathy—a stress-related heart attack known as broken heart syndrome. Steve said this condition, which usually occurs in post-menopausal women, is brought on by a shock so severe that the body floods the bloodstream with chemicals, and this chemical overload stuns the heart, causing it to falter or stop completely. The condition is rarely fatal—most patients recover rapidly and there's usually no permanent damage, but if untreated it could kill.

What could a motel maid, somebody Bernice knew and trusted, say or do to cause such a severe reaction? And Amanda was murdered soon after she'd gone in Bernice's room. Camille felt certain Amanda's killer was Jim Davis. He'd used Amanda to get to his mother somehow, probably by threatening her son—from the way she'd looked on the surveillance video she was terrified. He must have made her deliver a message to his mother. Whatever the message was, it was so horrific Bernice had gone into cardiac arrest. If Amanda had called an ambulance Bernice would have survived. But Jim Davis was holding her son hostage, so she didn't want to call anybody in. Yes, this fit. There was a huge motive in the seventy-two million dollars that Bernice had control of and that, no doubt, Jim felt entitled to inherit. It was safe to assume Jim was using fake ID, but she had his picture and would start showing it around; he had to be staying somewhere. The information she'd got from Andy and the recording Bernice made would be a big help. They could check cold cases around where Jim had lived and see if there was a DNA or fingerprint match, but first they'd have to find the asshole and get samples.

She gathered her things and headed across the parking lot. As she approached the front door, she saw a man standing on the sidewalk chatting with a street character. He took his wallet out and gave the guy a fiver, then turned toward the door.

It was Mace. He was wearing a loose chambray shirt over a faded black tee, and jeans. He looked more like some kind of office geek bumming around town on his day off than a cop. Camille figured he was packing, which was why he wore the loose shirt. With the sleeves rolled up on his forearms she could see what looked like a red scaly reptile tail snaking down his left arm.

They reached the door at the same time. "Hi, Mace," Camille said, and reached for the handle on the glass door.

"Good to see you, Camille." Mace let Camille hold the door for him and she followed him in.

The cashier looked up and smiled. "Mace! Go on back." She finished ringing up the customer at the register, grabbed a couple of menus and followed them through the crowded restaurant to the back, through swinging red doors into a separate, dimly-lit private dining room.

Mace crossed the room to a red vinyl booth and waited for Camille to take a seat.

"You both want coffee?" the waitress asked.

"Yes, thank you," Camille responded, sliding in with her back to the door—a courtesy.

"You know I'm gonna have some," Mace said. "This place has the best coffee in New Orleans."

"Yeah, you right," the waitress said. She was a middle-aged woman with orange-red hair done up in an old fashioned bouffant. Her name tag read Jodie. "I'll be right back with the coffee." Jodie placed the menus on the table and left.

"The food's great here," Mace said. "You had breakfast?"

"No. But pancakes slow me down. I'll take a couple of eggs, scrambled. Grits and toast."

"What about a Cajun omelet? Their sausage is the best. And you have to have the French bread."

"Okay, whatever. But I didn't come here to talk about food." She watched Mace from across the table. He looked almost feminine, with fine sandy blonde hair cut short, pale gray eyes with long lashes, delicate features, and a slight build. His looks didn't match his rep, except that his eyes looked intelligent, thoughtful.

"I like what you did last night," he said, "and I checked you out. You've got a good solve rate."

"Whadda you mean you liked what I did?"

"You knew something was wrong and you went in. That took brains, and some guts. I don't always work by the book. I don't like to work with people who care more about their careers and going by the rules than they do about solving murders."

"My career is solving murders. I wouldn't be doing this if I didn't care."

Jodie came in with a tray and a stand. She set them up with a carafe of coffee, two cups, a pitcher of cream, and sugar packets. "You two ready?" she said, pulling a pen out of her stiff hairdo and taking an order pad out of the pocket of her pink uniform dress.

"Yeah, we'll take two Cajun omelets," Mace said. "Grits and bread. You want cheese on your grits?" he asked.

"No."

"Plain grits for both of us. Thanks, Jodie." He handed her the menus and she left. He continued where he'd left off. "You probably figured out the NOPD don't like working with outside jurisdictions. But our cases are connected. I want to work this case with you. I guess I'm asking you to let me in.

The way I see it, we need to cut the bullshit and get this guy."

"How do I know you won't take my information then shut me out?" Camille asked.

"I'm asking you to trust me. This is the way I see it. You work the same as I do, the case comes first. And the perp's operating in both our jurisdictions so we need to work together on this, with or without department approval. We can bypass their bullshit and maybe solve the case. So, whadda you say? Are we a team?"

Camille had already thought about all this. She was here because she knew her chances of solving the case on her own were slim to none. She felt almost certain that the perp was hiding in the city of New Orleans, and that was out of her jurisdiction. And she didn't have any experience catching a serial killer, Mace did. "Okay, I'm in," she said. She'd come prepared to work with him if possible, and she felt the stress ease up as she handed him a copy of the file on Jim Davis. "I picked up the file last night. This copy's for you. It's about the suspect." She began to tell him about her meeting with Andy the night before. Mace was looking through the file. He looked up over her shoulder and she heard Jodie come in, the food smelled great and suddenly she was hungry.

12

He sat in his car watching the kids play through a pair of binoculars. The school building was a two-story red brick Georgian, set back on a lush green acreage studded with twisted old oaks dripping Spanish moss, magnolias, and flower beds bright with color. The school was having summer day camp. People with money to send their kids to schools like this expected things to be safe, and that they normally were.

The preschool kids were out with their teachers. A stocky woman with short, steel-gray hair was blowing a whistle and telling the kids to line up, and her assistant, a beautiful young woman with long shiny black hair, chased after a little redhead boy who was running away from the group towards the back of the fenced-in playground. The young one reminded Jim of his mother. That's why he was here. He noted she was wearing a wedding band. He snapped her picture with his digital binoculars, then set them aside and checked his watch—it was 11:10. Pre-school camp let out at 12:30. If she was a mother, she'd only be working half days. He would go get some early lunch, then come back and continue his surveillance.

He drove to the local Wal-Mart where he could eat and shop. He liked to browse big department stores looking for new gadgets. He knew they would have a McDonalds. He ordered a Quarter Pounder with Cheese and had them super-size it, then told them he'd be back to pick it up in a few minutes and took off for electronics.

A young woman—brunette with short curly hair—was pushing a cart with a toddler, a cherubic girl with big blue eyes, reddish blonde curls, and chubby legs dangling out through the knee holes of the shopping cart, feet encased in white sandals and frilly ankle socks. The child noticed Jim half an aisle back, staring at her. Her eyes clouded with confusion, then worry. Her face crumpled and she started screaming at the top of her lungs. The mother turned, saw Jim, and felt fear grip her in the stomach as she dropped the curling iron she'd been examining and fled, pushing the shopping cart and murmuring to her child. She looked back as she turned the corner of the aisle and saw Jim standing in the same place, watching after them with a wolfish grin.

He went over and picked up the curling iron the woman had dropped, stood holding it for a moment, thinking. He put it in his shopping basket, went through checkout and paid, then picked up his food and left. It was almost noon. He drove back to the school, parked down the street in a space where he could see the parking lot clearly but far enough away to avoid notice. Other cars were beginning to arrive—mostly nannies there to pick up the kids.

He spotted her exiting the back door and watched as she walked to her car—a Civic just like his. It was a sign that he was meant to have her. He snapped a picture of her license plate as she turned into traffic, then pulled out and followed. She drove to the same shopping center he'd gone to for lunch. He drove past, then made a U-turn and entered the shopping center's parking lot, keeping an eye on her car. After she parked and went in the store he also parked, as close to her vehicle as he could. The surveillance gave him a sense of ownership. He saw she had a child carrier in her back seat—this was good. He slapped a tracker under the rear end of her car then went back to his car and left.

13

Camille spent the day making the rounds with Davis's picture. There were hundreds of hotels, motels, bed and breakfasts, and rooming houses in New Orleans and the surrounding area. But she had to start somewhere. She decided to save the Quarter and the Central Business District for last. These would be expensive for a long-term stay. She started in the Faubourg Marigny. It was a historic neighborhood behind the Quarter, mostly one-story Victorians, but with a few big houses and mansions that had been converted to rooming houses and bed and breakfasts. She could eliminate these quickly. She showed his picture around to managers and front desk agents. Nobody remembered him but they kept her card and promised to call if they spotted him.

Next, she headed over to Tulane Avenue. Tulane could compete with any street in the world for being depressing and plug ugly. A bleak, shadeless wasteland of pawn shops, bail bonds offices, motels, strip malls and convenience stores, the worst part is the evil-looking stone and barbed-wire complex that occupies a few city blocks on Tulane and Broad—Orleans Parish Prison and Criminal Court. An inscription carved in stone above the Broad Street entrance to the courthouse reads, THIS IS A GOVERNMENT OF LAW NOT OF MEN. Camille always superimposed another inscription in her head: Abandon hope, all ye who enter here. Orleans Parish could make a decent person ashamed to be in law enforcement. She had to wonder, as she made her way down Tulane from one blighted poverty hole to another, if the prison complex had poisoned the surrounding area like a curse.

Out of all the hotels, motels, bed and breakfasts, and rooming houses she visited that day the only desk clerk who wasn't helpful worked at the seediest motel on Tulane, the Shady Grove. It was the next to last one on her list and this place made her want to have a shower after exiting the property. The desk clerk came out from a back room after she rang the buzzer five times, opened the sliding window to his dingy cubicle and said, "Yeah." He was fat and pale, with icy little blue eyes that peered out from his puffy face with suspicion and hatred. She noted with disgust that a booger hung out of one crusted nostril, and she suspected this guy didn't clean his nose on purpose because he liked being revolting. His thin, greasy brown hair was pulled back in a lank ponytail. He wore a purple T-shirt with black skulls, and rumpled shorts with a Hawaiian print of orange martini glasses and pink hibiscus. She could smell his B.O. a yard away.

Camille inadvertently stepped back from the window. "I'm a detective with the Metairie police and I'm looking for a suspect in a murder. I was hoping you could tell me if you've seen this person." She held up the print of Jim Davis.

"We don't give out information."

"This person may have been involved in the murders of a young mother and her child."

"You talking about that jig was killed in Mid City yesterday? Some of us think that was a community service. You're out of your jurisdiction. Get a warrant." He slammed the window shut and went waddling back to wherever he came out from. Camille couldn't think of what else to do and was glad to leave.

Some afternoons residents got a reprieve from the heat as the skies opened up and dumped rain on the steaming city. Just now the rain was coming down in buckets. Camille was sitting in her car outside the last motel on Tulane sipping a diet Coke and trying to put herself in Jim Davis's shoes. Where would he stay? Hotels and motels were essentially public places, but he liked to keep a low profile and blend in. Residents with means often left town for the summer, going across the lake to stay at their summer places and fishing camps, and a few of these people rented out their homes and condos while they were gone. Subletting a private residence would be ideal for somebody who wanted to stay below the radar. Where would somebody list for a sublet? Maybe Craigslist and the local papers. She needed to get the Craigslist back listings. And she needed the classifieds from the past six months, not just the Times-Picayune, because some people liked to list rentals in the Gambit, a local guide to arts and entertainment. She had friends on staff at both papers. She was about to call one of her friends when her cell rang. It was Mace.

"Mace, what's up?"

"We found a neighbor who saw somebody leaving Amanda's yesterday. It wasn't a positive ID, but she said it could have been the man in the picture. She said she noticed because Amanda didn't have many visitors and this guy was white, older, and didn't look like somebody she would know. The neighbor's nearsighted and lives down the block and across the street so she wasn't sure. She was outside potting plants when she saw him leave, around three. He had a backpack and he was walking. She saw him go up the block and turn the corner. I'm thinking you're right—it's the son. You got anything yet?"

"I've covered the Marigny and Tulane Avenue, but I'm thinking he might be subletting. I'm gonna contact the Picayune and Gambit to get the listings for the past six months. Can you get the ones on Craigslist? I don't even know who to contact about those," Camille said.

"Yeah, I can get somebody to check Craigslist, but I think we need another plan. Something to draw this guy out. You wanna meet for a drink in a couple of hours? We could get dinner while we're at it."

"Sure, what place do you have in mind?"

"Let's go to Mandina's. I'll treat."

"Mandina's sounds great. I haven't eaten there in years. But it's my turn to buy, okay? What about eight?"

"You got it. I'll see you at eight. Call me if you get anything."

"Okay." Camille was happy as she hung up the phone. She liked this guy. But though the feeling was good, it made her nervous. She reminded herself that this was business, but she still felt excited to be meeting Mace for dinner; he was the most interesting man she'd been around for a while. She checked her watch—four-thirty. She wanted to meet with Tyler from the Picayune in person. She had a plan. If she was going to contact both papers she needed to hustle.

14

Sylvie felt out of her element in Andy Sharp's law office. It was the richest place she'd ever been in—the view, the furnishings, the décor, everything was a statement about money and power. But one thing about money—it could provide security, like a fortress, and Sylvie had been scared since finding Bernice dead yesterday morning. Then today—finding out about Amanda and her son—Sylvie could not remember ever feeling this kind of dread, like something very bad was going to keep happening—except for on that night, eighteen years ago, when her mother did not come back from work.

They were seated in big, deep red chairs, with bottles of ice water on a glass-covered dark wood table, and Andy set out a cut crystal ashtray for Sylvie to smoke. Sylvie was trying to focus on what Andy was saying but she was overwhelmed and her mind kept wandering. She wasn't sure she could live with this kind of opulence and hoped she wouldn't be expected to.

"Are you okay?" Andy asked.

"Well, this is like another world. I'm not sure I can fit in here. I've always been poor, you know?"

Andy laughed. "I guess this office is a bit intimidating. We have some very rich clients, and they expect our law firm to play a role." Andy thought for a moment, then added, "It's kind of like stripping—it's an act. You don't go around town dressed like a tart, right? Well, when I get off work, I go home to a regular house in a middle-class neighborhood. I wear mostly jeans when I'm not working. I shop at the thrift store and Target like everybody else."

"I know some strippers who act like they're on the job twenty-four seven," Sylvie said.

"Yes, we have a few attorneys like that, too. The senior partners, for instance. They're as rich as some of our clients. We let them do most of the schmoozing. I'm just a junior partner and I have kids to support and put through college. I want them to have a normal life."

"I guess that's what I hoped I wouldn't have to do, I mean by accepting this trust to help kids. I just want to have a some-what normal life, and for the kids to have a normal life too, whatever that is. I mean, middle class."

"I think you'll do great. My motto is happy medium. We want to help kids out of poverty and danger, give them good opportunities, but without giving them aspirations that are hard for most people to fulfill. I'd have to question your judg-ment if you wanted to help the kids in luxurious surround-ings. We have enough materialistic assholes around, and most of them aren't very happy."

"Well, I don't expect to live a normal life, because the chance to help kids is more than I ever dreamed of. But I want to keep it as close to normal as possible, for the kids' sake and mine. Now, can you explain what a trust is to me?"

"A trust is like a legal container, only everything is on paper. It holds property. In this case, the money Bernice Davis put into it. The ownership of the property is split between a trustee and a beneficiary. Put simply, Bernice Davis named me as the trustee, or legal owner of the assets she put into the trust. But you are the beneficiary, meaning that you are the person who benefits from the use of the assets. Only in this trust she set up, you are to receive sixty-thousand dollars a year, with periodic raises at my discretion, as a salary, along with health insurance. The trust is also paying for your education, as much as you want, wherever you want. She also stipulated you'd pick out a practical car to drive and the trust would pay for your vehicle. As for the rest of the money, you are to use it to help children in danger and with me having the final approval of what you want to do, and who it will benefit. It's a job, a huge responsibility, and it will be an on-going one. So, if you don't want the job, Bernice wanted you to have a good education anyway, while I am to either find kids to help, or find charities that benefit needy children to donate the money to. Bernice didn't want the money spread so thin that lots of kids would get a little help. She wanted the children who get help to get all the help they need. She wanted somebody to work with individual kids, one on one."

"I totally want to do this," Sylvie said. "And I know a family in trouble right now. Where's the papers? I'm ready to sign!"

"Well, you know I have final approval of who you want to help, what you can use the money to do for them, and this is to protect you, too. Normally you don't have to sign anything with a trust, but I've prepared a contract stating that you understand our relationship, that we're supposed to work as a team, with you doing most of the work, but with me protecting you and the money. Just take a moment to read it and I'll answer any questions you have."

Sylvie took the contract and as she started reading, she

saw the numbers—$72,000,000.00, only it wasn't numbers any more, it was blood. A picture rose in her mind of sweatshops, ragged children worked to exhaustion, even to death, a misery so profound it was hellish. She saw Bernice lying dead in the bathtub. Giving this blood money back—using it to help children who were defenseless, it was like defying the evil power that ruled the world. She knew there would be consequences. No matter what circumstances she had found herself in over the years and no matter how scared she was, Sylvie never prayed. She had not asked God for anything since the night when her mother left for work and never came home. Sylvie closed her eyes and said a silent prayer for protection, then put the pen to the document and signed her name.

Andy went to the bar and took a bottle of champagne from the fridge. "Are you okay?" she asked.

"I guess so. I just think that this isn't the way the world works. Using an entire fortune to help people is like spitting in the face of the devil. You know the old saying, no good deed goes unpunished. I don't know—I just feel like this isn't going to be easy."

"Well, the more I get to know you the better I understand why Bernice chose you for this job." Andy handed her a glass of Taittinger, took her own and raised it in a toast. "Here's to spitting in the face of the devil!"

Sylvie touched her flute to Andy's, then drank.

After they toasted, Andy told Sylvie that Bernice's remains had been released by the medical examiner, and she was scheduled for cremation on the following day. There would be a memorial service a week from Sunday, to give family members time to attend.

"I thought Bernice was estranged from her family," Sylvie said.

"Well, her father did leave her the money. And I think they're curious about you. Anyway, it was her choice to stay away, not theirs. Besides, her son might show up. I mean, if he doesn't know he's a suspect."

"Great." Sylvie said. "Can I have another glass of that champagne? I think I need a sedative."

Andy grabbed the bottle and topped off her glass. "Now we have to talk about keeping you safe. You know Jim Davis is the primary suspect. Unless we find out otherwise, we have to assume he's out there. Bernice thought he was dangerous enough to hide from him for almost a decade. It's safe to assume he's gunning for you now. He may have me in his sights too, so I've had to hire somebody to watch my kids. Did you hand in your notice at work?"

"I offered to give two weeks' notice, but Bill told me that he can have his niece cover my hours 'til they find somebody. I think he wants to avoid more trouble at the motel. I just don't know how long I can do this. What if they never find this freak?"

"Money can buy a lot of safety, and we have plenty of that. You know my family isn't safe either. I have two teenagers who aren't very happy right now about having to stay home with a bodyguard." Andy thought about her kids, Corey and Brianna, and shuddered. She had spent so much of her life trying to create safety for her kids—she thought that making a lot of money would help protect them. The irony of the current danger being a result of her first pro bono case did not escape her.

"Okay, let's go to your place and meet Trey. If there's anything you need from the store we'll have to stop on the way there. I don't want you going out just yet."

"I feel like I'm in jail. How long is this going to last?"

"Let's give the police a chance to find him. If they can't do it, we'll come up with a plan B, okay?"

"I guess we don't have much choice right now."

15

Camille called Fran at the Gambit. She was an old friend from Loyola and it wasn't the first time their connection had come in handy. It was a long shot, but chances were that Jim Davis had sublet a place for a few months. It would be cheaper, and low profile. If he had sublet, he probably felt clever, which was good. Fran agreed to email her a copy of all the rental ads for the past six months. She said she'd have it to her by morning.

The Picayune would require a personal meet with Tyler, another old buddy who had helped her out in various ways, usually in exchange for an inside story. Tyler wanted to meet at an artsy uptown coffee house called Z'otz. He settled for Denny's out in Metairie. The entire state of Louisiana had three Denny's; Camille felt sure they wouldn't see anybody who recognized either of them at this restaurant.

Tyler was seated in a vinyl booth when Camille arrived at 5:30. He stood up to greet her and she smiled inside at the incongruous figure he cut, with his black framed glasses askew on his nose, long straggly blonde hair, goatee, and six foot-three frame on which a flowered tropical shirt and khaki pants hung in a way that suggested he'd pulled them out of his laundry hamper yesterday morning and slept in them. She told him to zip up his fly, for starters.

"What's the scoop?" he asked, zipping up his fly then squeezing back into the orange booth and almost knocking over his glass of ice tea.

Camille had long suspected that a big reason Tyler was so good at getting people to open up and talk was that his scruffy appearance and cheerful demeanor threw them off guard. She wondered if the disarming persona was calculated. Tyler was smart. He had a formidable talent for sniffing out the whole story, not just the version people wanted to appear in print. He was relentless in his quest for the facts and she wanted to keep him as an ally, not an enemy.

"I need you to do me a favor, maybe two. First, I'm trying to track down a man who might have sublet an apartment or house for the summer. He's a suspect in a couple of murders, and may have targeted a young woman as his next victim. It's complicated, but you can't print anything about the murders yet because we don't want to scare him into leaving town. I promise you'll be the first to know when things go down."

"Sounds interesting. What do you need me to do?" Tyler's blue eyes were gleaming.

A young waitress who looked overworked approached with menus, and Camille ordered a glass of ice tea and waited for her to leave. "I need you to pull all the ads for sublets for the past six months. We know who he is, but he's going under fake ID. We're using his picture to try to find out where he's staying."

"Is this about the mother and kid who were murdered in Mid City yesterday?"

"It is, and we think he may have targeted somebody else. Listen, it's complicated but I'll give you the whole story as soon as I can."

"So, he killed somebody else in Metairie or you wouldn't be involved," Tyler said, with his relentless instinct for sniffing out the facts.

Camille told him about Bernice, the money, and Sylvie Compton.

"Shit. This is great!" Tyler said, meaning that it would make interesting copy. "But you didn't call me out here to get the classified records. What else do you need?"

"Well, I have a plan to draw the killer out. I have to get Sylvie Compton to go along with it. We think he's after her, and calling him out will be better than waiting around while he plans an attack. But of course, it could be dangerous. What I need you to do, if I get her to agree to the plan, is to run a feature story on her, where she lives, and the trust. It's a great human-interest story but I need you to write it in a way that will provoke the son to attack. I also need you to not write anything yet about the murders being connected and play Bernice Davis's death off as a heart attack. Don't mention that she had any children. Just write the article as if the son doesn't exist. These psychos are megalomaniacs—that's part of the profile. So, ignoring him and giving attention to this young woman who controls his mother's money could flush him out from wherever he's hiding."

"I think it's a good plan. I'm in."

"Thanks. You'll get the entire story and the interviews once we have him."

"Same deal as always. I've gotten some great stories from helping you out, but this one's going to be the best. And of course, I want to see whoever killed Amanda and Adrian Butler caught."

"I think he's a serial. From the way the crimes went down

he's killed before, maybe a lot. Listen, I'll tell you the whole story as soon as I can. I have to run this past a couple of people, then I'll give you a call and we'll set up an interview with Sylvie Compton, okay?"

"Sounds good. Okay, I'm out of here." Tyler finished his glass of tea, and stood up to leave.

"I'll pay the check," Camille said as he reached for his wallet. "Thanks for coming. You sure you don't want something to eat?"

"Oh, well, it's tempting but I had a late lunch. And I've got a dinner date."

16

When they pulled up in front of Sylvie's building, Andy pointed out a young man standing in front of the souvenir shop downstairs. He was short—around five-six, dark-skinned, and handsome. His hair was pulled back into a ponytail that looked like a pom-pom at the nape of his neck. He was dressed like a street artist or tarot reader, in loose white harem pants and an embroidered kurti. He did not glance their way. His hooded eyes gazed across the street with a dreamy look as if he were meditating. "That's Trey," Andy said. "Ignore him. Just go up, and he'll be at your place in a few minutes. I'm going back to the office to park the car and take care of a few things. I'll be back in a cab shortly. I can bring up some of this stuff, if you like."

"Thanks, Andy. I'll bring up the drinks. I want to offer Trey something."

"Well, he doesn't drink alcohol on the job. He'll probably accept some water or a bottle of tea."

"Okay, see you soon." Sylvie got out of the car, grabbed a couple of bags from the back seat, and went in the gate. As she ascended the stairs she thought about Trey—he didn't look like a bodyguard, which was a huge relief. He was actually kind of cute and he didn't look like anybody's idea of a tough guy. As Sylvie unlocked the door, she realized she was glad he'd be coming up—she didn't feel safe in her apartment any more. Her first impulse was to check every hiding place possible. As she pulled back the shower curtain she felt like a kid again, looking in the closet and under the bed for monsters. She had since learned that the only monsters out there were people.

She began stocking the fridge with water, beer, and bottled tea, listening for Trey's knock. What she heard first was annoying. The singing street hustler downstairs had taken up his post again.

"Swing low, sweet chariot, coming for to carry me home, swi-ing low, sweet chariot, coming for to carry me home. I looked over Jordan and what did I see, coming for to carry me home? A ba-and of angels comin' after me, coming for to carry me home. Swing low, sweet chariot..."

Sylvie heard somebody had poured a bucket of piss on the guy from a balcony on Decatur, and it worked. He moved to this block of St. Peter, where he would sing the same song over and over again all night and into the morning hours. Living in the French Quarter had its drawbacks. She wondered if she could get Trey to persuade him to station himself somewhere else. At least until she could find another place to live.

There was a knock on the door and Sylvie asked who is it.

"Trey."

Trey didn't look dreamy like he did down on the street. His eyes shone with intelligence, and there was an edge to him, an alert and thoughtful quality as he stood looking at her in the doorway and, she suspected, sizing her up.

"Hi, I'm Sylvie, come in." Sylvie stepped back from the

door and allowed him to enter. "Can I get you something cold? Maybe a water? Or I have iced tea."

"Water would be good. Thanks."

Sylvie got him a bottle of water and didn't know what to say so she began to show him the apartment. He paid special attention to the bathroom window. He checked the lock, opened it up and looked up and then down at the courtyard. "This is a weak point," he said.

"But it's four stories up. It's too small for somebody to get in."

"Oh, believe me, they have kids and addicts can get in here. They go over the roofs. A lot of people think like you do, so if they live on the top floor, they think it's okay to leave the window unlocked. Some of these kids are like monkeys. That's how they make their money, getting in and out. You need to keep this window locked, okay?"

"Yeah, okay. But I'm going to be moving soon. I don't feel safe here anymore."

"There's no place safe. Your safety is in knowing what people do, and staying on guard. I know you got some street smarts. Andy told me you were in homes, and a stripper. Just use your brains. And don't go thinking you safe just because you have money. That only makes you a bigger target. Another thing." Trey paused and looked away as he unscrewed the bottle and took a long drink. "You do the same thing the same way every day, and you're making it real easy for somebody to get to you. You need to bust up your routine, take different routes, go different times. If there's some joker out there trying to get you, you need to be a moving target. I need to know when you leave, where you at, and when you're coming back. I'm going do my best to protect you, but we have to work like a team. Don't look like you know me on the street, neither. If I'm there, pretend like you don't see me. The way I see it, we draw this dude out quick, we can eliminate him. Then all you got to worry about are the rest of the freaks out there, and chances are they don't even know you're alive."

Trey set his water on the table, went in the bedroom, and lifted up the sheet over the window. "I need to go check this out," he said. He spent a moment checking the window lock and, satisfied, opened the window and crawled out to the roof. Sylvie crawled out behind him.

He pointed to the square opening in the roof where the fire escape stairs went down to the third floor. "I'm keeping the window to my balcony unlocked. If you hear somebody try to get in, just go out the window and come downstairs. Don't stick around to find out who it is. Okay?"

"Oh, I'm gonna run like hell, don't you worry about that. I'm not a tough guy."

He sized her up with those big, dark eyes, and his smile was back. "You're plenty tough. You're smart too. Just remember, stay smart and stay alive. This is the jungle, and there's a big cat out there trying to sniff you out, track you down. He's a killer with a taste for blood. We just got to keep you safe 'til we put him down. Remember one thing—you got an enemy, the worst mistake you can make is to underestimate him."

They could hear the singing droning continuously from the street. "I'm sometimes up and sometimes down, comin' for to carry me home. But still my soul feels heaven bound…"

"That street singer is driving me crazy."

"The dude's got some pipes on him," Trey said. "He's four

stories down and he sounds like he's in the next room. How long's he been out there?"

"Since last summer. All night, every night. Sometimes he starts early on the weekends. Singing the same song over and over again. I've asked him to go someplace else or sing something else, at least some of the time. But he says he makes good money here and that this song is the only one they want to hear. He has a license to perform on the street and nobody can do anything about it. He was on Decatur before he came here, in front of the Rebel Arms. Then somebody poured a jug of piss on him from their balcony, at least that's what I heard. Now we have him. Can you maybe talk him into going somewhere else?"

"I'm thinking. If he's out there all the time, I'm going to offer him some money to watch the street for us. I can't see shit from up here—it's too far up. And if I'm down there on the street keeping an eye on things, you're up here alone, and St. Peter ain't the only route to your place. Like I said, they go over the rooftops here in the Quarter. Buildings are close together, makes it easy to do that."

"But he's driving me crazy. I'd almost rather take my chances with a psycho than listen to him sing another night."

"You don't mean that. Listen, I don't know how much you know about this dude supposed to be after you." Trey turned toward her and looked at her dead on, then his eyes dulled for a moment as if he wasn't seeing her at all. "This dude likes to torture people. He likes to burn little kids. You better take this serious, because once he have you tied up, you going to wish you were dead, and he's gonna want to keep you alive and play with you for a long time. He'll make you wish you never were born."

"Okay, I guess I can just go back to sleeping with earplugs on."

"No, you can't do that. No earplugs. You need to hear what's going on. You need to hear if somebody's trying to get in. Listen, I'm here to protect you but like I said, I can't do anything without your help, and I'm not going to stick around and watch you get yourself killed. I got plenty of ways to make money besides trying to do a job that can't be done."

"How long do you think this has to go on? Do I have to live like this forever?"

"I hope not. This thing just got started. We need to smoke this dude out. We don't know where he's at, but he knows where you at, most likely. Our best chance is to get him to show up around here, without letting him know we're waiting for him. I grew up in the Iberville projects. It's like war. I have some experience with how these psychos think. They think they're smarter than everybody. And the smarter they feel, the easier they fall."

Sylvie's cell rang. She pulled it out of her pocket and answered. It was Andy. "I'm back. Buzz me up, okay?"

"Sure, just give me a minute. We're on the roof."

17

Lionel took a break from singing and surveyed the other people on the street. He stood halfway between the Square and Royal, his usual post and now the place he was paid to be. The narrow street was lined with Creole townhouses, antique brick and stucco. Many of them had souvenir shops on the ground floor. The sidewalk was shaded by balconies, supported by spindly iron colonnades that gave the appearance of being flimsy, though in reality this neighborhood had survived the worst of hurricanes.

There weren't many tourists out today, but the ones that were on the street were tipping. Lionel emptied the tip bucket for the second time in two hours. It was all bills, no change. He counted thirteen dollars this time, not bad for an hour in the summer heat. Somebody had thrown a fiver in the bucket, which was sweet. There'd be more people and more money once the sun went down. He needed to make enough money to chuck the phone and blow town for a while, before this psycho went off on him. Maybe a grand would do it. He was thinking of going out to California to work the beach for the rest of the summer. He'd never been to Cali, but he'd heard that Venice Beach was a good gig. It wouldn't be as much money as New Orleans—too much competition and not enough drunks. But he could survive for a couple of months, anyway. He'd have to come up with a different act, maybe pose as an artist. Nobody went for this Aunt Jemima shit anywhere but here. Maybe he could get some work as a movie extra, something.

He'd called the creep at 5:30, when he saw that white woman go up to her place. He reported that she got out of a silver Prius, went upstairs alone, and did not come back down. He didn't tell him that the woman who drove the Prius came back later in a taxicab and went up there too. Lionel would not volunteer extra information. He could always say he didn't know who the bitch had at her place. He had to get out of this. The last thing he needed was for the dude to get to the woman before he was gone. Because then, he knew, he'd be next on the list.

He removed a blue paisley bandana from his back pocket and wiped the sweat off his face as he looked up and down the street. The dude said he'd be around, checking up on him to make sure he's doing his job, and he was sneaky. A group of tourists were walking his way. He stuffed the sweat rag back in his pocket and started singing.

18

Though she always took cool showers in the summer, Camille wanted a hot shower and plenty of soap. She encountered all kinds of people in her work as a homicide detective, but her brief conversation with the desk agent at the Shady Grove left her feeling like she'd been touched by an unclean hand. Still, though he'd been revolting, this wasn't the type of person Camille feared. Truly scary people blended in, looked as normal as anybody else, were often charming and popular. They camouflaged their intentions, motivations, and feelings so that what you got was an act, well-practiced—an imitation of human kindness. They had no conscience; their boundaries were set by what they calculated they could get away with.

She took Metairie Road out to her place. Traffic was light for a Friday evening. She switched the radio on to WWOZ, where Art Blakey and the Jazz Messengers played "A Night in Tunisia," followed by John Coltrane's "Blue Train." By the time the DJ was back on, she was turning down her street. She lived in a moneyed section of Old Metairie; in a back house she rented from a woman who had moved with her family from New Orleans to Metairie to escape integration in the Seventies. The front house was a big two-story brick structure, expensive but with none of the charm of the mansions that studded the city of New Orleans like jewels—it was too new. But it was old enough that its yard was well shaded by large oak, maple, and magnolia trees, with a crape myrtle in back by the cottage Camille rented for a song. Ashley Ledet, the elderly woman who remained of the original family, liked having a cop living on the property. Camille would stop by the big house occasionally and check to see how she was doing, and in turn Miss Ashley would sometimes send her maid Faith back with fresh flowers, or a container of gumbo or beans and rice. Though Camille liked Miss Ashley okay—the rent was too cheap not to like her—she felt more comfortable with Faith. Both Camille and Faith were members of the group that Miss Ashley regarded as "the help," though Camille got the uncomfortable feeling that she was slightly higher up in Miss Ashley's ranking of social caste.

Camille was totally amped up. She always got excited when she had a plan to catch a killer, if it was a good one. In most cases, murders were crimes of passion and were committed by somebody who knew the victim. They usually took place on the spur of the moment and were not premeditated. Most people who killed felt remorse over what they'd done to another human being, either in a fit of rage or after having too much to drink, or both. Maybe they were sorry about getting caught, too, but they did have a conscience. What Camille believed to be true about most human beings, that people are all guilty of committing many acts for which they don't stop to measure the consequences, tempered her anger towards the killers she apprehended. Camille's idea of justice was a state of being in the afterlife where everybody would have to know the full consequences of their actions—

how what they did out of anger, greed, jealousy, fear, or some other poisonous motivation affected other people, not at a superficial level, but totally.

But there was a different kind of killer than the spur-of-the-moment passion slayer. These were killers who meticulously planned their crimes, then carried them out with full knowledge of what they were doing. Camille believed these were the true sociopaths. And of this group, the most dangerous kind were those who didn't kill for any self-serving motive such as money or personal gain—it was the act of killing itself that was the reward. They sought out victims they didn't even know, and had nothing to gain from killing beyond sadistic pleasure and the feeling of power and control they derived from taking another's life without mercy, usually after prolonged torture. She had worked only one case that involved multiple homicides, a gang-related series of killings that was about control of drug money and territory, and which the perpetrators rationalized as warfare and retribution, part of being in a gang. Though she'd read plenty about serial killer sadists, she'd never had the opportunity to track one down and bring him to justice. It wasn't that she was glad to have it now—she was horrified at the hard deaths Amanda and Adrian and Bernice had endured. But she had a new feeling, like a core of steel running through every fiber of her being, and she recognized this feeling as a need to go after and personally bring down a monster.

She took the hottest shower she'd had in months, then had trouble dressing. She wanted to look attractive, but also professional, because this was supposed to be a business dinner though it felt sort of like a date, and these feelings were both confusing and somewhat unwelcome. She finally settled on a beige silk blouse and loose-fitting black linen pants. She decided to skip the jacket and just bring a bag that was big enough to carry her gun, a Glock 17. As she placed the weapon in her purse, she thought that, even though she'd never killed anybody before, she could probably shoot and kill Jim Davis easier than she could squash an insect. And this gave her pause. The worst evil did to people was not infliction of pain and loss but the debasing, corrupting effects of hatred and fear. Camille had a deep reverence for life and her instinct was to be protective, but some beings were poison to everything they came in contact with, and their evil was beyond redemption.

19

Jim woke up from his nap. The amber light filtering through the wooden blinds told him it was late in the day. He had a long night planned. First, he would check on the woman he'd targeted today, start to know her routine. He needed to find out her husband's routine too, in order to plan the attack. He could drive by their place, tail the husband to work and put a tracker on his car. He needed to synchronize discovery of their bodies with his attack on the Sylvie whore. With local police diverted by the family crime scene, he would be free to deal with his real target. There was a lot to learn but he had time. He figured the whole operation would take two weeks, tops.

Tonight, he would eat at The Gumbo Shop, across the street from the Sylvie whore's place. He had a reservation for 8:30, window seat. He could check up on the tool while he was at it, make sure he was doing his job. Then, he was going hunting; he wanted to use his new curling iron. He had an arrangement with the owner of the Shady Grove, so that's where he'd take her. After, he'd just roll her up in the tarp and haul her out to the swamp. The alligators would do the rest. Streetwalkers disappeared all the time. He'd been doing them for years.

20

Little Z lit up a joint and surveyed the action down on the street. He needed to get a car, take it to the chop shop run by his homie. At least he wanted to be in the gang. He just had to prove he had the guts. And he had a plan. When he'd rented this place by the corner of Henriette DeLille and Kerlerec one of the main features was that it was a ho-stroll, with a steady stream of johns rolling by, mostly white dudes driving new cars. It was like hitting on a school of fish. But the action was low-key, not too many girls or cars at once. He was going to put his girl Junie down there as bait. Though Junie was nineteen she looked no older than thirteen. Any perv who was looking to pick her up would deserve exactly what he got, and most of these guys weren't too eager to go to the cops, cause what they doing out there in the first place? He was standing on the rooftop deck of his place, looking down. The street was deceptively quiet and devoid of traffic or people. But he'd been casing the action for days, and when he saw a fancy car drive by here in the hood, he pretty much knew what the driver was looking for. A lot of the girls down there came from the Walk-In Center over on North Rampart. They were runaways, scraggly, and many of them were used up with heroin or meth. Put Junie down there and see what he could reel in. Course nothing was as easy as it seemed. He needed a late model Acura or Civic, and most of these dudes 'round here drove big-assed SUVs—totally useless.

He went back inside to see how Junie was doing. She was putting on her makeup in the small bathroom, bouncing her fine little ass to Ice Cube and Dr. Dre. "Go easy on the paint, babe," he directed, handing her the blunt. "You got to look like a schoolgirl. Put on that clear gloss, no mascara."

"I know what the fuck I'm doing," she sassed him, her black eyes snapping. "I used to get come-ons from these pervs every day when I went to McDonogh." She was referring to the high school she'd attended over on Esplanade. Wearing an abbreviated version of her old school uniform, white blouse unbuttoned and tied under her perky breasts, the flawless honeyed skin of her slender midriff exposed, plaid skirt barely covering her bubble butt, glossy black hair done in two school girl braids, she was a pedophile's fantasy. Dr. Dre's rap fit her mood perfectly because she hated these white motherfuckers that disrespected her like she's a piece of meat, and she wanted Z to drag one out of his car and let her beat him to death with one of the shiny black five-inch spikes she had on.

She closed her eyes as she took a hit off the blunt, lost in her own fantasy. She handed back the joint, took a pot of clear gloss and fixed her lips, pursing them and then sticking out her tongue at her image in the mirror.

"Here's the plan," Z said, pausing to take a hit off the joint. "We're looking for one kind of car, a late model Civic or an Acura. You and me gon' wait for the right car to come by, then you step out and do your thing. When the motherfucker opens his door to let you in, he'll be looking at you, and I come up to his window and stick a gun upside his head.

You need to be standing on the side where his window at, and try to get the motherfucker to roll the bitch down, you got it? That way I get the gun right upside his head, and he can't just drive away. He gon' roll down his window, ask you if you need a ride or whatever these motherfucking perverts say, and you go round the front to get in the car, and make sure he be looking at you, not at the open window; I need to surprise his ass. That way we got the motherfucker cold."

"Z, I wanna beat his ass. Am I gon' get to slap him around? I hate these funky-assed perverts."

"Man, we got to be professional. There ain't no room for personal feelings in a job like this. Not good, not bad. We got to keep it simple and do what the situation say we got to do. If the motherfucker don't do what I say, I make him want to do what I say so bad he be begging for a chance to do it. We got to get the car, get his wallet, and get the fuck out of there. You got to do what I tell you to do. You got to do what I say and not one motherfucking thing I don't say. You got that? 'Cause trust and believe, if this gets blown because you screwed up, we're both going down. I gotta answer to my homies on this job, big time."

"What homies? You ain't in no gang. You a homie wanna-be."

"Yeah, but they promised me they'd think about lettin' me in if I show 'em I got some heart and some smarts. I told 'em I'd get a car and now I gotta keep my word. Besides, this is a money job. They get the car; I get the cash."

"Man, I don't know why I'm helping you out with this. Why don't you just get one of your homies to put on a motherfucking dress, or get one a they hoes to go down there. Huh?"

"Oh, man, ain't nobody gon' stop for one of those

skanky-assed bitches. You the queen bee. Everybody gon' be buzzin' around you. Sides that, you're my partner. Tell you what. You want to beat up one of those freaks, we'll get you a freak and you can stomp his motherfucking ass all you want. You can beat the motherfucker to death if you want. But that's for fun, okay? This is business, and we got to handle our business first."

"Okay, babe, we do it your way tonight. But I'm gonna have my night, too. You got to promise me that."

"You got it, princess."

21

Andy stayed long enough to see that Trey and Sylvie would be okay for the night, left Sylvie with enough cash to order food delivered and said she'd be back in the morning. She told Sylvie it would be fine helping Brittney and the kids, but not just yet. She gave them a copy of the old picture of Jim Davis and told Sylvie that a neighbor had spotted somebody who looked like him leaving Amanda Butler's house the day of the killings. And she asked Sylvie to consider just quitting the motel job, since Bill said it was okay.

When Andy left, Sylvie called and ordered pizza, and she and Trey watched the news broadcast on her computer. There wasn't much about Adrian and Amanda, just a picture of the crime scene and the report that police were still investigating. A gang-related shooting in Algiers was the big story today.

After they ate, Trey went downstairs to talk to the street singer. He put a twenty in the bucket to get his attention and told him there was more where that came from.

"What you need?" Lionel asked.

"I need you to watch the street. I mean, you're out here all night, and I need somebody to keep an eye on things down here for me. You got a phone?"

"Listen, I can't talk here." Lionel glanced up and down the

street then looked back at Trey. "Meet me in the men's room round the corner at La Marquise. I'm going there and get a cold drink."

"I'll be there in twenty minutes," Trey said. "I'll knock on the door twice, fast."

Lionel had trouble keeping his face blank when Trey showed him the picture—it was the white dude, only younger. He gave him a number and told him to call right away if he saw him hanging around.

"What's he done?" Lionel asked.

"He's dangerous. We think he's after somebody."

Lionel did not tell Trey that this same person hired him to keep tabs on the white woman. He had been on the street for ten years—ever since he'd got off parole, and he'd never had this kind of extra work, keeping an eye on things. He was going to stay neutral, play both sides against the middle and get the hell out of this. His cell rang. It was the psycho checking up on him, like he could see every move he made. He told Trey he had to talk in private, and waited for him to leave. The psycho asked what he was doing leaving his post. He said he had to use the bathroom and get a cold drink. He left the bathroom, looked around the front of the pastry shop and out back in the courtyard, wondering where the dude was at. The shop was almost empty and getting ready to close. Lionel knew he had to make up his mind quick—either tell Trey what was going down or leave town. He just needed a couple more days to get the money together. The brother gave him a hundred, and told him there was a hundred a night in it. So, he was up to four hundred a night. This was besides the tourist money, which came to around seventy or eighty on the weekends. It was maintenance money, enough to buy himself a little something for his head, maybe get a room once in a while. After a couple of days, the extra would be enough to bounce. He reached in his back pocket for the flask—the vodka was almost gone. He'd have to go to Rouse's for another half-pint if he was going to be out here all night. Shit man, make it a pint. This shit was getting creepy.

22

It was twilight when Camille arrived at Mandina's. The restaurant was located in Mid City—the same neighborhood where Amanda Butler had lived. It had evolved from a neighborhood grocery—one of the old-fashioned businesses where the family lived upstairs. Built at the turn of the twentieth century, the two-story clapboard structure was painted pink with red and yellow neon signs lighting up the large ground-floor windows.

Camille saw Mace standing at the bar as soon as she walked in. He was still wearing the clothes he'd had on that morning, and she supposed he'd been working nonstop on the case. He was drinking an Abita, so he must be off duty more or less, though Camille suspected he was never completely off duty with a case like this open. He waved her over as soon as she walked in, but he looked tired and his smile looked forced.

"Hey, how you doing?" he said. "You look great."

"Thanks." She stood next to him at the historic mahogany bar and told the bartender, a thin middle-aged guy with a deadpan look, to bring her a double scotch with a water back. "Anything new on the case?" she asked, turning to Mace.

"We've been working the neighborhood, seeing if we can come up with any more witnesses. Any neighbors who heard anything, any suspicious activity lately, people hanging around who don't belong. So far nobody saw anything besides the woman down the block. Ms. Savio. What about you?"

"Well." The bartender set Camille's drinks on the bar and Mace told him they wanted a table. After he walked away Camille resumed speaking, in a low tone that she hoped wouldn't be overheard in the crowded restaurant. "I have an idea I wanted to run by you. Looking for someone from out of town with fake ID, it could be impossible to find this guy, especially before he hurts somebody else. I spent the day just covering the Marigny and Tulane. There's hundreds of places he could be staying; he could be across the river or over on the North Shore. If he's subletting, we might get lucky. But if we can't find him within the next couple of days, I have a plan to draw him out. We'd have to use Sylvie Compton as bait."

"Yeah, I thought of that too," Mace said. "But it's asking a lot. The guy's a maniac. I'm not sure I want to be responsible for that."

"Okay, but he's going after her anyway, right? I mean, I'd be willing to bet that he isn't going to let it slide that she has control of the money. Has somebody checked out Bernice Davis's computer yet? If he went into it, he probably knows who she is, where she lives, and he can track her. So, we can either draw him out, or do nothing and let him pick when he wants to attack. And which one do you think will give us a better chance of protecting her? Not to mention the other victims he'll probably go after, maybe in the meantime. We're looking at a serial here, one who's killed before. These guys escalate when something major happens. It's called a trigger. But you know all this, right?"

"Yeah, you have a point," Mace said. "So, what's your plan?"

"Are we going to get a table?" Camille asked, looking around the crowded room. This was the first time she'd been in the restaurant since Katrina had shut it down. It looked like a newer version of the same place—straight out of the 1930s, down to the clock on the wall, the chalkboard for posting daily specials, the red-carpet runner that led from the entrance past the bar to the dining room. She saw a middle-aged waiter approach, smiling. He wore shirtsleeves and black tuxedo pants.

"Here's our waiter," Mace said. "Let's eat, then we can go somewhere else and talk strategy."

"Sounds good." They followed the waiter to a table by the corner window, the one that advertised "AIR CONDI-TIONED" in neon.

They ordered shrimp remoulade for an appetizer, and both decided on the catfish almondine. After the waiter left, Mace drew a corner of the café curtain aside and looked out into the night at the traffic going past on Canal. "He's out there," he said, dropping the curtain and turning to face Camille. "I can feel it. While we're sitting here in a good restaurant, he's out there hunting. Nobody in this city is safe."

"That's what scares me," Camille said. "I really think drawing him out is our best hope, and the sooner the better."

"Yeah, I guess you're right. Okay, we'll eat and then we go talk. Whatever we do, we need to do something quick."

"That's what I'm thinking," Camille said. "Well, here comes our appetizer."

The waiter approached with a tray and set out shrimp remoulade, two small plates, cocktail forks, and lemon wedges. Mace asked him if they could put a rush on the rest of the food, and bring the check. He said no problem, and Mace thanked him and turned his attention back to Camille. "I want this to look like a date, okay?" His gaze wandered the crowded room. "He could be watching us. It would be typical."

Camille wanted to tell Mace that she'd done her research on serial killers and knew they sometimes tried to be close to the investigation because part of the thrill was in fooling the police, but since she had a mouthful of food, she heard him out.

"You probably know all this stuff," Mace continued. "I guess what I'm trying to say is we need to go somewhere private and talk this over, but I don't want you to think I'm putting a move on you."

Camille could feel her face flushing red. She wanted to tell him that it would be fine if he did, but knew that her respect for him would take a nosedive if he tried to at this point in their acquaintance. She swallowed her food and said, "Wherever you think." She kept her eyes steady on his as she speared another shrimp and popped it in her mouth.

"I live around the corner and I've got beer in the fridge. Faubourg okay?"

"Sure. I like Faubourg a lot. My parents won't buy any other beer."

For the first time that evening, the sparkle returned to Mace's eyes, and Camille decided that respect wasn't everything. She had to wonder who this man was, really. "So, tell me about yourself," she ventured. "Where did you grow up?"

"Right here in Mid City. My father worked at Dixie brewing. He was a manager. Of course, he retired after Katrina. He was okay with it for a while. Said he never had enough time for fishing, so he did a lot of that, bought a boat and everything. Then they had the oil spill. It took him a couple of years to get over it, but he found something else to do. He volunteers at Catholic Charities, helping people learn to read. I think he's happier now than he's ever been. He's a tough old guy. No matter what happens, he won't stay down for long."

"He sounds like a wonderful person."

"Yeah, I'm lucky," Mace said. "I got good folks. The best. The longer I work as a cop, the luckier I feel."

"I know what you mean," Camille said. "My folks are pretty good too. And I get that a lot of crimes start before the perp is out of diapers. It can go on for generations. What we cops do is damage control. By the time we deal with a situation it's too late. What your father is doing, helping people be smarter and have a better life, it's the most important work there is."

"Yeah, you right. That's how he sees it. I think that's why he's so happy. He married young, right out of high school. So, he had to take whatever job he could get. But I've never seen the old man like he is now. I'm beginning to understand that even when bad things happen, good can come of it. It helps me to keep doing what I do."

23

Mace lived around the corner from the restaurant on Cortez, in half a shotgun double. Camille noticed the place was clean but cluttered, like the occupant didn't spend a lot of time there, was a bit distracted or just busy, and probably used a cleaning service. She took a seat in a bentwood rocker in front of the old coal-burning fireplace. Mace excused himself and went to the back for beer, and Camille used the time to consider how to present her plan. She decided to tell him the plan and get his reaction before mentioning that she had already arranged things with a member of the local press. The NOPD had a volatile relationship with the *Times-Picayune*, mostly because New Orleans cops had been caught throughout the years in numerous activities that were either blatantly criminal or just shady. The entire police department was currently under investigation by the Feds, and this wasn't the first time. New Orleans cops had been caught slinging dope, ordering hits, looting and killing during Katrina, armed robbery with multiple homicides, murder, rape—just about any street crime or form of thuggery imaginable. Considering that the percentage of criminals that are caught is small compared to what's actually going on, the record was scary.

Mace came back in the room with a couple of Faubourg longnecks, handed one to Camille, threw a stack of papers on the floor, and sat on the sofa. "Excuse the mess," he said, taking a swig of beer. "So, what's your plan?"

Camille told him about her plan to provoke Jim Davis to attack with a news story about Sylvie Compton and the trust.

"You think the story would be enough to draw him out?" Mace asked. "He might catch on to what we're trying to do. It could drive him away."

"It could, but I don't think it will. I think he's losing control. He didn't get what he wanted from his mother and now the money's gone. With this kind of trigger, he'll need to kill again. If we can get him to go after Sylvie, we can see him coming and stop him. Whatever we do we need to do it fast, because he's probably hunting now, or he's killed already."

"Okay, but how can we guarantee her safety?"

"Can't you get backup for this project? I mean, from NOPD?"

"Are you kidding? Look, if somebody I loved was in danger, these guys are the last people I'd call. A lot of them hate my guts, and most of them are dirty. I mean, there's a couple of people I'd trust with my life, but for most of them, you have to be doing something wrong just to fit in with these guys."

"Well, are you? I mean, how do you function with them?" Camille asked.

"I know what most of 'em are up to. At least enough to nail their asses. And they understand that if they just let me do my job my way, I'll leave them alone. I mean, within reason. But I know they don't like me. There's a lot of hard feelings because I didn't call for backup with the Pearl River thing. They think I wanted all the glory. But shit, I couldn't risk losing my chance at catching the guy by letting those assholes in on it. He had a schoolgirl out there. Snatched her off the street over in the Ninth Ward."

Camille said, "I remember the details. I read about it. So, if you think this is a bad idea, then I guess I'll go back to trying to find out where he's staying."

"No, I really think it's a good idea. I'm just playing the devil's advocate." Mace drank the last of his beer and held it up. "You want another one?"

"Sure, I'll take one more." Camille drained hers and handed him the bottle. "Then I have to be going. I've got to get some rest. I was hoping to get an answer from you tonight."

Mace took the empty and left the room without saying anything. He went back to the kitchen, then came back a moment later with two cold ones.

"So, can you think of a strategy to protect Sylvie Compton? I mean if we use my plan." She accepted a beer and took a swig.

Mace pulled an ottoman up to the other side of the fireplace and sat. "I like your idea. My only problem is how're we gonna protect her after we stir up the hornet's nest? Let me sleep on it tonight. I can give you an answer tomorrow, before noon. There's a couple of officers I can ask to help out. We'll maybe have to pull extra duty on our off time. But I'd rather keep this between us, okay? Our department has more leaks than the levee after Katrina."

24

Jim Davis waited in the doorway of the Gumbo Shop, then stepped out onto the sidewalk in front of a group of tourists. He didn't want the street singer, who he thought of as a tool, to see him. He'd been sitting in front by a window, watching the tool and the whore's apartment building while he ate. Now he was going hunting to satisfy his other appetite. He turned the corner at Jackson Square and walked up Chartres towards the pay lot. When he approached the intersection at Iberville, a young woman stepped out of a doorway, dressed like a streetwalker in a low-cut black shiny dress and five-inch heels. Her hair was teased up into a wild dark tangle and she sported heavy makeup, her pink lips curled into a half smile. She was about to say something to him, but whatever she had in mind, when she looked in his eyes, she ducked back into the club. "Fucking creep," he heard her say under her breath.

He crossed the intersection and passed another strip joint on the last block before Canal, pausing to look in the open door. The jukebox was blasting Coldplay's "A Sky Full of Stars." A girl was on stage wearing thong panties and nothing else, moving around in awkward, stiff motions, one hand holding the pole. The red stage light made her pale skin glow pink. Her head was down, long blond hair hung in her face. When she looked up, unsmiling, he saw that she was very young. Her clumsy movements just added to the impression that she was fresh meat on the table, maybe a runaway with fake ID. The bar was packed with men, eyes sharp with hunger as they watched her performance. After a moment, a tall, oily man wearing a black leather vest stepped into the doorway, blocking the view. "You like what you see?" he said with a conspiratorial gleam in his eye. "One drink minimum gets you in the club. You can spend time with the lady of your choice. There's a back room for private shows, if you know what I mean." This last part was said very low, almost in a whisper and Jim knew the huckster was trying to convey an impression that he could have whatever he wanted if the price was right. Jim walked on—they weren't going to like the kind of show he wanted to see.

He picked up his car from a pay lot and headed down Canal towards Rampart. He'd checked out a new website: wildsidehunt.com. For a small price you could type in the name of your city and a link to a chat room came up where you could talk to people who had been in the town you were in and knew where the action was. There was a neighborhood in back of the French Quarter which was supposed to be a good place to pick up young girls, off the beaten path and very quiet. It was reputed to be a good place to find runaways, since it was near the Stop-In Center for street kids and had a few abandoned houses nearby where squatters holed up.

He turned left on Esplanade and hung a quick right onto Henriette Delille. The neighborhood was strange—a mix of well-kept old houses and urban wasteland. On the right was a vacant lot, with the remainders of concrete foundations pale in the moonlight amid weeds and dead looking grass, a set of concrete steps leading to nowhere midpoint in the second block. A big trash dumpster stood in the middle of the broken-up sidewalk. On the left was a row of well-kept Victorians, fronting a sidewalk which was clean and smooth. There were no streetlights—what signs of habitation there were came from across the vacant lot on Rampart Street, where lights and traffic noise contrasted with the dark quiet zone. Jim had trolled for prey in many blighted neighborhoods, but this was one of the weirdest streets he could remember. It was exactly how the person he'd chatted with said it was. All you had to do was drive through, like going into the projects to buy dope, and the action would find you.

Halfway down the block a girl stepped out from between two of the houses and stood looking at him. She was dressed like a schoolgirl gone bad in a miniscule plaid skirt with a white blouse unbuttoned and tied under her breasts. Her hair was done in pigtail braids, her wet, pouty lips were sucking on a lollypop, the kind with bubble gum in the middle. She withdrew the lolly slowly and licked it before inserting it again, all the time looking in his eyes like she could suck on anything he had with the same sensuous pleasure.

He hit the brakes, rolled down the window and smiled. "You need a ride, honey?"

She crossed the street walking slow, and when she leaned down at his window her blouse opened wide so he had a clear look at her breasts. "Where you going, daddy?"

"I have a room over on Tulane. Or wherever you want sweetie. That lollypop sure looks good."

"It is good, daddy. I love sucking on candy. I can suck on just about anything. Mmmm." She inserted, then withdrew the lollypop, and licked her lips. "You got some candy for me?"

121

"Get in," he said, then unlocked the passenger door and watched as she walked slowly around the front of the car, giving him a naughty look and pulling the lollypop in and out of her mouth slowly like she was putting on a show. She was a naughty girl, and he was going to punish her.

He felt something hard slam into his ear, and a low voice said, "Put your hands up. Get out the car. Now."

Jim's insides turned to mush and all he could think was, he was caught and he would die, right here. "Please don't hurt me," his voice came out in a squeak. "I'll give you whatever you want, just don't kill me."

"Shut up, get out the car." He groped for the door lock but was shaking too hard. He felt an arm at his back, then felt the door swing open and a hand grabbed his arm and yanked him out of the car, then something hard slammed into the side of his head and he was shaking and sobbing because he couldn't do anything, and he was going to die at the hands of this pitiless stranger with the dark cloth over his face and the angry eyes.

The girl wasn't a little girl anymore, she was mean and rough as her hands ran over his body taking his wallet, his phone, his keys, and then she told him to get on his hands and knees and start crawling. "Not that way, bitch. The other way. Crawl down that street." She kicked him in the ass hard as he started crawling in the direction she told him, going into the dark neighborhood. "Okay, you can get up now. Get up and run. Count of ten I'm gonna shoot."

His bladder let go and a warm stream of urine darkened his trousers as he scrambled to his feet and ran, stumbling in a panic down the street, expecting to feel the bullet with every gasping breath.

25

Sylvie sat on the roof listening to the weekend party traffic and the incessant singing of the street hustler, now paid to watch the street for unusual activity, unusual having a whole different interpretation if you lived in the French Quarter. She could see the full moon over the rooftops, and the night wrapped around her like a warm, soft blanket. She was thinking about quitting work. She didn't want to spend her time in hiding—she'd go crazy. But she did have something better to do, if she could convince Andy to let her get started.

The more she thought about Brittney's situation, the more it seemed like a good idea to help Brittney and the kids now. It did not escape her that Brittney had turned a trick today in order to make ends meet. That's what she meant by somebody coming by to help out with the rent. For Sylvie, it was not a moral issue. A woman did what she had to do, and aging strippers don't have a whole lot of options. Getting paid to service a customer couldn't be any worse than, for instance, having to stay with an abusive man because you couldn't afford to move out. But what if the kids found out? What if Child Protective Services heard about it? All it would take would be a phone call from a vindictive ex. Four years in foster care had taught Sylvie that, except in the most extreme situations, kids were better off with their parents.

Brittney was in danger and so were her kids. Sylvie wanted to help her now, not later. She couldn't just sit around in hiding. Besides, she wasn't going to give anybody that much power. Some classes in self-defense would be good. Maybe she could get Trey to show her a few moves. And about using a gun, but Sylvie didn't have faith in guns. You'd have to be packing twenty-four hours a day; look what happened to Bernice. But with a combination of firepower, self-defense training, and brains, she should be able to put any attacker down. She could be just as mean and smart as anybody.

The shock of the last two days was beginning to wear off and Sylvie was getting used to the idea of the money and the responsibility that went with it. She wondered at Bernice's loathing for the money and the nefarious way her family had amassed it. How would it feel to be from a family you were ashamed of? Sylvie supposed it might be just as hard as having your only family, your mother, disappear suddenly without any warning, and never finding out what happened to her. She wondered if her mother had been murdered by a monster like the one who'd killed Amanda and Adrian. Sylvie knew that strippers, by the nature of their business, attracted psychos and pervs. Her mother was almost certainly dead or she would have come back. She thought about news stories of men who held women hostage in dark rooms, sometimes for years. She didn't allow herself to speculate long on any of it.

Sylvie remembered the night her mother didn't come home. She'd woken from her sleep and checked the clock. It was three a.m. and her mom was always home by then. She'd dialed the beeper number and waited for her mom to call. She spent the remaining hours of darkness calling the beeper and waiting. By sunrise her fear had grown into a big ugly thing, her worry transformed into the terrible knowledge that something bad had happened. As hope faded and died, she was left with the knowing, in that place in herself reserved for the worst thing that could possibly happen, that she'd never see her mother again.

Now she had an opportunity to help other kids, and Sylvie knew she'd found the one thing that could ease her loneliness. It was sad that Bernice could not be here with her, helping her to plan. Still, as she sat on the roof listening to the street noise which usually made her feel more, not less alone, she felt the gentle presence of Bernice's spirit, approving of her plans to get started right away by offering Brittney a way to pull herself and her kids out of their downward spiral.

Saturday

26

Z kicked back on the mattress and lit a blunt. "Sheeeit! That was easy pickings! We gon' be in the money now." He handed the joint to Junie, who was lying next to him. "Now I'm gonna get a piece of the action. And while I'm in the green, you gonna be my queen."

"Shut up with that." Junie handed him back the joint, sat up and took a swig of her coke, capped it, and lay back down. "You think that perv's gonna call the cops? Fuck. We shoulda killed his nasty ass."

"Who cares if he does? What he gonna say? Man, that dude was scared. Yeah, he gon' call the cops, but he ain't gonna tell 'em what really went down, 'cause he look like one a them chumps got a werewife waiting at home. He'll be more scared of her than he was of us. He gon' tell the cops some bullshit, like he went to bed and when he got up the car was gone. That way he can collect on the insurance."

They had dropped the car off at Mo's shop and taken a cab back. Z kept the computer, along with the gun he found under the front seat—a Beretta Nano 9mm, the backpack, the wallet, and the phone. The backpack was stuffed to capacity. It contained a tarp, shoe covers, latex gloves, a shower cap, a curling iron, handcuffs, nylon rope, a hunting knife with a gut hook, and a big roll of duct tape. When he saw the gloves, the knife, the tape and the handcuffs, his gut clenched up—what kind of freak was this? There was a pack of condoms in the backpack, too. What kind of freak used a tarp, gloves, and a curling iron for sex? Not to mention the handcuffs, the gun, and the other stuff.

Little Z, also known as Andre LeBlanc, got the car for Mo as a condition of being given a job selling in the Bywater. He was trying to get into the St. Roch Road Dogs. Their reluctance and skepticism were based on his previous clean record—his rep as a mama's boy who did good in school and stayed out of trouble. But he didn't live with his mother any more. She'd been killed by a rival gang, the Hometown Players, after agreeing to testify against the Player who'd shot a boy in front of the school where she worked. Z had been living with his grandmother since his mother's death. He couldn't take on the HTPs by himself, but if he joined the gang they were warring with, the Road Dogs, he could do some major damage. Stealing a car and delivering it to a Road Dog chop shop showed courage and loyalty, and placed him on the right side of the law—the outlaw side. He knew that in order to be accepted into the gang he'd have to endure a beat down and also help with a drive by. But he already felt as beaten down as dirt since his mother died, and there was nothing he wanted to do more than drive into Hometown Players' neighborhood and let loose with some firepower, take those motherfuckers out.

He'd given up his dream of becoming a police officer, he hated cops now. The DA promised his mother police protection, but the cops who were supposed to be guarding her house took off right before the gangbangers pulled up and sprayed it with bullets. It was a setup; Z was sure of that. His mother had died in his arms, her final words whispered through the blood bubbling out of her mouth, "Be strong." And what had strength and goodness gotten her? He'd seen her work as a cook at the school cafeteria all her life, coming home most days so tired she was limping. She'd never complained much, was in church every Sunday. All her hard work and decency hadn't even earned her the protection of the law she had believed so fervently in obeying. Z felt betrayed; he would now cast his lot with the other side of the law. If he ever got the chance, he planned to find out who shot his mother and also track down those cops who'd sold her out and kill them all.

Z took another hit off the joint, drawing deep and holding it in his lungs, as if the pot could assuage his anger. Junie was snoring softly beside him on the mattress, the only furniture in this tiny efficiency. She had been his girl for the past five months. He didn't know how deep his feelings were for her, because everything was scrambled up and confused. The only feelings he could register were anger and shame. Shame because he'd been home with his mother the night of her murder, in his room with his headphones on, playing a video game while she fixed dinner. He didn't even hear the shooting. His mother crawled back to his room to be sure that he was okay, gut shot and trailing blood down the hallway.

He didn't want to love Junie or anybody else. He wanted revenge, and that didn't leave much to offer a woman. He'd wanted to be with Junie in his other life, the one before his mother's murder, but she never noticed him back then or if she did, she looked down on him. She liked the outlaws.

Gaining her interest was a sign that he was transforming himself into a different man.

Z was too keyed up to sleep, thinking about the past and how tonight had brought him closer to his goals. He wondered what that stupid fuck had on his computer. Maybe there would be a clue about what kind of a freak he was, going around picking up whores with this freak kit he had. Z took the laptop out of its case, plugged it in and booted it up. It was a Toshiba, not the most expensive brand, but nothing about this dude had been flashy. One of those generic silhouettes came up, with the words, "Welcome Bob." He clicked the icon and it asked for a password. Z decided to go in the wallet and look for a clue. He found three credit cards, one an American Express with the name Robert Smith and the other a Visa with the name John Legitt. There was also a Diner's Club with a Master Card logo on the front under the Legitt name. There were driver's licenses for each card, the Smith license was an Oregon ID and the Legitt was Texas. They both had pictures of the same dude, the one he'd jacked. There wasn't much else, Chase Bank for the Smith and a Whitney for the Legitt, a Security Surveillance business card, and a few credit card receipts. He'd already removed the cash—four hundred eighty-three dollars. A lot of cash for the average guy to be carrying, but Z supposed he was planning to use some of it to pay for the sex. There were no pictures, and nothing to give a clue where the dude stayed. Unless he maintained the addresses on the driver's licenses, which Z doubted. Smith lived in Salem, Oregon, and Legitt gave a Houston address. Z started going through the pockets in the computer case. He found a short list printed on an index card—it had names and numbers on it, like somebody wanted to keep track of a few different codes. There was Bob, with ecneics83; John, with ecinreb38; Slavemaster, with niap72. Z wanted to know what that meant. He clicked on the 'change user' and typed in slavemaster, and a flame icon came up, then he typed the password, got a message that it was wrong, then typed it backwards, so that it read 27 pain. He was in.

Z was getting a creepy feeling; he thought about putting Junie out on the street as bait for this freak. What if something went wrong and the dude got to his gun before he could get him out of the car? Z thought about how he'd failed his mother, about how he could have put Junie into the hands of a sexual sadist. He glanced over at her, lying still on the bed in the glow of the street light coming in through the window. She was laying on her side curled up, her profile framed by soft dark curls, her pouty lips parted and partially hidden by one of her hands, long dark lashes shadowing the soft curve of her cheek. She looked like a beautiful child, vulnerable in sleep with her defenses gone—all the sass, the anger. Z realized there was a core of innocence in her that she guarded with her biting tongue and attitude. The thought of her in the hands of a sadistic monster made him realize that somewhere, scrambled in with a confusion of painful emotions, he had feelings for her.

He turned back to the laptop, curiosity supplanted by dread. But he was imagining things, he'd find out it wasn't that bad. This guy just liked to play bondage games, and from the cash he'd had on him he was willing to pay extra for his fantasies. Z clicked on the 'my videos' icon to see what kind of skin flicks this perv got off on. A list of dates came up. He scrolled down the dates, and saw there were 27, arranged from the most recent, 05/19/13 to the earliest, 10/31/93. He clicked on the earliest date and a picture came up—a woman, her eyes open wide in stark horror above a silver slash of duct tape wound tightly around the bottom of her face, her long blonde hair tangled and spotted with blood. She was on concrete in what looked like a big warehouse, backed up against a concrete block wall with her arms stretched taut above her head, wrists cuffed to a length of chain which was attached to something above and out of the frame. Her legs were tied together with a length of nylon rope like the kind he had in his freak kit. Her naked body was smeared with blood, covered with cuts and what looked like chew marks, and there was a blotch of red gore where one of her nipples was supposed to be. There was a circle with an arrow in the middle of the picture which would start the film. Little Z did not want to click the arrow but he did, the way you cover your eyes at a scary movie then peek. He knew that whatever images the film contained would be embedded in his memory forever, but he had to see.

A man in a black leather jump suit and chaps came into the film. He was a white dude, same size and build as the car freak, and a rubber mask covered his head. He turned to face the camera and the mask was a caricature of Ronald Reagan, smiling garishly with black holes for eyes. Z recognized the likeness, but it was before his time—Reagan was before his time. The picture was moving fast. The freak had a gas can in his hand and he turned back towards the woman and began pouring fluid over her head while she choked and cringed in terror. He moved down the length of her body, drenching her, and continued to pour in a trail which led out of the picture frame. The woman's eyes opened again, tears streaming down her face, jaws moving behind the tape while her body thrashed and strained wildly against the restraints. Z had never seen such frantic terror—it was way beyond anything he'd ever imagined or wanted to. The flame traveled towards her rapidly, engulfing her in seconds. Z switched the film off. He'd seen enough. He looked at the other 26 dated links. She was the star of the first film. What did the others contain? He didn't want to know. But he needed to punish himself. He was certain the monster was the white dude they'd just jacked. The one he had Junie approach.

27

Jim Davis had to break into his own place. He was badly shaken and, for the first time in his life, ashamed. How did it happen that somebody else got control? A nigger street punk. He was losing it. The past two hours had been a nightmare— slinking through a maze of back streets, staying away from traffic and lights, jumping at the sounds of people, of dogs barking, ducking and hiding, lost, stinking with his own urine, and scared, really scared for the first time in his life. He'd found his stumbling way home, creeping down the street like a thief who didn't belong and then, confronted with the absence of keys, going around back, dragging a trash can over to his window, then a ladder from the carriage house in back because the plastic trash can wasn't tall enough—they built houses high back in the 1800s because of the long, hot summers, the hurricanes, the flooding. He'd groped around the yard and found a rock, climbed up the ladder, shattered the window over the breakfast table where he liked to take his meals and, cutting himself on a shard of glass as he reached in to unlock the window, he opened it and crawled in, his body aching because he wasn't young any more. He was old and he was losing his power.

He felt like an intruder in his own apartment, like he should stay in the dark and continue to hide. He lowered the shade, switched on the light, found a bottle of water in the fridge and drank half of it down. Then he went to the sink and examined his hand. A shallow gash on his right palm and blood was everywhere in thick red drops and splotches—the sink, the floor, the windowsill where he'd come in. He made a sobbing sound as he examined the cut under a stream of cold water. He tied a dishtowel around the wound, then stripped naked, dropping the clothes on the kitchen floor. He proceeded down the hallway and through the bedroom to the shower, turning on the occasional light as he went through the apartment. He needed to wash off the blood, the urine, the street grime, the stink of fear and the shameful miasma of defeat. Then he'd be able to think this through.

28

She was with Eileen, sitting on the bed in her big sister's room, watching her pack for her return to LSU after winter break. She knew Eileen shouldn't go back to school but she couldn't speak. She could not tell her sister that death waited for her in Baton Rouge. Eileen was wearing a flannel nightshirt, her thick red hair wound into a sloppy knot on top of her head, brown eyes glowing, dimples flashing as she chattered away, full of the excitement of going back to college. "I love this sweater you gave me," she said as she held up the navy-blue pullover. "Synthetic fabric is soooo warm! You have the best taste in clothes. Hey, you remember the fight we got in over my black sweater?" Eileen said this as she folded the garment and put it in the suitcase. She stopped packing and walked over to the closet where she began going through clothes on a shelf. "This one." She held up the sweater. "I want you to have it, okay? It looks great on you and I can't fit it in my suitcase with all this new stuff. Here, Cami," Eileen held out the sweater, "I'm sorry for getting mad at you for wearing my stuff. Really, Cami, I mean it. What's wrong?"

Camille woke up sweating and panicky, her cheeks wet with tears. Eileen had been wearing the sweater she'd bought her for Christmas the night she'd disappeared. They found fibers from it in the torture shack after they arrested Radow. Her naked, mutilated body was found in a dumpster outside the cafeteria on the LSU campus. As Camille lay in bed with these memories, the panic she'd felt on waking was replaced with the old ache of missing Eileen, the horror of her death. Eileen would be middle-aged now and, as Camille thought about this, she missed the kids Eileen never had, the woman she never became.

She turned over in bed, her movement heavy. Her digital alarm glowed 3:17. Shit, she thought, do I really want to go back to sleep? But she knew she needed those additional few hours before the alarm sounded, so she groped around on her bedside table for the Benadryl, swallowed two pills dry. She found the water bottle and, after drinking, she held it against her face for a moment, trying to escape into the physical sensation of cool metal against her skin. "Please Lenie," she prayed, "help me to catch this monster. I know you're with me on this. I love you." She lay in the dark a long time before the pills worked.

29

It was almost four and the crowd was going strong. All kids, though, and they didn't have money for street musicians. Now, if he was out here slinging dope, he'd have all the business he could handle. He was about ready to call it a night. He reached in his back pocket, pulled out the pint bottle and drank the last of his vodka, watching as a tall dark figure turned the corner from Jackson Square. He was dressed like a character in a vampire flick, with a dark shiny top hat and a flowing black cape which was thrown back over a shoulder to reveal purple satin lining which gleamed in the light of the Victorian street lamps. His ebony walking stick had a silver wolf's head handle, the wolf's head contorted into an angry snarl and Lionel suspected that if you removed the handle a blade was concealed beneath. His face was heavily made up with black lipstick, kohl eyeliner, and pasty white pancake foundation. He stopped at the gate of the building where the white woman lived and rang one of the buzzers. Lionel thought about calling Trey and decided against it; this dude was one of the vampire tour guides, probably just got off work and was stopping to visit a friend. He didn't look out of place in this neighborhood.

As Lionel watched, a skinny white boy with long, matted, blonde dreads, rounded the corner from the square and ran towards the vampire dude, carrying what looked like a wooden broomstick which had been sawed in two and whittled to a sharp point at one end—a makeshift wooden stake! He was wearing a tattered wifebeater; his shaved skull, neck and arms were covered with geometric ink. His meth-crazed, bug-eyed face was contorted with fear and, as he neared his target, he let out a high-pitched scream, drawing his skinny arm back with the stake held high. The vampire tour guide lifted his cane and brought it down on the deranged guttersnipe's arm. Lionel winced as he watched the arm twist down, the stake clattering onto the slate sidewalk. The vampire raised his cane to strike again, but the kid dropped to his knees and threw up his good arm to shield his face. As the vampire lowered his cane the kid reached for a large silver cross he wore on a leather thong around his neck and held it in front of him, staggering to his feet and advancing, as if he expected the tour guide to cringe and fall back. Instead he entered the gate, shaking his head in disgust, and slammed it shut behind him with a clang.

Lionel decided to quit this scene just as the injured punk let out an anguished, high-pitched scream and the cop from Rouse's came running. A group of college kids had gathered, some of them holding up their phones, and a passing car had stopped, its occupants hooting and shrieking with laughter at the street drama. Then another car rounded the corner and started honking its horn, the occupants screaming profanity at the car stopped in front. Nobody asked the kid if he was okay. Lionel bent down, scooped up his empty bucket and took off towards Jackson Square, expecting to hear the cop calling out to him to stop. He rounded the corner with relief and walked fast up Chartres towards St. Louis. He would make the block and head up towards the Quartermaster, an all-night grocery with a take-out counter where he could pick up a sandwich and a fifth of vodka on his way back to the room. He needed a packet of headache powders too. The noise and foolishness of the Friday night crowd had gotten to him.

30

Junie woke to an empty bed and a keening sound coming from the bathroom. She went to investigate and found Z lying in the bathtub curled up, rocking back and forth, sucking his thumb, and moaning. "What the hell's the matter with you?" she demanded, squatting down beside the tub and shaking him hard. He squeezed his eyes shut tighter and stopped rocking, then opened his eyes and looked up at her, only his eyes didn't seem to be focused on her but on some hellish inner vision that had consumed his sanity.

"Mama," he whispered. "I want my mama."

"Boy, your mama's dead. What you want me to do? You look like you seen the devil. What're you on?"

"I want my momma!" he shrieked. Then he squeezed his eyes shut, started rocking and moaning, sucking his thumb.

Junie decided to go look through the place, see if she could find out what he took. Damn, she wasn't asleep three hours and he had to go get himself high on some damned thing and drive his self crazy. What kind of dope was he on? She went in the kitchen, switched on the light, and saw that it was as clean as it had been when she went to bed. She lifted up the half-eaten pizza in the box on the counter, looking for dope. Junie knew the guys at the bar sent something extra out under the pizza pie for special customers. It wasn't like Z to be taking stuff without telling her. He was always cool that way and besides, he didn't really mess with the hard stuff— just a little pot and a couple of beers, mostly. He'd tried smoking meth, snorted a couple of lines of coke, even done heroin with her once and neither one of them liked any of it.

She could hear his moaning as she moved into the main room, checking the mantle over the old coal-burning fireplace, taking out the fake electrical outlet that was really a stash box, looking out the window onto the roof. Everything seemed the way it was when she'd lain down. Then, as she stood by the window and looked around, her eyes fell on the computer which was closed, but plugged in. She crossed the small room, sat down on the floor and opened it, tapping the pad to wake it up. It asked her for a password and she found the index card with passwords on it and began entering them, using the same process of elimination that Z had used. When she entered pain 27, the circle of dots started whirling and then she was in. The image on the screen made her shriek out in fear and disgust. It was a young Hispanic girl, ten at most, handcuffed to the to the bedposts and spread eagled, lying on what looked like a bloody tarp covering a bare mattress, her legs stretched, spread, and secured to something off the screen, her genital area smooth as a baby's but bloody up between the legs, areas of her body gouged and bleeding, her chest and shoulders covered with what looked like dozens of cigarette burns. Her mouth was bound with duct tape which had been wound around her face tightly and secured in back, her eyes wide open in terror and pain, and tears had made streaks on her blood smeared cheeks. In the center of this picture was a film icon—a circle with an arrow in the middle.

Junie slammed the computer closed and ran back to the

144

bathroom, knelt on the floor next to the tub and leaned in, hugging Z as best she could in the cramped space of the tub, murmuring in his ear, "It's okay, Junie's here now. Everything's okay, baby. Shhh, it's okay."

While she held him, she was thinking about the computer and the video. The man wasn't just a pervert, he was a monster. Junie was scared, and she was mad. She wanted to go find him and put a bullet in his diseased brain. But she was more scared than mad. This was what he'd had in store for her last night. If she had been a streetwalker who really needed to turn a trick, she would have gone with him. She shuddered at the consequences—being held captive and tortured right at this very moment. Could he still get her? The idea of such a monster even knowing she existed was terrifying.

She wondered what other horrors were on the computer and decided she didn't want to know. What she felt like she needed was protection. But Junie had never called the cops in her life. The ones she knew were worse than street thugs—dealing, stealing, having people killed. She'd never felt protected by anybody. She was the one who looked out for her mom, who was gone on crack since before she was born, turned tricks for dope, and couldn't even get it together to feed herself without somebody making her eat. Junie had been the one to take control of the welfare check, the food stamps, her little brother, and all the housework, laundry, bills, grocery shopping—Junie was the adult of the household. Plus, she had to ward off the men her mother brought home and try to keep them away from her little brother.

She hated perverts and tricks with a passion, and it seemed like they had always been everywhere—like they sensed that she was a child unprotected and therefore maybe available. She wondered how many of them, the men who'd assaulted her with their eyes, their offers of rides, their interest in her, a girl young enough to be their daughter or granddaughter, were into this kind of shit. She wondered who in this messed-up world she could ever call on for protection. And now here was Z, helpless as a baby, and he'd almost got her in the car with a sick monster. Why did she always have to be the strong one? What was she going to do about him?

As these thoughts went through her mind, she soothed him like he was her baby brother, not her man. "Shhh, it's okay now, Z. Come on; let me help you out of the tub."

"Get my mama," he moaned.

"Okay, get out the tub and I'll call your Grandma Beverly. Come on now." Z was rocking himself again in her arms. She'd had plenty of experience with dead weights. Her mother was drunk when she wasn't high on dope, and there were many nights Junie had to get her off the floor and into bed. One time she'd had to get her mother out of bed after the dizzy bitch set the mattress on fire with her cigarette— she'd put the smoldering mattress out, put her mother back in the bed. Her mother remained comatose through the whole ordeal.

She managed to get her arms under Z and lift him to a sitting position, then he let her pull him up with her arms under his armpits and her hands clasped behind his back for leverage. After she pulled him up, he let her help him out of the tub. She guided him back into the main room and onto the mattress, helped him lay down, and covered him up.

She unplugged the computer, took it in the kitchen. She did not want to look at this thing and she sure didn't want him to see it. She stashed it in an empty cupboard and went back in the living room. He'd gone stark crazy and Junie didn't know what else to do but call his granny.

31

Camille woke to the alarm. She felt good, like the nightmare of a few hours ago had been erased by a couple of hours of dreamless sleep. She put a pot of coffee on and stepped outside for a moment, breathing in the morning air, the yard smells, and listening to the birds. This was a crucial part of her daily routine, fortifying herself before facing the sleaze and mayhem of her job. The sun was chasing the shadows out of the yard and a squirrel ran across the grass, which was covered with white crape myrtle blossoms around the entrance to her cottage. Beauregard, Miss Ashley's big yellow tom, slunk across the yard, pausing to turn and glare at her before he took up his station by the back door of the main house and began licking the night's grime off his fur.

Camille took the hint and went back inside. She fixed herself a cup of coffee and checked emails on her phone. Both Fran and Tyler had left messages. She opened Fran's first: Here's a list of sublets for the last six months. Let me know how things turn out, and if there's anything else I can do to help. She booted up her laptop and scanned the list—there were almost fifty entries. She printed it out, took a pen, a highlighter, and a legal pad to the kitchen table. She was going to narrow it down. Most of the ads were easy to eliminate. What she had left were sublets for one month or longer that covered the month of July, though she felt that this guy would have been in town longer, long enough to case out the Magnolia Courts and zero in on Amanda Butler. She would give the summer listings priority. She was certain that he was here now, that he wasn't finished because a guy like this would not just accept defeat and go away—he would need to do something to control the situation, even if it was only to wreak revenge on the person or people who now controlled the money he felt entitled to.

Limiting the list to sublets for the summer months, she narrowed it down to eighteen names. There were nine more for six months, and the rest were for longer or shorter periods or only for major events like Jazz Fest. There were a couple of ads for carnival season next year, some local residents left town for two weeks prior to Fat Tuesday, avoiding the time of year when the town became constipated with parades, crowds, and drunks. Thank God this isn't going on during carnival, she thought.

She went back to the computer and checked out the email from Tyler. There weren't many sublets listed and he'd winnowed out the short-term rentals and those requiring a six-month lease. There were eight sublets covering the summer months. Tyler added that he was waiting to move on her plan, and to contact him as soon as it was a go. She went over both lists, and was able to eliminate slum neighborhoods and the larger apartments and houses, bringing the lists down to fourteen possibilities, all with contact information, a good place to start.

After she'd showered and dressed, she thought about calling Mace. It was after eight. He'd had plenty of time to think things over. But he said to give him 'til noon. Still, she could use some help contacting the sublets, and with a killer on the loose they didn't have time to waste—they needed to locate Davis. She argued with herself as she fixed breakfast—a bowl of Life cereal with a fresh sliced peach. She finished breakfast and began calling the lessors.

The third rental was a hit. It was in the garden district on Chestnut and Second—a high-end neighborhood, but some of the owners of the old mansions had turned them into condos. The owner, Maxine Jordan, called back from San Diego where she was spending the summer vacationing. Yes, she'd rented to an older man, John Legitt, a retired teacher from Houston. He'd paid for the entire summer with his Visa. She was eager to look at a picture and make sure he wasn't a suspect, so they reconnected via Skype. When Camille held the picture up in front of her computer, Maxine went ballistic.

"Oh god, he's my tenant!" Maxine shrieked. "How do I get rid of him? What if he kills somebody? Shit! What do I do?"

"Calm down, Maxine. You've been a big help. And the best thing you can do now is do nothing and let us handle it. If this guy is our perp, you want to stay out of it. We need him to stay put until we have enough evidence for an arrest. I'll let you know when we're going to arrest him. Can we stay in touch?"

"Please do! Oh, please, please, I don't want him in my place. I don't want him around my neighbors. We're nice people in our neighborhood!"

"Just trust me, Maxine. The worst thing we can do right now is to alert him that we're on to him. You don't want to deal with this guy. I mean, if you tell your neighbors anything, and they react, he could be very dangerous. Listen, this guy is smart. He's not going to prey on people from around where he stays. If he's our suspect, he hunts for people who are powerless and your neighborhood is too high-profile for him. Okay?"

"I want him out!"

"Can you give us two weeks?"

"Okay. But not a day longer."

It was almost nine when Camille called Mace. Their agreement was to work together and the circumstances warranted an early call.

"Hey Camille, what's up? I have an answer for you if that's what you need. We can go ahead with this, but I need to arrange for backup to cover Sylvie Compton, that's why I asked you to wait 'til noon."

"Mace, I found him."

"Whadda you mean?"

"I mean I found Jim Davis. He's renting a condo in the garden district, going by the alias, John Legitt."

"Legit huh? That asshole."

"I'm going over to stake out the place now."

"Wait a minute—let's meet. You eat breakfast yet?"

"Yes. I've been up since seven."

"Can you meet me at the pancake house anyway?"

"I'm on my way."

32

Junie eyed Beverly from across the room. She was in awe of the woman and though she wasn't scared of her, she wouldn't want to tangle with her either. Beverly was small in size, just under five feet and wiry. What was big about her was her attitude and her mouth. She'd been in the apartment since five a.m. The place was tiny; there was no getting away from her. Now she was on the phone with the priest, Father Greg Lee. After arguing all morning, Junie finally caved and said she'd tell the priest what happened. She wanted to tell somebody. She wanted somebody to take the computer away and do whatever had to be done to catch the monster. But she needed to know that whoever she talked to couldn't tell on her, wouldn't go after the car because it was probably dismantled and there was no way in hell she was going to turn in a chop shop owned and operated by a Road Dog—that would be instant death to her whole family.

"No," Beverly said into the phone. "I don't need a deacon over here. My grandbaby's in trouble. I never saw him like this. Not even after his mama got shot. He's gone crazy and his friend won't tell anybody what happened but you, 'cause you're a priest. Okay then, I'll see you in a few minutes."

Junie handed her a bottle of water. "You sure you don't want me to run get you a cold drink or some coffee?"

"No baby, this is fine. I guess y'all went and got yourselves in trouble with a gang. That's why you can't talk to anybody but the priest. How's your mama been?"

"Drunk and loaded."

"That's a shame. Can't she get help?"

"She don't want no help."

"What about your little brother?"

"He'll survive."

"Yeah, but you're not over there to take care of them. You moved in here."

"Well, it looks like I'm moving back in over there. I can't keep this place by myself, and Andre's not his self right now."

"Well baby, you can come home with us. That is, if you want to. But I don't let anybody who stay with me run with no hoodlum gang members or be acting wild, you hear?"

"I'll think about it, Mama." Junie turned and looked out the window that faced the drive below. She had never in her life lived in a safe household with a strong woman in charge. She'd always had to take charge. It seemed like the stronger she got, the sicker her mother got. And she was beat down by the burden of taking care of her mother and her little brother. There were always creepy men around, always something bad to deal with and she just wanted some peace, some room to breathe. She'd been so happy to move in with Z because he wasn't a bad guy and he'd proved that he wasn't stupid about things either, like he was when he wanted to be a cop. He had some street smarts now. It was sad that his mother had to die before he woke up. What would it be like to live in a house with a motherly-type woman? Like the way a mother's supposed to be instead of a pathetic mess? Junie wanted to find out, but it sounded too good to be true and she wasn't going to get her hopes up, not until she found out how this was going to turn out.

She saw a black Acura turn in and park in the drive. The man who got out had a clerical collar on. "Mama Beverly, he's here. I'll go down and let him in."

"No, let me go down. I need to talk with him a minute. We're gonna get this mess straightened out. Then we're getting Andre to a doctor."

Junie watched Beverly go down the stairs, heard her open the door and say, "Fr. Greg. Thanks for coming." She went to the window and watched Beverly and the priest as they stood talking. A boy zigzagged down the street on a bike, followed by a tan and black shepherd. Other than the boy and the dog the street was quiet, but there were plenty of places for somebody to hide. She wondered if the monster was out there; looking to find out who they were, get his movies back. She wasn't staying in this apartment any more. Z moaned in his sleep and she glanced down at him lying curled up with his thumb in his mouth, another dead weight.

After a few minutes Fr. Greg looked up at Junie standing at the window. He was elderly with short cropped white hair, tall, thin and dark. She could see concern in his eyes, and something else—uncertainty, or maybe fear.

He came up the narrow stairs first, and when he stepped into the room his head almost touched the ceiling. "Hi. Junie, isn't it?"

Junie was relieved that he didn't put on a Mr. Nice Guy smile. "Yeah, and you're Father Greg."

"You can just call me Greg if you like."

"Father Greg is fine."

He looked down at Andre on the mattress, which took up

almost half the floor space. "We can take him to a hospital," he said to Beverly, "or we can take him to your house and call Louella Jackson, see if she can come to your place and give him a sedative. She's a doctor. We don't want to check him into a psych ward if we can avoid it. It's good that he calmed down when you came over but we need to find out what happened to upset him like this." The priest turned to Junie. "Beverly said you agreed to talk to me."

"Yeah, I'll talk. But only if I can be sure you won't tell anybody. I mean, you're a priest, right? So the police can't make you tell 'em what somebody tells you, right?"

"That's right. Is there somewhere in here we can talk?" He glanced around the tiny space as if he was doubtful there would be. "Or do you want to go sit in my car?"

"Let's go to your car." Junie turned to Beverly. "Mama, I know you're curious, but you don't want to know. It's real bad. Just trust me on this."

"Do I have a choice?"

"Yeah, you got a choice. You can look around while we're downstairs talking. You might find a computer with some bad movies on it. And if you find those movies, you might regret it. Ya'll don't want to see this stuff."

"Are you telling me he got a hold of some bad movies? Like what? Snuff films? Child pornography?" Beverly's eyes narrowed, she glanced at Fr. Greg, then down at Z, curled up sucking his thumb.

"Mama, you don't want to know. Andre's a good boy. But he's a little mixed up, on account of his mama getting shot. Now if you don't want him to get in the kind of trouble that don't go away, let me tell Father Greg and see if he can do something to handle it. Okay? This is too big for us. We need help. God's help."

"Junie, you are one smart girl. Where'd you learn about God? Your mama?"

"No, ma'am. I don't know nothing about God. I just know when something's too big for me, so I was hoping there's a God can handle it. I've had to deal with stuff that's too big for me all my life, but this is the worst thing."

"Well, you two go on and talk. I won't be looking around your apartment. Just go on." She waved them towards the stairwell.

Junie told Fr. Greg about the carjacking.

"What did you do with the car?" he asked.

"You can trust and believe that car's gone. But we took some stuff out the car, off this pervert who wanted to pick me up. One of the things we took is a computer. After we came back last night I went to sleep, and when I woke up I heard Z—I mean Andre. Z's his street name."

"Street name?"

"Yeah, you know, they all got street names. Gang members. Andre picked Z because he went from A to Z when his mama got shot."

"I see."

"Okay, I hear him in the other room. He was moaning, all crazy like. Crying out for his mama. I went in there and he was in the bathtub, like he was hiding, moaning and crying out for his mama and rocking his self back and forth. I didn't know what was wrong, and I was looking around, like maybe he took something bad and it drove him crazy. I couldn't think of nothing else that would make him act that way, but he don't take hard drugs, at least not around me. Anyway, I was looking around and I saw he'd been looking in that computer we got out the car. So I checked the computer and there was a bad movie on it. I ain't never seen nothing that bad. I don't want to talk about it, neither. But I think the man we jacked is worse than a pervert. I think he kills people, like little kids."

Junie paused and looked out of the car window at the morning sky, electric blue with a few wispy clouds. A white butterfly was flitting around the passion flower vines that grew up over the wooden fence on the side of the drive and she wished that she could believe in another reality, a different reality than the one created by people.

"I can't go to the cops," she continued, looking out the window as she spoke. "But somebody needs to take that computer and bring it to whoever's gon' stop that bad man from doing what he's doing. I think that somebody's gonna have to be you." She turned around to look at him. "Can you do that without telling on us?"

"As long as this is considered confessional, what you tell me is confidential. Unless you tell me you're about to harm yourself or somebody else. Is this a confession?"

"Yeah, that's what it is. And I'm real sorry for what I done. But I hate them perverts always tryin' to get in my pants. They been bothering me my whole life. Doing nasty shit, like pulling up next to me in a car and they asking for directions, and they be in there jacking off, and I'm just a little kid, and they following me home from school and stuff." Fr. Greg winced. "I wanted to kill this freak last night. I ain't too sorry about taking his car, neither. What I'm sorry about is my whole life, having to be around bad people, and hating them so much I think it's making me bad too."

"Well, maybe we can help you with that. That's what church is for. And Beverly wants you to stay with her. You won't find a better person. I think she believes that if you're there it will be good for Andre. You should give it some serious thought. You could do worse. It sounds like you're doing a lot worse right now." The priest glanced out the window and saw Beverly watching them from up above. "I want to talk more with you. I'm hoping you decide to come to church, but even if you don't want to come, I'd like to talk again. Right now, we need to take care of Andre, and you need somebody to take that computer off your hands and give it to people who are trained to deal with that stuff."

"We got some other things, too. There's a wallet and a phone. And he had a backpack with some weird stuff, like maybe he was gonna tie me up. And a gun. But I want to keep the gun, only I don't want to lie to you. I have to lie to everybody and it's good to have somebody you can talk to and you don't have to hide nothing."

"You can do better than me, Junie. You can talk to God any time. God loves you."

Junie did not reply to this. She wondered why, if God loved her, did she have to grow up in the hood with an addict mother and all these grown-up problems that she couldn't do anything about.

33

It took a few minutes before Jodie noticed Camille standing in front by the register. "Hey hon, Mace is in back. I'll be there in a few to take your order." This said as she rushed past with a tray of food.

Camille made her way back through the crowded dining room, careful because there wasn't much space to maneuver between the tables. Mace was in the same booth they'd shared yesterday. When he looked up and smiled, Camille saw the haggard look was gone and his eyes were sparkling.

"You look like you got some rest," Camille said.

"Yeah, well it's a relief to know where this guy's at."

He had his iPad with him and they pulled up the address on Google Earth. The front of the house faced Second Street, but the apartment Jim Davis nee John Legitt occupied had a different address on Chestnut. Camille guessed it was the door that was accessible up the iron stairs on the side of the house. The house was raised, the first floor built high with a double curved stairway in front flanked by Doric columns, two on each side. There were potted petunias on the wide portico, and a veranda on the top floor fronted with cast iron lacework which ran between the columns. A lot of houses were built high in New Orleans, but this one was different because where most of the old houses had enclosed the space under the main floor after the pump system was put in, this house left the space open, screened by latticework painted white, green with moss in places. The dark space behind the lattice caused Camille to think about dead bodies, big spiders and rats.

Mace ordered breakfast to go and they headed across town to begin surveillance. They parked down the block on Chestnut and sat there for an hour and a half before something happened. They watched a cab pull up and Davis came out of the door that Camille had guessed was his apartment, locked up, went down and got in the cab. He was wearing a plaid cotton shirt and khaki pants, gray hair cut short, and he wore wire-rim glasses. He looked so innocuous—the kind of guy you wouldn't notice, or if you did you would not think of as being dangerous. It was chilling. They waited until the cab was a block down the street then Mace started the car and followed.

"I wonder why he's taking a cab?" Camille asked. "He couldn't have pulled off Amanda and Adrian's murders without a vehicle. Or maybe he could. Could he have been using a rental?"

"Beats me. I want to go in when he's gone and have a look around. But we need to follow him for now, get a handle on his habits and see what he's up to."

34

The 8th district PD is one block over from the Louisiana Supreme Court building on the corner of Royal and Conti. The two-story building is peach with white trim, fronted by big columns and a flagstone courtyard with palms and potted plants. Aside from the cop cars parked on Conti and the motorcycles in the courtyard it looks like a tourist information center. A sign on the wrought-iron gate advertises NOPD T-shirts for sale.

Officer Fred Garvey was on the desk when the priest came in carrying a big cardboard box. He was a tall, muscular, Nordic looking guy with a red face and brush cut blonde hair gelled into spikes on top. Some might find his Ken-doll features handsome, but his cobalt eyes were arrogant and he looked mean. "What can I help you with, Father?" he asked.

"I had a parishioner bring these items to me to turn in." The priest heaved the box up onto the high counter. "They're stolen goods. The computer may contain evidence of a violent crime. They all came from the same person, and I believe the wallet contains ID."

"What do you mean you think the computer contains evidence of a violent crime?"

"The person who gave me this stuff said there are bad

films. I'm not free to disclose the details. It's information obtained in the confessional."

Garvey gave the priest a hard look. He was contemptuous of clergy, especially priests. Part of Garvey's discomfort was the vague sense of culpability he felt around these people, as if they could read him like a book and discern that he was a rogue cop and as dirty as the French Quarter streets on Ash Wednesday.

"So, have you looked in the computer?"

"No, I did not. I offered to turn all of this in to the police."

"So, you're telling me that the person these things belong to has maybe committed a crime and the evidence is on this computer?"

"Yes, that's what I'm saying. The person who stole this stuff found some bad films on the computer and asked me to turn all of this in."

"Well, thanks for coming in, Father. We'll handle this from here. Can we be in touch with you?"

"What for?"

"We may need information about how this was obtained."

"I can't talk to you about that. It's privileged. Listen, it doesn't matter, because the wallet and the computer are tied together, so you have an ID right there of whoever owned the computer. I would be willing to testify to this, but that's as far as I can go. I had to persuade the person that gave me this stuff that they wouldn't be involved. I'm leaving now. You can reach me at my office. St. Brigid's over on Rampart. Goodbye." He turned and walked across the marble-floored lobby, which featured a vending machine for the souvenir T-shirts and a rack of tourist brochures, and exited back onto Royal.

Garvey watched the priest leave then took the box back to the locker room. He was excited. The procedure was to hand over the evidence to one of the detectives, but he wanted to see this stuff first. He set it down on a large table, took out the wallet and went through it. Two sets of ID? Maybe he could work things out to his advantage, get a promotion or something. Good thing everybody was gone. A convenience store on Esplanade had been robbed right before the priest showed up. He was mad when they told him to stay behind at the station, but now things had changed. He booted the computer, looked through the bag and found the passwords, then got into slavemaster.

He reviewed the links quickly, one after the other. Snuff films! What would they bring? He would burn them to sell on the black market. He shut down the computer, put it back in the box, carried the box out the side door and put it in the trunk of his squad car. He'd think of something to tell his supervisor about why he couldn't turn this stuff in right away. Or maybe he wouldn't turn it in. He was tired of taking protection money, shaking down dealers and whores and moonlighting as security. If he played this right, it could be his ticket to early retirement. He'd seen a movie where a rich man paid his lawyer a million dollars to have a snuff film made.

35

Camille and Mace followed the cab to a Honda dealer out in Metairie. They watched from across the street as Davis got out of the cab and sent it off. He left the dealership an hour later driving a new silver Civic. They followed him to Wal-Mart, went in behind him, and watched him buy a backpack, a curling iron, a wallet, an extension cord, a roll of duct tape, a tarp, heavy duty garbage bags and some nylon rope. Next, they followed him to Mike's Firearms on Airline Highway. He went in and came out thirty minutes later. So, he had a gun, duct tape, rope and a curling iron? He was putting together a murder kit. The curling iron was creepy. Camille tried not to speculate on what he was planning to do with it. He put the bags in his trunk, and went to Best Buy where he bought a laptop, a throwaway phone, and a computer bag.

By now it was getting late in the day. They watched him take off in the direction of his place, and decided not to press their luck. They went back to the Pancake House, switched to Camille's car.

"How long do you feel like staying on him tonight?" Mace asked.

"He's about to do something. But we'll both have to get some sleep. We can take turns napping in the car. What do you think?"

"I think we need help. We can only watch him for so long. I know a couple of people I can trust, if they don't have other duty. I have to get authorization, but that shouldn't be a problem. We'll stay on him 'til about midnight, and I can make some phone calls. I may have to go in and talk to somebody. I don't want to leave you by yourself on surveillance."

"I'll be alright. If he makes a move, I can call you."

They drove through McDonalds, and got sandwiches and coffee then parked around the corner from his place on Second. The Civic was parked in front of his entrance on Chestnut. Shadows from the big oaks that lined the block played across the car as the afternoon light mellowed. A man rode down Chestnut on a bicycle, and a uniformed maid swept the porch of a mansion up the block. She looked at their car as if she saw everything and wanted a category to put them in. Camille and Mace talked about how they were going to maintain surveillance in this neighborhood without blowing their cover. They decided that, if need be, they would get the cooperation of somebody who lived here, maybe get a maintenance crew over. It depended on how long it would take to gather evidence and make an arrest. They decided that at this point, the newspaper interview wouldn't be necessary because he was already planning something. And he wasn't looking for anybody to be watching because he obviously felt that he was above suspicion. He was the hunter, not the hunted.

"So, what do you think happened to the other car?" Mace asked. "I mean if he had one. Maybe it had trace evidence and he dumped it."

"If we can get the record from the dealership, we can track his license and registration, maybe find the car if he sold it.

They won't tell us anything unless they see ID. You wanna go out there or should I do it? I mean in the morning."

"Metairie is your jurisdiction. You go."

"Okay, but he may try something tonight. God, I just want to nail him now." Camille pounded her knee with a fist to punctuate now. As she said this, Jim exited his door and started down the stairs. He had the backpack and the laptop in its carrying bag. He put the equipment in the backseat of his car, got in and drove off down Chestnut.

"Shit, there he goes," Mace said.

Camille's answer was to start the car. She watched him drive down past First Street and turn the corner onto Philip then she drove down Chestnut after him. When they reached Philip, they could see him a couple of blocks up, heading for St. Charles Avenue. "Five dollars says he's heading for the Quarter," she said.

"I'll buy you a drink if you're right."

"You're on. See? He just turned right on St. Charles. Let's see what the asshole's up to."

Everywhere on the Avenue Camille saw the relaxed bonhomie of people enjoying the lazy rhythm of Saturday afternoon, looking forward to the night. Traffic was heavy and people were out jogging and walking their dogs, sitting at tables in front of cafes and bars. A streetcar rumbled past clanging its bell. And a predator moved among them, hunting. Somebody nobody would look twice at or see coming.

36

The torture videos were a turn on for Garvey and now that he was off work, he was going to do something about it. He sat in his squad car at the corner of Iberville and Rampart, looking for a working girl. When he saw Brittney get off the bus on Canal, he started the car and followed her. He didn't plan on paying for anything—one of the fringe benefits of protecting the public was getting freebies from the local pros. She looked tired, and her shoulders slumped like she carried a bigger load than her dance bag. She was headed down Canal to her job at the Last Call, a strip-dive a couple of blocks from the Mississippi on the opposite edge of the Quarter. Garvey made a U-turn on Canal and pulled up a block ahead, waiting for her approach. He especially liked doing Brittney because she already looked beaten down and hopeless. He leaned over the seat and rolled down the window as she approached, then called out, "Hey, Brittney, get over here." The fear in her eyes excited him. He opened the door and said, "Get in babe. We're going for a ride."

"I'm late for work," Brittney said, her eyes moving around as if she were hoping for escape.

"Get in the car. I'll give you a ride." He winked at her and grinned, eyes sparkling with meanness.

Brittney threw her bag in the middle of the seat before getting in, as if the bag would protect her.

"Move the bag. This won't take long. Jesus, I'm hard as a rock."

The first time Garvey had made Brittney get in his squad car he'd put it to her this way, "Look, bitch, I know what you do in that club. And so does everybody else in this town. So, either you take real good care of me or you're going downtown on a crime against nature. And who do you think they'll believe? Look, it's traditional for the local whores to take care of us cops."

Garvey started the car and unzipped his pants. He threw a jacket over her head as she took him in her mouth, so if anybody looked in the car, they wouldn't be able to nail him for lewd conduct. He turned the corner and drove up Burgundy. The look of revulsion on her face had him ready to come. He wondered if he could take her somewhere—do the kinds of things he'd seen in the films. The thought of what he could get away with doing to somebody like Brittney made him groan with pleasure and he grabbed her hair and twisted hard, forcing her head down and ejaculating in her mouth. Then he laughed at her. "You know you liked that. I might be by after work to take you home, if you know what I mean."

Brittney did not reply to this or even look at him. He rounded the corner onto Iberville and pulled to the curb. She opened the door, grabbed her bag and left, slamming the door. She was headed to the liquor store on Royal for a fifth of whiskey to disinfect her mouth and to sedate.

Garvey continued down Iberville, thinking of who he might contact about selling the snuff, which he'd copied to a flash drive. Traffic was getting heavier as he neared Bourbon and the sidewalks were crowded, mostly with people who were already half drunk, he surmised. He was glad he didn't have night duty any more. It was like babysitting at a frat party, especially on the weekends.

He saw the man emerge from the parking garage a block off Bourbon and couldn't believe his luck—could it be the same guy? It was! After years patrolling the streets, looking at IDs, mug shots, people, people, people Officer Garvey was very good at pairing faces with photos. It was the slave-master. Damn, this was his lucky day! He turned on the bubble light and stopped the car in the middle of the street, unsnapping his gun in its holster as he opened the door and got out, moving fast and knocking a tourist out of the way in his haste. He grabbed the man's arm from behind, just above the elbow, spun him around, and threw him up against the brick wall. "YOU'RE UNDER ARREST! PUT YOUR HANDS OUT AND SPREAD YOUR LEGS!" he yelled, kicking the guy's legs apart. "HANDS ON THE WALL!" He patted the man down and removed his parking ticket, his phone, wallet and car keys, then jerked his arms back and secured his wrists with a zip cuff, tight enough to hurt. He grabbed his elbow and yanked him around, knocking his glasses, which were askew and hanging from one ear, completely off his face and onto the sidewalk. He reached down and picked them up, put them back on Davis's face. Yeah, he was the one. He grabbed him by the elbow, marched him over to the squad car, opened the back door and pushed him in rough so that he fell sideways across the seat, then slammed the door.

He got in the front seat, went through the wallet and found another set of ID with a different name. "Hey," he said, turning to face the man in the back of the car who stared back evenly, a cold disdain in his pale blue eyes that Garvey wasn't used to seeing in people he had in cuffs. He swallowed hard, hesitated before going on. "You wanna tell me which one you are? I mean, this is the third set of ID we have on you, buddy. Is it Henry Lewis, John Legitt, or Robert Smith? By the way, I liked your home movies. You wanna tell me about those? It's gonna go a lot easier on you if you cooperate, starting right now."

"I demand an attorney," Jim Davis replied.

37

Mace and Camille watched the whole thing from a bar across the street. They had parked in the same parking garage and gone across the street for beverages, all the time watching helplessly as Garvey handled their suspect. "That Garvey's a dirty cop—one of the worst on the force, and stupid as shit. Whatever he has on Davis, he's going to blow it." Mace glared out the window as he spoke quietly to Camille. "He's used to bullying the street people—bottom feeders who hustle in the Quarter, dopers, homeless, prostitutes. People who don't even know they have rights. He don't know how to deal with a regular person who knows his rights—somebody with money to hire a lawyer or knows to ask for one. I swear to god if he blows this and somebody gets killed I'm gonna have his badge and his ass."

"Can you talk to him and see what's up?"

"Fuck no!" Mace spat out. "This guy hates me—hates any cop who isn't as dirty as he is. If I let him know he's got my suspect he'll fuck it up on purpose. He doesn't give a damn about public safety. Shit. I'm sick of his kind. They're worse than all the other criminals put together cause they have a badge to hide behind and pull their shit. Its guys like him keep us in trouble with the Feds. Sometimes I think they're the majority here, too. Jesus, I'd rather deal with a gang member any day than some a these cops; at least with gangs they have a few rules. Some of these NOPD assholes don't have a bottom."

"I don't see how you can put up with it, Mace. Why don't you just work for a different force, like in Jefferson Parish?"

"Yeah, I've thought about it. But JP isn't exactly clean. This shit's all over the place. And I can't just give up and leave my hometown to the thugs. Somebody's gotta do something to keep things safe here. Whadda you do? Just run away and let the bad guys take over? My family lives here, my mother."

"You're a good man. Hey, will you let me buy you a drink? I mean, what do you want to do now? It's almost six and if we can't do anything else right now, I'm ready for a drink."

Mace turned away from the window and smiled, though it was obvious this took effort. "Yeah, let's get a beer. Then I got to tie up a few loose ends. Or maybe I should just call somebody at the station and find out what they've got on him. I want to keep in the background on this one."

"Well at least everybody can breathe for the rest of the weekend. He isn't going to be arraigned 'til Monday. We need to find out what they've got him for though."

"That's what's worrying me," Mace's mouth was tight, the anger returned to his eyes as he turned back to the window in time to see Garvey take off down the street, speaking into his radio as he drove. "Because whatever they have on him, even if it's the murders, Garvey's going to fuck it up so he walks."

38

Sylvie was looking forward to the night. Today had been her last day at the motel. She cut a deal with Andy that she wouldn't return to work if she could offer Brittney help now. She had not seen Brittney during her shift, but she usually didn't see Brittney unless her rent wasn't paid, and then she stopped by the office to work something out. Sylvie had checked her payment record and saw she was paid up today, but not for tomorrow, so she'd most likely be at work tonight.

She had seen Brittney's two youngest kids, the girls, getting cokes and junk food out of the machines earlier. The oldest, a pale girl with long blonde hair who looked around ten but with the serious, watchful eyes of somebody older, noticed Sylvie looking out of the lobby window and yanked on her little sister's arm then whispered in her ear, probably telling her to hurry up and make her selection from the machine. Sylvie recognized the behavior, a wariness which came from too many bad experiences with adults, and she left the window and went back to the video monitor to watch the girls go back to their room.

Sylvie had just come out of the shower and was trying to decide what to wear as a customer in the bar where Brittney worked. They were going to buy her out of the club for a couple of hours and take her to dinner. They planned to get to the club early in the shift in order to talk to Brittney while she was relatively sober. She picked a blue cotton wrap-around skirt and a loose-fitting white tank that was opaque and showed no cleavage. Management was always looking for new talent on stage and she did not want to encourage them. She dried her hair and applied a little makeup. There was no way they could really communicate at her job. Andy had called and told her Jim Davis was arrested so at least for the weekend they could all relax. She finished getting ready, called Trey, and stopped by to get him on the way down.

39

The Last Call didn't have a day shift. It was open from six to six, so dancers had the option of starting early and leaving before closing, but like most of the clubs, dancers showed up when they felt like it and left if there wasn't any business. Brittney was one of the girls who kept regular hours because she had the kids and no help. She'd gone to the store, bought a fifth of V.O. then called her connect to come by and drop off something to keep her on her feet and balance out the booze later on. She sat at the counter in the dressing room applying makeup and drinking from a full highball glass of whiskey. Usually, she got a coke from the barman and spiked it, but tonight she didn't give a damn. She was the only dancer there, which was another reason she liked to show up early. Things got crazy in the cramped dressing room with ten girls getting ready at the same time.

The door opened and Buddha, the barman manager stepped in. He was a short, stout Vietnamese with a shaved head, a body covered in dragon ink, and a ring in his nose which reminded Brittney of Ferdinand the bull. "Hey Britt, there's a couple in front to see you. It's a buyout, get out there."

"Tell 'em to wait. I'm not ready yet."

"Hurry up babe. The club needs the money."

"Alright, goddammit, give me ten minutes." Brittney liked Buddha; he usually wasn't pushy. Buddha was a big reason she worked at Last Call. But business had been so slow this week they'd closed early the other night, and he had a point. She didn't feel like dealing with a buyout tonight because a buyout usually meant going with a customer to their hotel for sex and she wasn't up for it after being raped again by Garvey. And she didn't like couples. They were unpredictable and usually wanted something kinky. The fact that things were dead meant she didn't have the choice to turn down the money and not go unless she wanted to make it up to the club with a hefty fine. But buyouts were good money, especially if the customer wanted something out of the ordinary, and she planned to stick it to these people all the way. Maybe she could make enough tonight to get the kids out of the motel and into an apartment. She applied red lipstick, toned it down with a layer of pale pink gloss, texted her connect in code to hold off on the delivery, then downed the whiskey, stubbed out her cigarette and left the dressing room.

The Black Eyed Peas' "Rock That Body" blasted her ears as soon as she opened the door to the bar. "Hey, Buddha, it's too early for that shit!" she yelled, crossing the room fast and going behind the bar to push the eject button on the jukebox. She stood there a moment, poised to eject the next number if it wasn't to her liking. When "The Beautiful People" came on she selected "Nightclubbing" to follow it, then turned and scanned the bar, looking for the couple who wanted to buy her out. The room was dim, with black walls and red lights behind yellowed shades. It smelled of stale smoke, spilled booze, and something undefined which, if Brittney wanted to bottle the odor to sell as a scent, she would call it Sleaze

Bar. There was a red tile floor with tables in the middle and high-backed wooden booths along one side. The main attraction was a long stage along the back wall with a pole, footlights, and a black tile floor with potholes next to the pole which dancers had gouged out with their stilettos, a mirrored wall behind, and a short runway extending into the room that had seats on both sides and a black Formica counter that was scarred with burn marks running around it.

The booths were designed so that it was hard to see exactly what was going on in one unless you were right up on it. Buddha came over and told her the couple was in a booth by the side of the stage. "They already ordered you a double so get over there. They've got plenty of money."

"Okay, but I need a shot of Jäger first. It's been a rough day and I'm not into this yet."

"No problem." Buddha poured her a double and told her it was the only one she was getting out of him that night which was fine—Jägermeister turned her into the Jäger monster fast; she'd learned the hard way to limit it to a shot or two for rapid sedation. "I'm gonna play the music a song at a time in case they want to see you do a set. Try to close the deal before the change their minds, okay?"

Brittney drank the shot down like medicine, dropped the glass into the dishwater behind the bar and said, "They ain't gonna change their minds." Then she crossed the room as Marilyn Manson's shrieking voice blasted from the sound system. Brittney had long suspected that stripper clubs set the sound system volume at full blast because the dancers and customers would be more attractive to each other if they couldn't actually hold a conversation. When she saw it was

Sylvie sitting in the booth with a dark-skinned handsome man, the shock snapped her out of her sedation.

"Hi, Brittney."

"Sylvie? You're the last person I expected to see in here. This your man? He's fine."

"Actually, we're friends. This is Trey. Trey, Brittney."

"It's a pleasure," Trey said.

"Likewise."

"We're out celebrating tonight," Sylvie said. "We stopped by to see if you want to come out to dinner and celebrate with us. We can pay the buyout if you want to come. And pay you for your time, of course."

"Sure I want to go with. What's the occasion?"

"Well, I'm not at the motel anymore, for one thing. And the rest is a surprise."

"You're not coming back to stripping full-time, are you?"

"No, I've got something better to do. So, let's get out of here and go eat. I made reservations at the Crescent House. You like that place?"

"Yeah, I do."

"So go get dressed. Our reservations are for nine. If you hurry, we can stop on the way and get something better than this rotgut champagne." Sylvie was referring to the requisite B-drink she had bought Brittney's time with.

"I'll be right back. But I didn't wear anything nice to work. Just jeans and a t-shirt."

"Here," Sylvie handed her a bag. "I hope you don't mind. I brought you a dress. Nothing fancy, just something to wear out. What are you, like a six?"

"Yeah, four to six." Brittney pulled out the dress, a silk shift with a muted abstract print, and there was a pair of silver metallic flip flops and a matching cross body bag. "This'll work fine. It's real pretty Sylvie. Man, this is sweet. I'll be right back."

As Brittney slid out of the booth, she noticed that Buddha was talking to Sapphire, another dancer who'd just come in and was still in her street clothes. Buddha waved her over. "You get the buyout?"

"Yeah, I know her. She danced at Sugar Daddy's sometimes. We're going out to eat."

"She want a job?"

"Nope. She don't dance anymore."

"Okay, I'll go collect the money while you get ready. Make it quick. I don't know how many girls are going to show up. We may get some business in tonight. It's Saturday."

Brittney looked at him deadpan, her voice taking on the quiet, careful tone which signaled she was trying not to blow up. "Buddha. They're buying me out of this dump to go eat at a nice restaurant, and I get to wear clothes. I'm not going to be in a hurry to get back here, right?"

"Sure, babe, as long as they pay for your time."

"Oh, they will."

She went back to put on the dress and Sapphire was right behind her. "They friends of yours?"

"Yeah, sort of."

"Maybe they want another girl. What do you think?"

"It's not that kind of a deal, Sapphire." Brittney was annoyed. Sapphire usually approached her customers as soon as she left to go back to the dressing room or the bathroom. She was an average-looking girl, not too bright, but she was young—eighteen. The fact that she was barely legal was her main marketable quality, and while her age alone was enough for certain men, it only went so far to make up for other deficiencies with a lot of customers. She was a relentless backstabber, and customers frequently told Brittney what she said to them in her lame attempts to cut in on Brittney's action. Brittney had worked with girls like Sapphire in the past—they didn't last long in this business. They got older and what appeal they had evaporated with their youth. If they were allowed to stay, they wound up giving cut-rate hand jobs and the like. It was bad for business. Nothing made Brittney angrier than a customer who sat and watched her perform without tipping while some girl who didn't know how to hustle jacked him off in a booth. She changed clothes, checked herself in the mirror and left the dressing room, just as another dancer, Randy, was coming down the hall.

"Brittney, you look nice. You off tonight?"

"No, I'm going on a buyout."

"Sweet. Hope I get a money date, too."

"Well, so far it's just me, you and Sapphire."

"In other words, I won't have much competition with you going out." They chuckled, then Randy went in to get dressed and Brittney continued down the musty hall to the bar. Buddha was just leaving the booth and he looked happy so he must have gotten a hefty tip. Brittney usually told people to take care of her bartender but knew she wouldn't have to say anything with Sylvie being a stripper. Sylvie knew how things worked.

"You look pretty, Britt. You ready to blow this dump?" Sylvie asked, smiling big.

"What do you think?" They all laughed as Trey and Sylvie slid out of the booth.

"See you, Buddha!" Sylvie called out, opening the black

vinyl padded front door which was still closed since they didn't have anybody performing yet. The weathered brick of the old warehouse buildings which now housed bars, restaurants and tourist junk shops cast deep purple shadows and the muggy heat had relented, helped by a slight breeze that came off the river. They walked down Decatur toward the back of the Quarter and came upon the open French doors of Kerry's Irish Pub. Sylvie checked her phone and saw it was eight o'clock. They had time to stop for a drink, but this bar was too crowded. There was a bar two doors down, Al's, that was almost empty. "Okay we have time for a quick one. What are you drinking, Britt?" Sylvie was thinking Brittney was already too plowed to make a serious decision. Maybe they could just talk about it a little tonight, then more in the morning.

40

There was plenty going on at Jimmy's Corner on a Saturday night. A working-class bar in Mid City, Jimmy's was a place where people could get whatever they wanted—a couple of beers, in on a poker game in back, a little something extra to keep the party going all weekend, a warm companion for a lonely night. Mace didn't care about the petty vice—it was unstoppable, and Mace had known most of the people that hung out at this bar all his life. He liked coming here when he was feeling bad because the seedy atmosphere matched his mood, and everybody knew him. In here he wasn't a cop so much as he was one of the neighborhood boys. Phil was tending bar, looking at people cross-eyed from behind his perpetually crooked black-rimmed glasses, like they were all crazy which they mostly were, but so was he being half drunk all the time but never all of the way drunk so he couldn't do his job. The bar was busy, people were talking loud and joking, a couple slow danced on the floor to Aaron Neville's angelic voice singing "Crazy Love."

Camille was sitting across from him at one of the wobbly tables. Her features were soft in the dim bar light, her face framed by luxurious, thick brunette hair which danced with auburn highlights and smelled faintly of mint, her brown eyes glowing with a warmth and humor that made Mace feel like a moth attracted to flame. "You wanna dance?" he asked her.

"Yeah, sure." As he escorted her to the tiny dance floor, his heart began to beat faster, like he was an adolescent boy at a High School dance. He turned to face her, placed his hand lightly at the small of her back, and he started to take her other hand in his, but she moved in close and wrapped her arms loosely around his neck, rested her head on his shoulder, and he felt her tension ease as he took her in his arms and they began to move slowly around on the floor, swaying to the rhythm of the song.

When they sat back down at the table, she asked him why he became a homicide dick, then blushed as if using the old-fashioned noir term was a slip of the tongue. So he told her about his mother, how she loved crime shows on TV, how they'd watched them together—Columbo, The Rockford Files, Quincy, nights while his father was sleeping because he had to get up early for work. It just seemed natural that he would want to grow up and solve murders in real life. And he knew his mother would have wanted to be a detective, too, if she hadn't gotten married young and wasn't a woman because back in her day women did not work as police officers in New Orleans, and even now with a few women on the force, they had a tough time on the job. He liked to talk shop with his mother because she offered him insights about cases that he couldn't see because he was too close. His father made fun of them in his good-natured way, but it was obvious he was proud of Mace, and happy that he and his mom were close buddies and always had been, though he joked that he felt like the odd man out.

Sitting here now, across the table from Camille at his

neighborhood bar, Mace felt like it fit, really fit. He'd gone with plenty of women, almost married one, but he'd never felt this way. Camille Hebert's was not the fashion model kind of beauty, but she was pretty and smart and she liked the same thing as he and his mom did—crime, or solving murders anyway. He really didn't like being in a serious relationship where he couldn't talk shop. Mace wanted a woman who was like his mother, smart, savvy and didn't want or expect to be protected from knowing about the hard realities he faced on his job. He was attracted to Camille in a way that he'd never before felt around a woman, like he could be himself and relax around her, and he knew she liked him, too. But he also sensed that it would be best to wait for her to make the first move, so he was hugely relieved when she drank the last of her beer, looked at him in a way that made his heart skip and said, "I hope you don't think any less of me as a cop, but I don't want to be alone tonight. Will you spend the night with me, Mace?"

"I was hoping you'd ask. Let's get out of here."

Mace put his arm around her and walked her outside to the passenger side of the car then turned toward her, looking in her eyes so she could see his hunger was for more than a body to lie with for the night. He placed his hand on the side of her face with a gentleness that was almost reverent, drew her into his arms and held her for a moment with his cheek next to hers. He turned into her and she felt him kiss her hair, pausing to inhale and nuzzle, then her ear, and then she turned her face to his and they kissed long and slow, savoring the flavor of each other and the feel of skin on skin, the promise of the night to come and the feeling of not being alone because they both had felt very much alone for a long time and now that empty feeling was gone, maybe for a night or two, maybe for keeps.

41

Mid-summer in New Orleans is a peak season for crime. People are hot, broke, mean-tempered and desperate. Central lockup was especially busy this Saturday night—the holding cells were crowded beyond capacity and they kept bringing more in.

Jim Davis had never been in jail before. He had always been treated like a privileged, educated white man. Now he was in a crowded, filthy twelve-by-nine holding cell that stank of urine and body funk along with an interesting mix that included two young blacks, one with a shaved head and one with long braided hair and a black T-shirt with HTP stenciled on the back, both wearing low-slung pants, boxers showing, eyes burning into each other and everybody else in a way that let you know that you'd better watch out because you were going to get hurt bad if you made a wrong move or looked the wrong way or said the wrong thing; a derelict white bum with matted, tangled salt-and-pepper hair and an untrimmed beard dressed in layers of filthy clothes who'd wet himself and was intermittently mumbling gibberish that nobody could understand; a preppy redhead in cargo shorts and a Tulane jersey handcuffed to the drain in the center of the concrete floor crying and yelling until one of the blacks kicked him in the side of the head and told him to shut his face; an elderly white with watery eyes, papery skin and shaky hands, nose and cheeks flushed red with a roadmap of purple veins, oily black hair with gray roots, wearing a shabby, wrinkled seersucker suit; and a Hispanic with longish curly hair, sporting plenty of ink, his face bruised and swollen with a couple of teeth broken off in jagged spikes and his Metallica T-shirt was ripped and covered in vomit and blood. It was early in the night. The cell was kept freezing cold and the fluorescent lighting was glaring bright so that the filth, graffiti, blood and weird spots on the walls seemed to be etched behind Jim's eyelids even when he closed them. People were screaming, crying, farting, laughing and cussing in a hellish cacophony that echoed off the concrete walls.

Jim stuck out in the crowd like the deviant he was so that the gang members eyed him with suspicion and one of them finally asked him what he was in for.

"I don't know," he replied. "I think it's a case of mistaken identity."

"Yeah, right. I bet you in for molesting kids. You look like a schoolteacher. You one of them nasty motherfucking diddlers. Shit. I hate bein' in here with your trashy ass. You stay the fuck away from me. Go sit over there." He pointed to the corner next to the steel toilet. Jim got to his feet and obeyed the order, careful not to look at the man directly, hunkering down on the floor between the toilet and the steel bench which did not have any space left for him to sit. The toilet gave off a foul odor, its surface encrusted with dried shit, piss and vomit.

All his life he'd dressed and tried to act in a way that caused him to be so nondescript he was almost invisible—it was how he'd stalked his prey, how he'd gotten away with it for so long. But now, in this town, in this jail, he stuck out like he had a sign tattooed on his forehead: DOES NOT BELONG. People were looking at him, sometimes staring like he was the most visible person here. Two uniformed cops came to the window and looked around, found him, and stared at him with deadpan expressions for a good minute. As they turned away one cop shook his head in disgust. Jim felt like an animal in a zoo.

42

The Crescent House is at the back of the Quarter on Governor Nichols, off the beaten path near Rampart. A remodeled Victorian mansion, it features private dining behind screens or, if you can pay, in small private rooms. The décor is Victorian and the cuisine is a blend of traditional and contemporary Creole. The restaurant serves dinner 'til one a.m. then switches to breakfast for the late-night crowd and closes at eight most mornings. It's a favorite of strippers who want a place to eat after their shift. Also, you can meet a special customer there for private dining and nobody has to know about it if you arrive separately. Seeing customers outside work is against the rules; the clubs are like pimps who want their cut of the action.

Brittney passed out in the cab on the way to the restaurant. She was leaning up against Trey snoring softly, her mouth half open and drooling. Then she started mumbling in her sleep, "lemme' lone, lemme' lone." Sylvie shook her when they arrived at the restaurant and she screamed, "DON'T TOUCH ME!" and punched Sylvie in the side of the head.

Sylvie and Trey exchanged a worried look. Maybe picking Brittney up at work wasn't a good idea. "Brittney," Sylvie said. "It's me, Sylvie. Wake up. We're at the restaurant."

Brittney's eyes opened and Sylvie could see a nightmare

of terror reflected in them that she had never seen in Brittney's tough girl demeanor when she was awake. "Are you okay, Britt?"

Comprehension crept into Brittney's eyes as she came to. "Oh. I just had a bad day. I'll tell you later." They could hear conversation and occasional laughter, the clink of silverware and the soothing notes of a Chopin nocturne as the maître d' led them down the red carpeted hallway lit by flickering electric candles in gilt wall sconces to a small dining room behind a heavy red and gold brocade curtain. Sylvie felt like she was in a nineteenth century novel in the private room, with its oak wainscoting and flocked gray wallpaper with a design of cherubs and leaves along the borders. The round table was set with white linen, gleaming white china trimmed in red and gold, and silver cutlery polished to a shine. There was a centerpiece of gardenias and candles floating in a crystal bowl, ornate silver candlesticks on a sideboard and all of it reflected in a huge gilt-framed mirror which hung on one wall and made the small room seem a lot bigger and almost ridiculously romantic. She'd been here with other dancers a few times but never in one of the private dining rooms, nor had she ever imagined paying to dine in such luxury, but this was a special celebration and talking to Brittney about maybe sobering up and getting training for a good job needed privacy.

"This room must've cost a fortune," Brittney said while they sipped Cristal and waited for their crab-stuffed artichoke and oysters on the half shell. "What'd you do, win the lottery?"

"Not quite," Sylvie answered. "I took a new job, and this is going on my expense account. I want to make a business proposition to you, but you don't have to decide tonight. I can tell you've had a rough day, and honestly I've never seen you drunk like this."

"Yeah, well, I just didn't have time to connect with something to balance out the booze. I'm not used to getting bought out this early in the shift. But hey, I'm not complaining. Thanks for all this, Sylvie. I mean, I can't imagine what kind of business you have in mind that I could do, so why don't you just tell me? If it's risky, I probably can't do it because of my kids. If something happens to me, they won't have anybody."

Sylvie had to wonder what could be riskier than stripping. She thought of her mother with a pang of grief. "My new job is to help kids. I don't know how to put this besides being straight up with you. Somebody put me in charge of a lot of money and I'm supposed to use it to help out kids in trouble. I'm being paid a generous salary to find kids who need help and spend the money helping them."

"So, what're you saying?" Brittney's eyes clouded with suspicion and the beginning of anger.

"I'm saying that I know you and the kids are in a bad situation living at the motel, and I feel the best way to help your kids is to help you. In other words, help you get training to have a regular job, something that pays enough to support you and the kids without having to strip or rely on men. I mean, we both know stripping is a dead-end job and men are unreliable."

"Who're you calling unreliable?" Trey affected an injured look.

"Sorry, Trey. I wasn't talking about you."

"You're talking about men. What you think I am, a lesbian in drag?"

"No, of course not. But there's a lot of creeps out there. Especially if you're a stripper. Women aren't the only gold diggers."

"Yeah, man, that's just what I been looking for. One a them naked mamas bring in the big bucks. You girls got any friends you can hook me up with?"

"I could introduce you to a couple of fine-assed girls," Brittney offered. "But you're gonna have to kick me back some of the profit."

"Stop it you two. What I was saying, Trey, I mean nothing personal but especially if you have kids you can't depend on anybody else to take care of you and the kids. Everybody plays nice at first, then after you're involved you get to see what they're really like. It's impossible to have a good relationship if you're a dancer." Sylvie paused, lit a smoke, took a sip of Cristal. "Obviously, you're dancing naked in front of a roomful of men every night—most men can't handle that. Unless they don't care. The ones that don't have a problem with it are like pimps—they just want somebody to support them. I mean, most of the women I worked with in that business, if they have a man, he doesn't work half the time, and if he is working its dealing drugs to the other dancers or something. Strippers get used by everybody, including their men."

A door opened in the seamless wall and an elderly waiter in a tuxedo came in, carrying a stand and a large silver tray of food — stuffed artichoke, a big platter of oysters, a bottle of Tabasco, a basket of warm, sliced French bread and a plate of butter. He took the champagne out of the ice bucket on the sideboard and topped off their drinks, asked if there was anything else he could bring them.

"We're fine for now, thanks," Trey said. The waiter

retreated with the serving equipment, disappearing behind the hidden door.

"Man, I could get used to this," Brittney said. "You're spoiling me. But I don't think I can go to school." She doused an oyster with Tabasco, tilted her head back and downed it. "I mean, it's real nice of you and all, but I dropped out in seventh grade. I'm way too behind to start now."

"Brittney, I'm in charge of a trust fund of millions of dollars. If you want to do something else for a living, I have the resources to support your family for as long as it takes while you go to school. I'd be happy to do this. Don't you have any dreams? What would you do if you could do something else?"

Brittney stared at Sylvie open mouthed, then lit a cigarette, blew smoke and said, "Hey, this isn't funny. You got to be kidding. It's not nice joking like this with somebody like me."

"I swear I'm not joking, Brittney. But there's a catch. You have to sober up. I'll do whatever I can to help, but you're the one who will have to work at this. You can't make it through school and have a regular job unless you're sober. No more stuff, no more booze. What would you pick if you could do whatever you want?"

Brittney thought about it for a moment as she drew on her cigarette. "I don't know. I mean, I never thought about it. I always figured I'd find a job tending bar when I got too old to strip, but I never thought about doing anything out of the clubs. I guess an office job, or maybe a nurse. But I could never be smart enough to make it through college and be a nurse."

"Well, what if you could? What if your only job was to go to school and get the training to get your nursing license?"

"I got too much catching up to do at my age."

"Nonsense. If you could do it, would you want it bad enough to stay sober?"

Brittney looked at her as if just the thought of having hope had already sobered her up. "I'd do whatever I had to do, I mean that's it. If you're serious about this, I'll quit drinking right now. Get the waiter to bring me some coffee. When does all this start?"

"You don't ever have to go back to work as a stripper again. I'm serious, Britt. Did you leave anything at the club you need?"

"Just my outfits and makeup. I don't need any of that shit. I don't want to go back there." She thought about the rapist cop saying he'd be there to take her home tonight and she felt her stomach clench up. "But how do I know you're not shitting me?"

"Why would I do that, Brittney? Look, let's eat, then I'll take you home and I'll be by to get you in the morning so we can look for a place for you and the kids. You can go to rehab if you need to, but you still have to have a place to live. How are the kids doing?"

"It's hard for them at the motel, but they're happy to be away from the asshole. I can't afford a babysitter so Kevin, my fourteen-year-old stays home and watches the girls. Truth is, they're used to doing without. Brandon didn't work half the time. I had to support his lazy ass along with the kids. When he did work, he blew the money, mostly on himself. I had to catch him on payday before he drank and smoked it all up. He's one of those paid-on-Friday-broke –on-Monday losers."

Sylvie thought about how right she'd been that Brittney would be a good candidate for a hand up. "Brittney, I don't want to go into all the details tonight, but know that things are about to get better for all of you. And thank you for letting me help out. I'm really just doing my job, but if this works out for you and the kids, I can't think of a better job to have. I mean, having a job where you get to help people. You'll see once you're a nurse. It beats hell out of working the clubs."

"I've been wanting out of the clubs for as long as I can remember," Brittney said, "but with the kids it's hard and I don't have any school. The older you get the less you make and the harder it is to find a regular job. I didn't think there'd be an out for me. I feel like I'm stripping on a treadmill. Sooner or later the motor's gonna die and I won't have anywhere to go when it stops. Jesus, just thinking about it makes me want another drink. I still can't believe this is happening. Something in me says I'll believe it when I see it."

"You can drink tonight, we're celebrating. But tomorrow we take care of business and you need to be sober."

43

Sometimes life is like a puzzle—like a big heap of jigsaw pieces that look like they're part of the same picture, but you don't know how to begin to fit them together and you don't have a clue what the picture will look like once it's finished. This is what Lionel was thinking as he stood on the corner of Governor Nichols and North Rampart and watched Trey and Sylvie come out of the Crescent House with one of the local strippers and get in a cab. They were flanking the girl, like they were steadying her, and she looked snockered. What the fuck? Lionel watched the cab pull away from the shadows of a church. What are they doing with that girl looks like she been drugged? The situation was getting increasingly spooky. Lionel thought about a rumor he'd heard a few years ago, that a team of serial killers was preying on the local strippers. And there had been a few dancers who disappeared from the clubs and the streets. People were talking about it in whispers. Nobody ever found the missing girls but the disappearances stopped and people speculated that the killer or killers found another town to hunt in when things got hot. It was thought the killers were a team, somebody from the clubs like a doorman and a stripper.

Lionel had done some checking and found out Sylvie worked at Sugar Daddy's one night a week. He didn't know what else she did. And the brother who hired him to watch the street was a glassblower who did bodyguard work on the side. They were both so low-key it was hard to know what they were up to in New Orleans, a city that was like a small town in that it was hard to go anywhere without seeing somebody you knew. Lionel knew where the drugged girl worked. He decided to find out if she showed up for work again.

He screwed the lid off his Smirnoff and took a drink. He was thinking he ought to leave town now while he's ahead. But he didn't have the money to leave town yet—the psycho was supposed to meet up with him and pay him today, but he hadn't heard from him. Tonight was his last night at the Alexandra, and he was going to have to pay more rent. He figured with all the weirdness he'd be safer at the motel than on the street. Trey had given him a hundred earlier and told him to take the night off. The white dude didn't pay him today so he didn't owe any time. He'd made seventy-one dollars and change off the street crowd, knocked off early and gone to see his connect. He was headed back to his room when he saw this shit. Now he wanted to know more but he was cautious. Curiosity killed the cat, he thought, and this cat ain't about to be killed. His cell showed 11:30. He decided to head back to St. Peter and see what he could find out. Maybe he should call the psycho, see what's up with his money.

44

Detective Charles Burell was an old dog in NOPD homicide. He was a dedicated cop, one of the good ones, and skilled at sniffing out evidence and solving murders. He'd been assigned to Garvey's suspect, but with three sets of ID they didn't even know his real name. Burell didn't trust Fred Garvey. Garvey was dirty, and he was also stupid. He'd arrested the suspect without Mirandizing him on the basis of an illegal search. Burell was certain the perp was going to be back on the street as soon as he was arraigned. The only good thing was that, because his arrest was on a Saturday evening, he wasn't going to see a judge 'til Monday. It was already after eleven on Saturday night, so that still wasn't much time. He had a hunch this sicko was connected to the Butler murders, a crime that had most of the NOPD, even the dirty cops, sickened and enraged. He had watched the films, at least as much as he could stand of them. Part of this guy's MO was torture with burning, which was what had been done to Adrian Butler. How many people could there be in this town who enjoyed burning little kids? Why did the evidence have to fall into Garvey's hands, of all people? Burell fumed. Dammit to hell. He knew Mace Delaroux had the Butler case and that he wasn't about to let anybody else in on it with him unless they could show something good.

Burell had been trying to contact Delaroux ever since he'd looked at the evidence, but Mace was off the radar tonight. And time was running out. He left an urgent message on his cell and didn't see what else he could do. He'd sent a cop down to Central Lockup to observe the suspect, and the officer reported back that the guy looked like the last person you'd ever suspect of committing the atrocities on the videos, except his eyes. He said looking into this guy's eyes was like glimpsing the void: it was what was absent that was creepy, like the guy was a walking dead person. Burell wondered what made those dead eyes come alive. Torture? Though he was a seasoned homicide detective who'd stayed in town during Katrina and had seen more than he ever wanted to, he shuddered when the images on the videos came to mind. He would never be able to get them out of his head.

He was sitting in his cubicle with the computer and other evidence when the perp's phone rang. Could this be a partner? But the videos pointed to a lone sicko. He picked up the phone and pressed the record app, then answered. "Hello."

"Hey, who's this?"

"It's Charles, who're you?"

"Bob there?"

Burell's mind was working backwards and forwards and he recalled the Robert Smith ID. "He's busy. Can I have him call you back?"

The phone went dead.

Burell logged onto the tracking app. The call came from St. Peter, a half block off the square. He would have the number checked later, but knew it was a throwaway. Now what? He'd spooked the guy. All he could do was go to the location, dial the number and see if a phone rang. It was almost midnight. He rang Mace's number again as he headed down to his car, and this time Mace picked up.

"This better be good."

"Hey, it's Charley Burell. I need feedback."

"What about?"

"We have a suspect in custody. I think he's tied to the Butler murders."

"You mean the one Garvey brought in this evening?"

"How'd you hear about that? You went off duty at six."

"Yeah. With a case like the Butlers there's no such thing as off duty, right?"

"I was supposed to sign off at ten, but I can't let go of this thing."

"I watched Garvey arrest the guy," Mace said. "I was already tailing him. So, we're on the same page about the Butlers and this asshole. What can I help you with?"

Burell got off the elevator in the parking garage and headed for his car. He told Mace about the box of evidence, the films, and the three sets of ID. "I don't know if we can use this stuff. Garvey went in the computer without a warrant then arrested him and interrogated him in the squad car without Mirandizing. We might only have a day before this creep walks. So I was hoping we could find enough new evidence to keep him in custody."

"Yeah. I want Garvey's badge, and if somebody gets killed over his stupid shit I might get it. The Feds want names. Just so you know."

"Hey, I'm with you on Garvey. I'll back you all the way. But right now, I have the fruit of the poisoned tree. I mean the evidence. We tried to get the perp to sign the Miranda form and he wouldn't do it. He said Garvey arrested him and then questioned him in the squad car, no Miranda. Anyway, his cell just rang. I don't know who called but I have a location. St. Peter, by the square. I'm on my way there."

"You want me to meet you?"

"How soon can you be there?"

"Twenty minutes."

"Front of the Cathedral. If I'm not out there I found the caller."

Mace hung up and turned to Camille, who was sitting up in bed listening. "I have to go."

"I heard. What's happening?"

Mace told her about the evidence and the phone call.

"Oh, now you're working with Burell instead of me?"

"How fast can you get dressed?"

"Hey, I'm a homicide cop, too. You wanna race?"

Mace had to fight the impulse to take her in his arms as she threw back the sheet and jumped out of his bed naked, sweat from their lovemaking shining on her skin in the moonlight. He marveled as he watched her rapid movements—she was just like him, married to the job.

"Hurry up," she barked, glaring at him from across the rumpled bed as she fastened her bra.

"You sure are bossy." He grinned as he groped for his scattered clothes, finally giving up and switching on the lamp because she'd flung his garments all over the room in her haste to have him in bed.

Two minutes later they were in the car, heading down Canal for the Quarter. "So what do they have?" Camille asked.

"There were videos on a computer belonging to Davis."

"You mean films of Amanda and Adrian?"

"No others, lots of them. From what my source told me, it's bad."

"You've known about this for how long?"

"I called somebody earlier. Look, I don't know the details yet either. Apparently, they have his cell, a wallet with two sets of fake ID and credit cards, another wallet with fake ID he was using when Garvey arrested him, and he had a murder kit, kind of like the one we saw him put together today, including a gun. That's all I know."

"Why didn't you tell me about all this?"

"I was waiting for more information. They're checking out Garvey's story. He said a priest came in to the station on Royal and turned over a box of evidence to him earlier today. He checked it out. After seeing the ID and the films he saw Davis in the Quarter and arrested him on the spot. He claims he had the box in the trunk of his squad car because he was going to turn it in on Broad. Then he saw Davis and arrested him without calling for backup. We saw that."

"How did the priest get the stuff?"

"He wouldn't say. Said it was from a third party and that person's identity is protected by the priest's office."

"What about Garvey? How do you think he botched the arrest?"

"He didn't Mirandize him and he didn't get a warrant for the computer. The guy's a loose cannon. I don't think he knows the definition of probable cause. Look, everybody in the country who knows anything about criminal justice knows NOPD has a rep. Katrina made it worse, but with the Consent Decree things are finally changing, only it's slow. There are still plenty of dirty cops who haven't been caught with their pants down. Could be people are afraid to complain. Or it could be that, like Garvey, they mostly interact with people who nobody will listen to anyway, and they know it."

They drove through downtown, past the Saenger, the fast-food places, the hotels, the bars and stores. The street was alive with people, some in evening wear, most dressed casual. Almost all had glittering strands of souvenir beads hanging around their necks and carried go cups of booze. A middle-aged couple passed in front of their car at the signal, he in an orange velveteen pimp suit with a matching musketeer hat; she in a short sequined purple dress with a boa of green chicken feathers draped around her shoulders, the green feathers marking her tottering trail like bread crumbs on the street. Apparently, they'd shopped for evening wear at one of the ubiquitous souvenir shops that feature loud Cajun music, gigantic dead alligators, high-priced hot sauce, refrigerator magnets and t-shirts.

"When were you planning to tell me all this?" Camille asked.

"When I got confirmation; like first-hand info not third. The guy we're going to see is the man. Right now's he trying to come up with some other evidence that incriminates Davis. Garvey didn't bother getting a warrant for the computer."

"What about calling ViCAP?"

"I was planning on it. From what I understand the videos are evidence he's been killing for years and in other jurisdictions so the Feds can pick up the case if we have to do that."

Camille lit a cigarette she'd fished out of her purse, turned to face him in the car. "You were planning on it? I will not be shut out of this case."

"Okay, I'll do anything you ask. I was gonna talk to you. Just try not to smoke in my car. Deal?"

Camille put out the cigarette in an empty coke can. "Tell me about the films."

"I called a friend on swing shift, a good cop who's trying to break into homicide and wants me to mentor her. I've already decided to do it but she doesn't need to know that yet. Anyway, she gets what she can for me without anybody knowing. She talked to somebody who was in the room when Burell opened the computer files. Like I said, this is third-hand. Look, we're almost there, so let's get it from Burell, okay?"

"What's he gonna say about me being with?"

"Nothing if he wants to play ball. He's a good cop. A smart cop."

They turned down Chartres. The crowd was mostly college aged, a few older tourists, some homeless, and the ever-present doormen and strippers around the Iberville intersection. At midnight on Saturday things were just getting started. They found a space a block up from the Square in a no parking zone. Mace checked his cell—they'd made it in nineteen minutes.

"Mace, Sylvie lives here. She's a half block up St. Peter."

"That's exactly where the call came from. Davis must have somebody else involved."

"Andy Sharp hired a bodyguard for Sylvie and rented him the apartment below hers. Should I call him? Maybe he's seen something."

"Let's talk to Burell first."

They crossed the Square, scanning the street while trying not to look too obvious. There were still a couple of tarot readers out, along with the homeless who hung out on the benches in front of the Cabildo at night. A woman was getting her fortune told at one of the setups by the side of the park, her companion standing next to her listening as she sat in the circle of light cast by a portable lamp, the fortune teller pointing at her palm as he talked. People crossed the Square in small groups headed to Decatur or Bourbon, most of them with go cups. Burell was standing in front of the Cathedral by the mouth of Pirates Alley, watching them approach.

Camille saw he was older, tall and thin with café-au-lait skin, white short cropped hair, a rumpled suit, and eyes that saw into her and also seemed aware of everything going on around the perimeter.

"Who's the lady?" he asked Mace, covering his surprise with a smile.

"She's from JP. We think the Butler killings were tied to one of her cases, so we're working together. But this is just between us, okay?"

"Sure," Burell said. "I'm Charley Burell." He held out his hand to Camille and she grasped it, giving a tight smile.

"Camille Hebert. What do you want to do? About the phone call."

"I think we missed the guy. There's still a cop in front of Rouse's. Let's go see if he saw anything."

45

Lionel was thinking about chucking the phone into the Mississippi, but didn't want to throw it away until he found out what happened to the psycho. He saw a cab pull up in front of Trey's building and watched Trey and Sylvie get out. Trey was paying the driver and he looked up and saw Lionel watching from down the block. He waved a hand and then they went in the gate. Lionel waited until the cab pulled off and turned onto Royal, walked up to the gate and took out his ID to pick the lock. He could hear them ascending the stairs, up at the top. He was quiet like a cat when he wanted to be, despite his hustle singing loud enough to disturb everybody on the street. He crept up the old winding staircase, reaching the third-floor landing as Trey rounded the corner heading back down.

"What are you doing in here?" Trey demanded in a soft voice that carried menace.

For once Lionel was out of stories. "I was wondering the same thing about you. I mean, you hired me to watch the street, but you didn't tell me what for, so I thought I'd just check things out. You know? I was thinking if you going to keep paying me to watch the street and I already do my singing gig here maybe I could rent a place." Jesus, I need to go back to the room and smoke some dope, he thought. I ain't cut out for this shit. "Well, you know if they got any places for rent?"

"No. Are you going to be downstairs tomorrow? I can try to find out."

"Yeah, I'll be down there 'round four. Where you live in here anyway?"

"You're standing right next to it. But they have a security gate here for a reason. Next time you stop by, why don't you ring the buzzer?"

"Hey man, no problem. I just didn't know which one to ring. Number six yours? I'll ring you next time for sure. Well, I'm gonna go back to my place, kick it for a while. You need me to watch things tomorrow?"

"Yeah, I'll be down." Trey stood on the landing and waited for Lionel to turn around and walk downstairs then he went out to his balcony and watched until he saw him heading back up the street towards Bourbon.

46

The temperature had cooled to a tolerable eighty-three degrees but it was still muggy out on the roof where Sylvie sat smoking and enjoying the comparative silence when her cell rang. It was Andy Sharp, wondering how the night had turned out. Sylvie told her about Brittney's resolve to stay sober and work with them to climb up out of the hole she'd been sinking in with the kids.

"Wait a minute," Andy said. "She's going to stop drinking cold turkey? Alcohol withdrawal is dangerous. If she's been drinking for years, she could die from withdrawal. She might need a hospital stay, or you can just monitor her and help her taper off with beer, but there's liability if something goes wrong. You need to go over there with a six pack tomorrow and arrange for her to be hospitalized for a few days. And we have to do something with the kids while she's in. I would say you could watch them, but what if Jim Davis gets out of jail Monday and comes after you while you've got the kids?"

"Are you telling me that the New Orleans police department is so messed up they can't protect us? What're they good for anyway?"

Sylvie heard Andy exhale a long sigh of exasperation. "Listen, I'm going to make a few calls and we'll work something out," Andy said. "These things are complicated, but it sounds like it's all going to be worth it."

"Andy, there's a part of me that feels like if I help Brittney, I'll be helping my mother. I was too young to help and I know if she had a safer job, she'd still be here."

"Well, just don't get your hopes up too much. My motto is hope for the best but plan for the worst. Listen, I won't be over in the morning. I need to spend some time with my kids. I'll have my cell on me if you need anything. We need to come up with a plan to get Brittney some help, and take care of her kids. It's good that its summer, so we have time to get them stabilized before school. Just remember, you don't have to solve everything in one day, alright?"

"Yeah, but I want to get them into a better hotel at least. The Magnolia's depressing and it isn't suitable for kids. Can I call you in the morning before I go over there?"

"If you have to, but no earlier than ten unless it's a life-threatening emergency."

"Gotcha."

After Sylvie hung up, she went in the main room and booted up her computer. Her temples were beginning to throb and she felt dehydrated from the champagne. She got a water out of the fridge and swallowed some ibuprophen. Then she went back to the computer and googled alcohol withdrawal. She found the Web MD link and read that alcohol withdrawal needs medical attention. The symptoms can begin anywhere from two to twelve hours after the last drink. She determined to go see Brittney early with a six pack of beer, before serious withdrawal kicked in.

In bed she drifted into sleep picturing gardenias and candles floating in a crystal bowl.

Sunday

47

Officer Owens was a rotund fiftyish man with gray hair and a cheery demeanor which was amazing in itself considering the characters he usually dealt with at night, including students, derelicts, tweakers, hookers, tourists, and residents of the Quarter, many of them night workers who needed something from the neighborhood grocery on their way home. He was keenly observant of everything that transpired within sight of his post in front of Rouse's on St. Peter and Royal. He'd noticed that the street hustler who sang halfway up the block left earlier than usual and came back around eleven-thirty, then disappeared again after he made a call on his cell. It was unusual for him to be around if he wasn't singing for tips. Owens was happy he was gone because his repetitious singing was torturous to listen to and there had been numerous complaints from local residents. Now three detectives were here, asking about him.

Burell said, "We're looking for somebody who was here right before midnight and made a phone call. That person's connected to a suspect we have in custody. We have the suspect's cell and somebody called it from right over there. Sounded like a male but there's no telling around here." He pointed across the street and down the block.

"Well, the singer's the only one I remember hanging over

there around then," Owens said. "Most people don't stop on that block. They walk past headed to Decatur or Bourbon." Now he recalled the habits of the annoying street singer. "The guy's been around for at least nine months. He stands over there all the time." Bowens pointed a stubby finger towards the mid-block point of St. Peter, right by the Gumbo Shop. "He sings the same song over and over for ten or twelve hours. People who live around here complain, but he has a license to be out there. Some people moved because of him. The guy's a druggie, homeless, and he looks like he don't eat. He comes in here at night," Bowens jerked his finger over his shoulder at the grocery, "but he don't buy food, only booze. You want me to, I can keep an eye out, let you know what he's up to."

"Perfect. Here's my cell number." Burell handed him a card. "I want to know about any suspicious activity on that block."

Bowens snorted. "You wanna know about everything goes on around here I'll be on the phone witcha half the night."

"So, you're a smart guy. Just tell me what you think is important to this situation. If I need more, I'll ask you."

"Sure thing, Cap."

As they stood looking down the block Lionel appeared from in front of the corner restaurant across the street. "That's him, right there on the corner," Burell nodded his head in Lionel's direction. He was shambling along in a daze and didn't notice them as he crossed the intersection. Burell took out the cell that belonged to Jim Davis, pushed callback, and Lionel's shirt pocket vibrated just as he reached their corner. He came out of his reverie, reached for the phone, and they surrounded him. Mace took him by the arm and steered him over to the side of the grocery store.

"We need to talk," Mace said. "We can do this right here, or we can go downtown, your choice."

Lionel's eyes were popping scared. "Man, I ain't done nothing."

Camille took the cell out of his pocket, and Mace continued to grip his arm as he guided him across the street towards the shadowy entrance of Pirates Alley. "We just need to ask you a few questions. If you cooperate, we'll be okay. Okay?"

"Yeah, man, whatever you want. Hey, why we got to go in here?"

They walked up the narrow alley which was bordered by the Cathedral on the left, shops on the right. The light from the street lamp on Royal grew dimmer the further they went in, but moonlight shone on the pale statue in the park, a stone Jesus atop a pedestal, his arms outstretched in welcome.

"This is confidential," Mace said. We're not gonna hurt you. But that freak you're working with might. You have any idea who you've been dealing with?"

"Oh, man! That's what this is about? I'm scared of that dude. Where he at? He see me talking with ya'll, he's liable to kill my ass."

"That's what I'm talking about." Mace stopped in the entrance of a walk-through behind the Cabildo that ran from Pirates Alley to St. Peter. He said, "Now I'm going to let go of you and we're going to talk. You need to make up your mind right now that you're going to be straight with us. Otherwise, we'll have to take you in, and we can book you into the same holding tank we've got him in. Is that what you want?"

"Shit, man, that freak needs to be locked up. I didn't want

nothing to do with him. But he ain't the kind takes no for an answer."

"How long have you known him?" Mace was standing in front of Lionel, who was backed up against the Cabildo wall, right under one of the high barred windows, with Camille and Charley at his sides blocking him in. He looked at Camille, then at Charley, then back at Mace. They were serious, but he didn't get the vibe he got from some of the thugs in uniform around the Quarter. He decided he didn't have a thing to lose.

"I was round the corner Thursday, doing my gig, when this freak comes up, pokes me in the back with a knife and tells me he got a job, gonna pay me some serious cash." Lionel let out a long sigh. "Look, I need a drink. You mind?"

It was Camille who answered. "What did you say your name is?"

"Lionel, ma'am."

"Lionel, we have a reasonable suspicion to search your person, and what I think is you're holding. An open bottle is a misdemeanor and we can take you in. If you have something else, you might not want us to find it. Now, let me see your ID."

"Aw, shit!" He reached in his back pocket and pulled out his wallet. Burell took it out of his hand, flipped it open, and saw that his name was indeed Lionel Scruggs.

"Okay Lionel," he said. "Go ahead and have a drink. Then we need the story. We don't have all night here."

Lionel pulled out a pint of Smirnoff and took a long pull, then screwed the cap back on and put it back in his pants pocket. "Okay man, this dude offered me a job, making three hundred a day, to watch the white woman who lives across the street from my gig. But I don't want nothin' to do with it. He's creepy. Real square looking but there's something fucked-up about this dude, and when I said no he stuck me with a knife, made me go to his car with him. Then he pulls out a gun and makes me get in the car."

"When did this happen?" Mace said.

"It was Thursday evening, bout four-thirty, five o'clock. I was just getting back to work again after the rain."

"You have a regular job around here?"

"Man, that's what he say. My singing gig's my regular job. I got a license to perform. I be out there every day, same time, same place."

"Okay, go on. Where was he parked?"

"He was over in that lot next to Jax on Decatur. He drive one a those Honda Civics. He pulled a gun over there in the lot and made me get in. Oh, there's a white woman lives across the street from my gig. She came down one time and told me to quit singing or sing something else. Anyway, we was walking through the Square and she walks by. The dude pointed her out, sneaky like, and told me she's his daughter and he want me to watch her. I think he's full of shit. This motherfucker be stalking her. I don't want nothin' to do with it. I don't need money that bad. But the dude's a psycho. I been thinking about leaving town behind this shit." Lionel pulled out the pint and took another long swig, replaced it in his pocket, took out a paisley kerchief and wiped the sweat off his face.

"So why did you call his phone tonight?" Mace asked.

"Man, the dude be spying on me, calling me up and shit. That's what he been doing. Then today I don't hear from him. I just want to know where he's at. I ain't stupid. I figure if I do what he wants, this freak's gonna kill me when he's finished with his business. But at least when I hear from him, I got an idea where he's at. If he don't call, that might mean he's done with me, and then I need to shag ass, or at least watch my back. But I been watching my back the last three days cause of this motherfucker." Lionel looked at Camille and said, "Scuse me, ma'am. I'm just stressed out."

"Please do not treat me different because I'm a woman." Camille enunciated each word slow. "I'm a police officer to you, a homicide detective. If you have to you can think of me as one of the boys."

"I don't mean no disrespect, but there ain't no way I can think of you as a boy. You're one fine woman." Lionel kept his eyes on her face, which Camille appreciated, and she smiled big and easy at him.

"Thanks Lionel. Now let's get back to your story. What are we going to do with you?"

"Well, no offense, ma'am, but I'm wondering how long you gone have this dude locked up. I don't want nothin' to do with his funky ass. I don't give a shit about the money. I'm a two-time loser but I ain't never done nothing to disrespect a woman; at least not on purpose. Truth is, I'm scared shitless. I been trying to figure out a way to shake him off."

Burell cut in, "You should have called the police right from the start. What's wrong with you? If you have knowledge of a crime in progress and you don't report it, that makes you an accessory."

Lionel turned and looked at Charley like he was crazy. "Man, don't give me that shit. I know how ya'll look at us homeless. You all ain't never done nothin' to protect me. No offense, but most of the cops I see around here would be just as happy if some psycho killed all us homeless, and maybe half the folks in the projects, too. That be the first thing this freak pointed out to me. He say ain't nobody give a shit about me, especially not the cops. You tell me to be straight up with you, don't run that shuck on me."

Both Mace and Camille turned to look at Burell. To his credit, he didn't have a comeback. "Listen," he finally said, "I hear you. I can't do much about what other cops do, and I know we have some bad apples. But I'm a homicide detective, and I didn't earn this position by dissing informants. You work with us, I guarantee you we keep it quiet, and we'll have your back. You have my word on it."

"Man, that's great. But you still didn't say how long this freak gone be locked down for. What you got him on anyway?"

The detectives exchanged a look. "We can't tell you that right now," Charley said. But he saw Lionel's face close up, like he wasn't going to play by those rules. "Alright, he's a suspect in some homicides. But his arraignment's on Monday and he could walk. If that happens, he may try to contact you. Look, where were you going, anyway?"

"I was heading back to my room. I had a long-assed day. I need to chill."

"Yeah, just don't chill too much. I'll need to be in touch in the morning. That okay?"

"Yeah, 'cept folks 'round there see me coming back with the police, they might take it the wrong way."

"I'll just drop you off in the neighborhood. Where you staying?"

"Right now I'm at the Alexandra over on Ursulines. But this is my last night there, and I don't got the cash to pay for more time."

Mace took the hint and pulled out his wallet. "Will fifty cover another day?"

"Yeah, that'll work." Lionel took the money.

Burell said, "Come on, I'll give you a ride to your place."

"So he did target Sylvie" Camille said, as they drove down Canal to Mid City. "If he walks because of Garvey, somebody's going to die. He could just disappear. He can get more IDs, and he's got money. From what you said about those films, he's been traveling, preying on people and staying under the radar. We really need to call ViCAP, get the Feds in on this. Can they get a warrant to go into the computer and tie the crimes to him?"

"Damned right they can. He's been killing in different states, and serial murder's federal jurisdiction. So's preying on kids, not to mention kidnapping."

"Let's call them in the morning."

"We will."

"Can they work fast enough to keep him in jail? I'm worried he'll go on a spree."

"They have resources. But they still have to go by the rules. It's going to take time to tie him to the computer and the films. There were twenty-seven videos, going back to '93. But most serials start killing early, like in their teens or twenties. The best chance is to find something to tie him to an early crime—some forensic evidence he left before he got good at it. You can bet your ass they'll have his DNA before he leaves jail. They just need to tie him to an unsolved. They can start by checking to see if there were any around the area he grew up in. Don't worry. They'll come up with something. In the meantime, we just do what we can to hold him."

Mace's cell rang, it was Burell. "Hey, Charley."

"Hey. I just dropped him off a block from his room. I'm thinking if the perp gets out of jail Monday, he'll leave town. But he might contact Lionel first, so we need to keep Lionel on our team. I'm going home. Tomorrow's a long day. But we should get together in the morning."

"I was thinking the same thing. Why don't we meet at Canal Pancake House around ten?"

"Let's make it nine. We may only have one more day."

"Can you bring the computer?"

"No, I don't think so. Well, yeah, maybe. Let me see what I can do."

"Okay, see you tomorrow."

Mace put his cell on the console and glanced at Camille. "You're staying with me tonight, right?"

"I'd like to, but I have to go home early and shower."

"Yeah, we'll probably have another long day." Mace pulled into his drive. He checked the time—one-twenty, less than two hours since he'd received the call from Burell. They'd have to be up by seven. So, if they could just go to sleep, they'd get five hours. Not bad for a case like this. But the challenge would be to actually sleep once they were in bed.

As if she could read his thoughts, Camille said "I need to sleep. We both do."

"Yeah, I'm beat." Mace was relieved. Maybe this would work for the long haul.

48

The morning sky was the same color as the slate sidewalks and the weather app showed fifty-percent chance of rain. Of course it would rain, probably all day long since she'd be helping Brittney and the kids move. A riverboat calliope piped out a tune and Sylvie could hear the clop-clopping of a mule-drawn carriage four stories below, the driver's nasal spiel a reminder that this neighborhood was a tourist attraction. It was like waking up in a theme park—one a customer at Sugar Daddy's had labeled, "a theme park for the depraved." Sylvie stubbed out her cigarette and crawled in the window. She was thinking about her day as she put water on to boil for the French press. First, get Brittney some maintenance beer, and then get her and the kids into a healthier place.

She googled 'family hotel suites new orleans' and found one in the warehouse district. It was far enough from the Quarter to be away from the stripper clubs and nobody would know where Brittney was. It had suites with kitchenettes, sitting areas, and enough sleeping space for everybody, with a fold out couch for Kevin in the sitting room. This would do for a temporary space while they planned the next step. If Brittney still wanted to give up drugs, it would be like a different world for them—a clean, wholesome family place with a pool, weight room, breakfast buffet, movies, and vacationing families instead of addicts and people in trouble. She called the hotel and booked a suite for a week. They could check in at three, so that was the project for the day—going over to Brittney's with a six pack and getting everybody into a better place. If Brittney needed to go to the hospital, Sylvie and Trey would stay with the kids, right there at Springhill Suites.

She left Trey at a diner up the street and went on in the cab to the motel. Kevin opened the door. He was a heavy boy with longish straight brown hair and big dark eyes that looked sad and guarded. "Mom's sick, he said."

"Well, I thought she might be. Do you mind if I come in and see her anyway? She's expecting me."

"Just a minute." Kevin shut the door and Sylvie could hear him talking with his mom. He opened the door a moment later and stood aside as Sylvie entered. The room was dark, with only the flickering light from the TV which was running without sound. Brittney was lying in one of the beds and the two girls were in the other bed, watching a muted cartoon in a coma of dazed boredom. Sylvie got the impression this was the regular morning routine in this family, at least while they were holed up in this motel. Brittney needed to sleep it off but couldn't allow the girls to go outside here because it was too dangerous.

"Hi Brittney, how you feeling?"

"Alright. How're you?" she croaked, propping herself up on an elbow and squinting toward the doorway.

"Pretty good. I brought something for you." Sylvie held up the six-pack. "Is there anywhere we can go talk?"

"Yeah, the bathroom."

As soon as they were in the bathroom Sylvie handed Brittney a beer. "You're going to need this. I did some research and you can't just quit drinking cold turkey. So, it's one beer an hour today, then we'll see how you feel tomorrow."

"Thanks." Brittney took the beer and popped the top, drank with relief, like it was the medicine she needed in the morning.

"How long have you been drinking, anyway?"

"What do you mean?"

"If you've been drinking a lot for a long time you can die from withdrawal."

"Jesus Christ," Brittney said. She took another drink, then turned around and threw up in the toilet. "Sorry. I do that every morning." She grabbed a cup, filled it with tap water and rinsed her mouth. She spit the water and took another drink. "Maybe I can hold this down."

"Look, Britt, if you need to go to the hospital for a few days, I can stay with the kids."

"Thanks. I'd rather not leave my kids though. Just let me try it this way first, okay?"

"Whatever you think. But if you get sicker, you have to go to the hospital. Hey, I got you guys a suite downtown. It's in the warehouse district. I hope you don't mind. I just thought you'd like a better place."

"Are you serious?" Brittney's eyes showed a sparkle of life.

"Reservation's for three this afternoon. You have the suite for a week, or as long as it takes."

"I haven't told the kids anything yet. I can't believe this is happening."

"I know you don't want to get their hopes up. So, what if I go rent a car, get some luggage for you to pack, and some breakfast. You need anything else while I'm out?"

"Yeah, water."

After Sylvie left, Brittney finished the beer, opened another, and went out to talk to the kids. "That was a friend. You know her, she worked the front desk. Listen kids, how would you like to get out of this dump today? Sylvie rented us a better place downtown."

The girls looked at their mother like she was crazy. It was Kevin who spoke up. "What do you have to do, Mom?"

"Whaddaya mean, Kev?"

Kevin thought for a minute. "I mean nobody does something without wanting you to do something for them. What does she want you to do?"

"She wants me to go back to school and get a better job; nursing or something like that. She used to work in the clubs before she worked here. That's where we know each other from. Somebody hired her to help people. It's hard to believe, but her job is to help people now. She's getting paid a lot of money."

"How much money is she getting for helping us?" Kevin sounded weary.

"Look, I know it's hard to believe. We went out to dinner last night and she explained it to me. I didn't say anything to you kids because I can't believe it either. It seems too good to be true. But she's here today, just like she said she would be. Anyway, what do we have to lose? If it doesn't work, at least we'll be in a nice place for a week and I can always go back to stripping. She brought me some beer because I have to drink a little and cut back gradually. If I quit drinking all at once, I'll get sick. But I promise if I don't have to go back to work in the clubs, I'm quitting drinking. It's what I have to do. My end of the deal, you know? I have to stay sober if she's going to help us."

"Cool!" Kevin's eyes lit up.

The girls were up now, paying attention. Stephanie, the oldest, wasn't saying anything. She looked skeptical, like this was just another one of her mother's crazy schemes to get a better life. There had been other people, all men. Things were always going to be better, and they were all nice at first. But things kept getting worse and nobody was nice, they were just pretending.

"Are we going to get an apartment Mom?" This was Allison, the youngest. She was sitting up, her face serious, her green eyes confused and a little scared. She wore a pink Dora the Explorer nightgown, and a few strands of her long blonde hair stuck to the side of her face because she sweated a lot at night and had bad dreams.

"We're going to stay in a hotel suite for a while and look for another place. Maybe a house with a yard."

"What's a hotel seat?"

"Suite, honey. It's like this, only nicer; we'll have a kitchen and more space. I won't have to sleep all day so you guys can play and stuff. Look, I know it's hard to believe, but this is an adventure, okay?"

"How are we going to have money if you don't work?"

"I am going to work. I'm going to school, just like you guys. I'm going to learn how to be a nurse. Nurses make more money than Sylvie's making for helping us. After I finish school, we won't need help. Now you girls get in the shower. We have to wear our good clothes because we're gonna be staying in a nice place."

Sylvie determined to drop off the food and luggage and go rent a car. She had bought six cartons of coconut water—

Brittney needed rehydration. She brought Trey with this time to help, so when she knocked on the door of the room, she decided that if the kids looked scared, she'd have to ask him to wait in the cab because she guessed the kids were scared of men. They looked scared of her too—scared of people.

Brittney answered the door this time. She looked better, like she believed this was really real and was starting to have fun. Kevin walked up to Sylvie and said "I'm Kevin." He smiled, but it was a careful smile. When he turned to Trey and introduced himself, they bumped fists and this seemed to put Kevin more at ease.

Stephanie looked like a version of her mother before the world chewed her up, with pale features, long blond hair, and intelligence and dignity which shone in her light blue eyes. She introduced herself to Sylvie and Trey, holding out a hand to each of them in turn, her eyes asking questions.

Allison homed in on the bags of McDonald's Sylvie was carrying and asked, "Is that for us?"

"Yes, breakfast. You like McDonald's?"

"It's my favorite! Thanks! Are we going to stay in a hotel seat?"

"It's a suite, and yeah, if you want to stay there," Sylvie said. "It's nicer than this place. They have a bigger pool, a better TV, and lots of other fun stuff."

"Yeaaay!"

49

The dragon's tail she'd seen below Mace's sleeve led to a tattoo which covered his back and trailed down his left arm—one of the most intricate, colorful tattoos Camille had ever seen. St. Michael the Archangel slaying a red devil with a human body and the face of a man in torment, dragon's wings and a tail that snaked up Mace's back and down his arm, almost to the wrist. The tattoo bore the Latin inscription Non Timebo Mala—I will fear no evil. They'd slept like stones and woke early, made love to birdsong as the light crept in through the sheer curtains and changed the room from dark to silvery gray. Their morning sex left Camille feeling like she could face anything the day threw at her.

They went over to Camille's where she showered and packed a bag, then they made it to the Pancake House early to have breakfast before Burell showed up with the computer. If they were going to check out the videos they wanted to eat first or they might not be able to.

The restaurant was packed and Jodie motioned them to go back as she rushed by with a tray of food. Camille saw that the outdated do was askew on her head and a curly strand of brunette hair had escaped at the nape of her neck. It's a costume! Camille realized with delight. The whole getup was a take on that TV sitcom from the 1970s. What a fun idea.

Camille liked her all the more for her role as quintessential hash house waitress. She suspected that if you met her on the street you'd have to look twice to see she's the same person.

They each had a pecan waffle with scrambled eggs and sausage, and they shared a plate of watermelon, cantaloupe, grapes, and pineapple. The workout in bed gave Camille a big appetite and the food tasted better because she was happy. Burell came in just as they were starting on the fruit plate, Jodie following with a pot of coffee. He was carrying a cardboard box. "Hey, ya'll." He set the box down in the booth then slid in.

"Good morning. You brought the evidence," Camille said.

"Yeah, I had to check it out and give 'em some bullshit about questioning the priest. It's everything—the laptop, the phone, the wallet, the gun and it looks like a murder kit. This guy's a sick fuck, you know? I mean, what's he do with a curling iron, fix her hair up after he kills her? He likes to burn people, at least that's what the films show, so I have a pretty good idea what he was going do with it. It makes me want to put him in an interview room, plug it in and shove it up his ass. I got sisters."

Jodie spoke up, "You want coffee?"

He looked over his shoulder, saw her standing there holding a coffee pot and was embarrassed. "I'm sorry. I forgot you were there."

"Aw forget it. I hear all kindsa stuff on this job. Can I get you some food?"

"No. Pour me a cup of that great-smelling coffee. This scum we have to deal with can ruin your appetite."

"You got it. By the way, breakfast's on the house if you change your mind," this as she poured the coffee. "If there's somebody bad out there, you need to eat. It'll give you the energy to go after him."

"Thanks, ma'am, maybe later."

"So let's take a look at this stuff," Mace said, pulling a pair of latex gloves out of his pocket as he stood up.

"Look, you don't want to see the films. We got a couple of good prints off the stuff so maybe don't handle it unless you absolutely have to. I had nightmares last night." Mace sat back down as Burell continued talking. "He's going to try to deny this crap is his. He'll probably try to say somebody else put the films on the computer. We need to find out how this stuff got from him to the priest. We can't make the priest talk, but if we offer immunity maybe the third party will come forward. We need the missing pieces, but this is the kicker—no matter what we have it's illegal to search his computer without a warrant unless he relinquished it voluntarily. So, Garvey arrested him on the basis of an illegal search. Then he questioned him in the squad car without Miranda. While he needs to prove the illegal questioning, it would be a reasonable assumption he's telling the truth based on Garvey's behavior. A good investigator could come up with witnesses to validate that Garvey violates people's rights all the time. The good thing is we can have Garvey's badge over this. But that's chicken shit. We need this guy to stay in jail."

Camille said, "We have to call ViCAP. Can't the feds get a warrant to nail him with the computer? If the films show murders in different states, it's a federal jurisdiction, and no matter what we did wrong they can step in and prosecute, right?"

"Right," Burell said. "But they may not have probable cause for the computer. We need to talk to whoever gave it to the priest."

"There's another thing," Camille said. She explained the connection with Bernice Davis, and the film Bernice left. "There's a good chance he's been killing for decades. If we can get the unsolveds from the areas he lived in before he started traveling, maybe we can find evidence and nail him for one of those crimes. This is where the feds can help."

"Let's do it," Burell said. "Hey, I think I got my appetite back. Where's the waitress?"

"She'll be back. So, what's the plan here? Why don't you send the prints to IAFIS and contact ViCAP? I'll go talk to the priest. What's his name, anyway?"

"Fr. Greg Lee. He's rector at St. Brigid's over in the Lower Nine. The church started from a tent he set up after Katrina. Now they're in an old diner up by the Industrial Canal on St. Claude. Here's the address." He handed Mace a piece of note paper. "I'm going to talk to Scruggs first, while I can catch him in his room."

"Listen," Camille said. "You need to contact the feds this morning. We'll go talk to the priest now, and you have to call the feds. Can you do that before you talk to Scruggs?"

"I don't know. We need Scruggs and I don't want him to bolt. The guy's scared."

They came up with a plan. Mace and Camille would go talk to Fr. Greg, Charley would go see Scruggs, then they'd meet back at the headquarters on Broad and contact the feds together. They decided the NOPD would not like them bringing in the feds, especially since they had yet another rogue cop in the mix, but they'd cooperate because of the Consent Decree.

Jodie came back and took Burell's order, two fried egg po-boys to go, one for Scruggs. After she left, Mace pulled on the gloves and began going through the contents of the box. He looked at the stuff that was in the backpack first. The things were smeared with black fingerprint powder and he left them in the evidence bags.

"Did somebody impound the car he was driving?" Mace asked.

"Not yet. It must still be in that parking garage."

"We followed him yesterday and saw him buy a curling iron, duct tape, rope, a gun—everything in this box. He was replacing the murder kit, and we can tie him to this one because he put together another one that's almost identical and it's in the trunk of that car. The car is a silver Civic with a temporary license plate FXY 396. We trailed him all day yesterday and watched him drive it off the lot. He was arrested right outside that parking garage by Iberville and Dauphine. The car should be in there. You want to go over, or should we?"

"Let's decide after we contact the feds. Maybe give them a call and tell them not to do anything with the car."

Jodie came back with the go food, and Mace and Camille stood. Camille dropped money on the table and Mace said, "We're gonna get started. We'll call you in a while."

"If I don't call you first."

50

Jim Davis got the number for a good lawyer from a drunk in intake. The man he asked looked somewhat respectable, which to Jim meant middle class on up, and he'd said the lawyer, Avery Heckler, was a top criminal defense attorney who had plenty of juice with local politicos and always won but his price was steep—$800 an hour. Jim made his phone call around four a.m. and left a message on the lawyer's answering machine. Now he was waiting to hear back. They'd transferred him from intake to the main jail on a chain with nine others early in the morning, not long after he made the call. The dormitory was rectangular, with thirty bunks to a side running down the long walls and steel picnic tables in the middle. At the back were toilets, urinals and showers in open brick stalls which allowed no privacy. His body ached climbing up to the top bunk, but he didn't have the jailhouse status to get a lower one.

He approached one of the guards, a meaty redhead with braces on his teeth and a bored look in his pale blue eyes, after 6:00 a.m. roll call. Jim picked this guard because he was white. The guard's eyes came alive with humor at the request. He sneered and answered loud, "You want a bottom bunk? Look, granddad, this ain't the Hilton. Get the fuck outta here." Jim heard the room go quiet. As he turned away from the guard, every man in the dorm stared, deadpan, and continued staring as he walked back to his bunk, their cold eyes a gauntlet of malice.

He understood the extent of his mistake when he went to the back to pee. While he faced the steel urinal, they surrounded him quietly. The gangbanger who made him sit in the corner in intake was the first to speak. "You wanna be in a lower bunk? We gon' put you all the way down." The open-handed slap was fast and powerful; when it connected with his left cheek Jim felt like his jaw came unhinged. The next blow came from his right, a punch that landed square on his mouth, and he felt a tooth break off. He put up his arms to shield his face as the blows landed from all sides. His ears, his ribs, his back, and then as he huddled on the cold tile somebody grabbed him by the hair, dragged him over to a steel commode which was full of shit, like a dozen inmates had used it without flushing, and forced his head into the slimy, foul-smelling contents.

51

Junie had no basis for comparison because this was the only church she'd ever been in. The room, formerly the main dining room of a restaurant, was packed. The AC was broken and the heat was smothering, except for ceiling fans and a couple of box fans in the windows which spread the smell of BO through the room. The metal folding chair stuck to the backs of her thighs and her whole body was slick with sweat. The congregation was a mix, a few rich, some homeless that she recognized from the street, and everybody in between. Still, despite the heat and the close-packed bodies, Junie felt like she belonged here. She listened with rapt concentration to every word Fr. Greg said.

She sat between Beverly and Andre—she would not dare call him Z in his grandmother's presence and he didn't act like Z anymore. He wasn't like the old Andre she'd known from school and around the neighborhood either. He seemed weaker, yet somehow stronger, and this transformation had happened while he was talking to Fr. Greg in private. The priest had spent hours with him in his bedroom at Beverly's house after he woke from the sedative that doctor woman came over and gave him.

While they talked, she and Mama Beverly had a wonderful time just doing nothing. It was the way Beverly LeBlanc lived, in her white stucco house with red trim. The house had a front porch, screened to keep out bugs, with soft old chairs where they'd sat sipping iced tea with fresh mint from the garden in back and watched the shadows grow long as the light faded to purple, and finally dark. There was a tree planted in the narrow strip of grass in front that hung heavy with big yellow bell-shaped flowers that filled the air with a sweet, spicy scent at dusk. Beverly said the tree was a Datura, but people called it Gabriel's Trumpet.

They'd feasted on pork chops and biscuits with butter and honey and collard greens from a can. After they'd done the dishes, Beverly pulled out the sleeper sofa in the front room, made it with fresh cotton sheets which she sprayed with lavender scent, and brought out big feather pillows from a closet. Then she'd placed a stuffed rabbit on the bed which made Junie tear up because it was a thoughtful gesture, and nobody had ever shown much care for her comfort before. Comfort was a way to describe Beverly's house, which seemed filled with everything a person would want or need. There was a refrigerator full of food, to which she'd been instructed to help herself, and shelves full of books and music and movies, flowers from the garden in back, and a kind of cluttered yet orderly comfort and simplicity that a person could relax in.

Junie felt like she was in a different world at Mama Beverly's, and now here, where Fr. Greg stood behind a podium which served as a pulpit by the window in back of the room. He wore a long green robe with embroidery on the edges that lent dignity to his tall dark frame. His face shone with sweat he wiped periodically with a handkerchief he pulled from a fold in his vestment. His eyes glowed with a fire that belied the dispassionate cadence of his words. As Junie listened, she felt like a veil had been pulled aside so she could sense beneath the bleak surface of poverty, addiction, violence and fear which had surrounded her all her life, that there was an energy pulsing with light and hope.

After the service they went back to the house, ate cold turkey and avocado on French sourdough and mint chocolate chip ice cream with shortbread cookies. Then it was nap time, Andre and Beverly in the back rooms, and Junie on the sleeper in front which was left unmade that morning at Mama Beverly's suggestion. "It's Sunday honey, and there isn't any point in making that bed because you might want to take a nap. I know I will. This is my day to do whatever I want, and I want to stay in bed all afternoon if I feel like it." Mama Bev suggested she might like to watch a movie or listen to music, and Junie had drifted off listening to Mahalia Jackson belt out a song about helping somebody in her powerful, soothing voice.

She woke to the sound of the knocker, peeked out the window and saw Fr. Greg standing on the front steps wearing khaki pants, a short-sleeved blue cotton shirt and his clerical collar. His forehead was shiny with sweat and he looked agitated. Junie let him in, apologizing for the unmade sleeper. "Everybody's resting," she said. "Can I get you some water or ice tea?"

"Ice tea sounds good." He followed her into the kitchen. "It was good to see you in church this morning. How'd you like it?'

"I've never been before and I never wanted to go." Junie spoke as she filled a glass with ice. "Just a minute, I'm going out back for some mint." She exited the kitchen door and walked to the back, thinking about how to answer the question. Her initial impression was that she loved church, but she wasn't ready to commit to anything. She'd heard bad things about church but there had been no browbeating about hellfire and damnation, nothing weird and no pressure to accept Jesus Christ as her personal Lord and Savior. She decided to be straight up with the priest.

"This is what I think about church." Junie rinsed off a sprig of spearmint, put it in the glass and poured tea. "Do you want sugar?"

"Please."

"I think I'd like to come back to church, but I don't want to commit to anything yet." Junie put a jelly jar of sugar and a teaspoon on the counter as she spoke. "I've heard some scary things about religion, so I need time to decide if it's for me."

"That's perfectly reasonable Junie. Feel free to come as often as you like, there's no pressure to join. Anyway, you're just the person I came over to see, and it's not about religion. Can we talk?"

"How about if I make up the bed and we go in the front room? It's too hot on the porch."

Junie went in the living room, folded up the sleeper, and put the pillows back in the closet. As she worked, she thought about what Fr. Greg came here for, and decided it had to be the stuff she gave him to hand over to the cops. But she felt she could trust him, and he'd given his word he wouldn't tell where he got the evidence.

She motioned the priest to take the easy chair by the fireplace, and she sat on the sofa. "Is this about the stuff we got off that man?"

"Yes, it is. As I told you, I don't have to tell anybody who gave it to me. And you can count on my silence. But two detectives came to see me in my office today, before church. I thought you'd want to hear what they said." Fr. Greg paused and took a long swallow of tea. "This tea is delicious. I want you to hear me out, and it's your decision what you think we ought to do."

"That's fair. I want to know what's happening anyway. I want the police to catch that man. I been scared of running into him on the street."

"I can only imagine. I didn't watch the films, but whatever evil is recorded on that computer needs to be stopped. This is what they told me today. They have a suspect in custody, he was arrested yesterday evening. The officer who took the box of evidence made the arrest. The problem is that some of the police in New Orleans make mistakes. This doesn't surprise you, does it?"

"You can call it whatever you want, but most of the cops I've met don't care about the law or protecting people. They're the scariest people out there. Andre's mother was shot 'cause the cops who were supposed to be protecting her sold her out."

Fr. Greg agreed, but he told her that not all cops are bad, that the detectives who he'd talked to that morning were okay. He told her about the probable cause issue, the illegal search of the computer, and that they might need somebody to testify about how the evidence came to be in police custody. He said likely the feds would get a warrant to search the computer, but they still needed probable cause, and this would require a witness to testify. He said the feds offered immunity to whoever came forward.

"But why does all this matter if they can't use the computer in court?"

"This is what they're going to do. Those films are evidence of serial murders, as well as crimes against children. So, a different jurisdiction, in other words the federal government, can get a warrant and search the computer. They've already contacted Quantico and a team is on the way down here. The goal is to keep this predator in jail, so he can't harm anybody else. We don't want him to walk out of jail after he's arraigned tomorrow. You follow me?"

"Loud and clear. We learned some of this stuff in high school civics, about the Bill of Rights and all. But most police don't respect folks' rights anyway and if you poor, what you gonna do about it? They supposed to get you a lawyer and maybe they do, but the lawyers they get don't do anything to defend you, least not if you're poor. They treat us all like criminals, like it's a crime to be broke!"

"Well, you're right about that too, Junie. But if you read the Hebrew prophets, it's the way things have always been, for thousands of years. There's always been injustice. But God sees everything, and I believe that things are going to be set right one day. If I didn't, I'd have to get another job."

"What do they want from me? Not to be rude, but you might as well say it."

"They want to offer you full immunity to talk to them, and testify in court, if it comes to that. What they want is for you to agree to go to court and say that you took the computer from this man then turned it over to me. He's going to try to say that whoever had the computer put those bad movies on it. But some of those films are older than you are. You know that, right?"

"I don't know nothing. I saw what was on the screen that drove Andre crazy, and I turned it off. I don't want to look at stuff like that."

"And you shouldn't want to. You did the right thing. Now, I'm asking you to make another choice about what the next right thing to do is. But I understand I'm asking you to trust a system that hasn't treated you fairly. Whatever you decide, I'll respect your decision."

"Thanks, Father Greg. I want a night to think about this. When do you need my answer?"

"It won't be right away. Hopefully the feds are going to arrest him again tomorrow, and since the FBI has a lot more resources for an investigation, you might not need to testify in court at all."

"Listen, I want this sickass monster in jail just as bad as anybody else." Junie's eyes were flashing with anger and fear. "Sorry 'bout the language."

"Oh, that's okay, and I agree with you. It's hard to describe evil without cursing."

"But how am I supposed to believe that this whole thing won't backfire? I can't go to jail; my family needs me. I help take care of my little brother, and I have to take care of my mother, too."

Fr. Greg didn't answer the question right away. He wondered why she got involved with the carjacking in the first place if she needed to stay out of jail. But he was thankful she'd committed the crime. He thought about the truth in the old cliché that God works in mysterious ways. "I don't have the answer to that," he finally said. "It's something you have to decide for yourself."

52

Sylvie and Trey left the family to pack, took a cab to the airport and rented an SUV. The clouds had cleared; the day was hot and muggy. She called Andy on the way in, and Andy authorized the rental, but told her she'd need to move buying a car up on her list. Andy approved the rest of the plan, though she voiced her misgivings about Brittney detoxing out of the hospital. If this didn't take, they would kick it up a notch. Both Andy and Sylvie respected that Brittney wasn't going to trust anybody with the kids just yet.

Sylvie got a Dodge Caravan for three days, with an option to rent longer if she had to. It would be just big enough for the whole crew. It felt good to be driving again, and as she sped along Airline Drive headed back to the motel, she wondered how she'd been able to put up with public transit for the past four years. The experience was already receding in her memory like a bad dream. Back at the motel they parked in front of the room and Sylvie went back by the office to talk to Bill about checking Brittney out. "I hope you don't mind that I'm taking your guests," she told him.

"Honey, I didn't want to rent to them in the first place. They didn't have anywhere else to go, so I figured this would be better than the streets. We aren't set up as a family place, and she couldn't even get one of the back rooms with a kitchen, because they're all taken. At least they were until Thursday." They both thought about Bernice Davis, and Amanda and Adrian Butler. "I told her to keep the kids indoors because we have some characters. I hope this works out; I really do. Please keep in touch."

"You can't get rid of me," Sylvie assured him. "I have to go. Let me know if you get more families in trouble. I'm not promising anything, but I might be able to help."

"Will do. Just a minute." Bill went back to the storage room and came out with a gift bag. "I got you a little something." He looked embarrassed as he handed her the bag. "You were a big help, but I'm not sorry to see you go. I think you're going to do a lot of good. Good luck."

Sylvie took the bag and gave Bill a hug and a peck on the cheek. "I'm going to miss this place, and you."

She left the lobby and walked back to the room. She looked around the grounds and felt a twinge of sadness because she'd grown fond of this motel and the people who lived here, on the edge but still doing what they had to do every day in the best way they knew how. She noticed a big wheel truck parked in back by the better rooms, black with dark tinted windows, and dismissed it as a visitor.

Trey and Kevin were bringing suitcases out to the Caravan as she walked up. It was almost three o'clock—they could finish loading up and get going.

"They're all packed," Trey said as he hefted the big suitcase Kevin had rolled out up into the back of the vehicle. "It didn't take ya'll much time to get ready," he said to Kevin.

"Yeah, we're used to moving."

"I know what you mean, my man. I grew up hard, too. But we're going to try and see that things get better."

"I guess," Kevin said, his words noncommittal, but his eyes showed the beginning of hope. "We going soon?"

"Soon as we load things up. It's almost check-in time."

Brittney and the girls were dressed and ready, and they'd straightened the room so it looked neat, which was amazing from a family of four with kids who were cooped up inside most of the time and an addict mother. Sylvie took in the order of the room and the way the girls looked, all pretty and dressed in matching shorts sets with their hair fixed nice. The whole family was trying hard. She determined that, no matter what she had to do, they were not going to be disappointed. "Is everything ready to go?" she asked Brittney.

"Yeah, we're ready. Hey, kids, you ready to get out of here?"

"Yeah!" Allison shouted, jumping up and down. Stephanie just smiled and nodded, but she seemed more relaxed and Sylvie gave Trey credit for fostering this cautious trust. She wanted to keep him on. She needed help and he was great with kids. He was also attractive, but Sylvie would not allow herself to go there with him. She was still recovering from her last relationship.

They loaded into the Caravan, Sylvie driving and Brittney in front while Trey sat in back with the kids. Nobody noticed that the big black truck left a moment later, turned onto Airline and followed several cars behind.

"How are you feeling?" Sylvie asked Brittney.

"Better than when I got up. That coconut water's great. I never tried it before."

"Yeah, I heard about it from a girl I worked with who drank all the time. I'm going to get you situated today and tomorrow, then I'm gonna look for a car."

"I bet that feels good."

"I left my old car in Dallas with my ex. Sometimes it's best just to leave, butt-naked if you have to. I've been on the bus four years."

"And I've been on the bus for a month," Brittney said. "I don't know what I would have done when school started up."

"You have to have a family car. After you're feeling better we'll get you one."

"Great. But will you let me pay you back when I get on my feet?"

"Sure, but it might not be in money. I might open a home for kids. I don't know yet, this is new. I was thinking after you finish school you could maybe help out as a nurse. Anyway, we'll figure something out. The thing is the more people give back, the more resources we'll have. You know what I'm saying?"

"I do. That's a great idea. And I would love to help out. You're saving us, Sylvie."

"Yeah, having the opportunity to help is saving me, too. I didn't realize how depressed I was 'til I wasn't. I mean, since you agreed to this I've been feeling better for the first time in years. We'll talk later." Sylvie glanced at the kids in the rear-view mirror. "Hey, kids. Have you ever stayed at a downtown hotel?"

"What's a downtown hotel?" Allison asked.

"A big one, sort of fancy, but not too much. Only it's way better than the Magnolia."

"Can we play outside?"

"That's up to your mom. But it's nobody's business at the hotel if you've never stayed at a place like this. So, we'll be there soon, and you might be surprised because it's nice. But you need to act like you're used to staying at nice places. Can you do that?"

"What do you mean?" Allison asked.

Kevin spoke up. "She means no talking 'til we get to our room. If you can behave, I'll take you swimming. But if you don't, we won't leave the room today."

"Mom!" Allison shrieked. "Kevin's bossing me again!"

"And he's right," Brittney said, turning around in the seat and smiling at her youngest. "You have to be on your best behavior at this place. We need to fit in with the other people there, okay?"

"Ow-kay." She made a face at her brother as soon as Brittney turned her head. "Hey, Mom, what if the other people there are naughty. Do we get to be bad, too?" Allison had to have the last word.

53

Lionel sat on the bed in his room, trying to get his head on right before facing the day. Man, this shit's getting old, he thought as he loaded his pipe with the last of the ice and lit up. They want me out there if this psycho walks. What they gonna do to protect me? He had one day to make up his mind before it went down. But he didn't have the money together to leave town, and even though he was scared, he wanted to stick around and see how things turned out. It was the craziest thing he'd ever heard of in his life—using millions of dollars to help people. Especially for a stripper to do something like this. Those broads all got an agenda. He'd never heard of no stripper doing nothing for nobody without getting paid up front. But this Sylvie broad was getting paid. The broad was slick. Front desk at a motel! How in the shit did she get that job? Lionel had a few ideas. Good looking broads got it made. Even the ugly ones got an edge. She had to be some smart to work the motel desk without getting caught. Lionel knew what he'd be doing with such an opportunity, but without a way to keep the boss happy, like a woman's way, he'd be buying himself a one-way ticket back to Angola, this time for life. Jeezus—cash, credit cards, rooms, drugs, girls—he got dizzy just thinking about all the scams he could run behind a motel desk job.

The cop told him they'd keep him in the Alexandra and also that he would continue to get his hundred a day if he stayed out front on the street and reported back to them. But this was bullshit. He wanted an assurance that they'd have his back if things got rough, whether or not they needed him anymore. And nobody had ever had his back if they didn't need him for something. Still, this could be the score he'd been waiting for. He didn't expect to get rich, but he wanted off the street and maybe to be comfortable, like a job he could do that wouldn't interfere with his pleasures. He decided the best thing to do was to play by their rules, and find a way to make himself useful so they'd want to keep him around.

Trey said he'd get back with him today, so it was getting time to head out. Besides, on Sundays people were generous. He finished the smoke and put the glass pipe in his pants pocket. Then he decided not to carry it with him, so he took it back out, wiped it down with toilet paper, and hid it between the mattress and box spring. Then he realized if they changed his sheets, they could find it. He went into the bathroom and put it in the toilet tank. He'd gone out earlier and bought a change of clothes at the second-hand store over on St. Claude. This was what he did every few days, go get a change of clothes. It was easier than doing laundry and carrying shit around. He needed to be free to move and stuff was nothing but a ball and chain. He'd had enough of confinement in Angola. Give him a pipe, a money bucket and a flask for his pocket and he'd be a happy man. He took both phones off the chargers—the one from the psycho and the one Trey gave him. He had the psycho phone on ring and the other on vibrate to keep track. Life was getting complicated and it was beginning to seem like work. Okay then, just so long as the money was right so it was worth his while. He checked the time—three o'clock. There was time to stop at the store for supplies on the way in.

54

Fr. Greg left after their talk but he called Junie back twenty minutes later. He asked her for a quick decision. The feds were on their way in, and they needed a warrant for the computer. They would grant full immunity.

Junie wanted to talk to Andre before making a decision, but he was sedated and would be sleeping for hours. She went in and talked to Mama Beverly instead, and it was Beverly who gave her the idea. She called Fr. Greg back, told him that she would agree to talk, but in addition to immunity she wanted justice for Andre's mother, Valerie LeBlanc. She wanted a full investigation into her death, the gang involved and the cops. She wanted the feds, not the NOPD or any state investigators. She would not talk with NOPD present in the room, and she did not want her identity disclosed to local authorities. Fr. Greg called back ten minutes later and said it was a deal. He would pick her up at four and take her to the FBI field office out by the lakefront for the interview.

55

The initial meeting would be held in the conference room at Andy Sharp's firm. Andy offered this option via Camille. Quantico made the final decision because they wanted to control the situation and hide the meeting from the press. They would hold a press conference at NOPD headquarters on Broad after Davis was re-arrested the following day. Camille would make sure Tyler heard about it first and got updates ahead of time. It had been decided that Garvey would be the scapegoat—he would be history by the time the public got the story. He had already been suspended without pay, and he would be fired after the press release.

A team of FBI agents had flown in, and IAFIS was running the prints against unsolveds around the country. Andy made a choice that, regardless of whether she got to spend time with her kids this weekend, Jim Davis needed to stay locked up or he was liable to target everybody involved, including her and her family. She went to her office early and compiled all the information, made copies, and copied the pictures and the video Bernice had made for law enforcement. She included the investigator's report on Jim Davis, and a list of every place he had lived before going to ground, including where the family had lived while Jim was growing up. Camille asked for this info and Andy had it ready when she arrived at the firm at two, carrying the murder book from the Bernice Davis case. Burell was bringing the computer and the other evidence Garvey turned in. Mace brought the Butler murder book.

Usually, people who were jailed over the weekend were arraigned Monday morning, but Mace called the DA and arranged for Davis's arraignment to be held off until afternoon court, to give them as much time as possible. Davis was already lawyered up, having contacted Avery Hekler, one of the best criminal defense attorneys in the state. Hekler had a rep for getting the guilty off, and his specialty was white-collar crime. He had represented some of the state's top politicos and his fees were upwards of $800 an hour. The joke going around town was that Hekler, not the voters, was responsible for keeping the wheels of government turning in Louisiana. He could smell publicity and he'd signed on pro bono to represent Davis. He no doubt thought he had a slam dunk and would be walking his client out of court Monday.

They got a hit from the prints an hour before the federal team arrived for their meeting. The case was in the Oak Cliff section of Dallas, in 1972. On a sweltering July night almost forty-five years ago to the day, an entire family was murdered in their home. The mother was a known prostitute and heroin addict. Her two small children aged three and five were also dead at the scene. The assailant had used washrags secured with duct tape to silence the three victims before the attack. The mother, Scarlett Long, died first—beaten to death in front of the children with what appeared to be a claw hammer. It was speculated that he had the mother tape the kid's mouths first, then gagged her before attacking her with the hammer. It was likely the same weapon he'd used on three-year-old Catherine. She was the first of the children to die, bleeding out after a sexual assault which included a large foreign object being rammed repeatedly into her little body so that her insides were scrambled like eggs. William had been doused with gasoline, set on fire, and burned alive. He was too badly burned to determine if he'd also been raped. A good fingerprint and a partial had been pulled from the aluminum screen door handle. The rest of the crime scene had been wiped down. If the killer had doused the house with gasoline instead of just the boy, the hard evidence they did collect would have been destroyed in the fire. They'd collected hairs from the bathtub drain, including hairs that did not belong to the family. That hair and the semen from the girl was being run for DNA analysis, but even prioritized, the analysis would take a few days.

Dallas was used to violent crime, but the brutality of the murders had shocked, sickened and scared the community. Police spent months combing through criminal records trying to find a match to the prints, but it seemed like a demon had come out of the void and then disappeared. Nobody had seen anything and there were no leads. At the time the case went cold most cops assumed that Scarlett, who was known to bring men back to her house occasionally, had brought home the wrong person that night. According to neighbors, she would put her kids to bed in the evening, then slip out and work the streets, sometimes operating out of nearby bars, but nobody had seen her out on the night of the killings.

The lead investigator on this case, Herbert Stanley, had entered the prints into IAFIS back in '99, right before he took retirement. As soon as he heard there was a national fingerprint database available and that cold cases were getting solved from old evidence, he knew that his role as an investigator wasn't over. The last thing he could do for this family was to enter the prints that were found on their screen door, like putting a message in a bottle and throwing it over the side of a ship, hoping the right person would eventually get it. His dedication to eventually solving this case which had haunted him for his entire career—his refusal to give up had led to finding a match to the prints fourteen years after he'd entered them into the database, and forty-five years after the murders. The prints came back as a match to Jim Davis. He was sixteen years old at the time the Long family was slaughtered. The youngest victim, Catherine, would have now been forty-eight and perhaps a grandmother. William would have been fifty. There was also residual blood in the shower drain that the killer had washed off, presumably right before setting the boy on fire and leaving, which established that he had showered after killing the woman and the girl. DNA tests were being rushed, but the fingerprints already gave Dallas authorities probable cause to issue a warrant for murder. Texas was infamous for the number of people it executed, and because of the brutality of the crime it was highly unlikely the prosecution would cut a deal in exchange for information on other murders. Ted Bundy, perhaps the most notorious serial killer, had doled out information to Robert Keppel in hope that his date with the chair in Florida would be postponed again, but that didn't work and he was finally executed as scheduled. He had managed to postpone execution for over a decade because mistakes in police procedure bought him numerous appeals that cost Florida taxpayers millions, and put the families of victims through a prolonged and hellish ordeal.

56

Camille went through the files on Bernice Davis as soon as she found out about the Dallas case. Here it was! Bernice taught kindergarten at Crockett Elementary in Oak Cliff at the time of the murders. It was the first job she'd landed out of college, and she worked there for twenty-two years. Somehow her son Jim had targeted this family through his mother's connection with one of the children. Camille began backtracking through old Dallas Morning News articles using an academic database she'd got through Loyola. She found an article dated July 14, 1972: ENTIRE FAMILY MURDERED IN OAK CLIFF! A photograph of the victims filled the front page between the headline and the fold. They were standing in front of the brick house where they had been killed. Scarlett Long was a younger version of Bernice Davis. In the picture she was dressed in cut-off shorts and a paisley halter. Her hair was long and dark, worn parted in the center. She held a baby on one hip and a small boy stood at her side, his smile bright as the afternoon sun. At that time, two years before they were killed, she had the picture taken to send to her husband who was serving a tour in Vietnam. He would be the first one to die in this young family, coming home in a body bag later in the summer when the picture was taken.

His death was the beginning of a downward spiral which ended the night of the murders.

By the time the Behavioral Analysis Unit agents arrived at Andy's office, Camille had already connected Jim Davis with the murdered family, using the files Andy had on Bernice along with the newspaper article. But the fingerprints on the door and the fact that Bernice was little Billy Long's kindergarten teacher could be construed as coincidental, especially with a lawyer like Hekler. Even with a rush on DNA from the semen and hair they'd recovered from the crime scene, there would be a delay of almost a week to nail Jim Davis to this crime beyond a reasonable doubt. But they had probable cause for an arrest. He could also be charged with fraud for the fake IDs.

57

There were six FBI agents–two each from BAU-3, Crimes Against Children and BAU-4, Crimes Against Adults, a forensic psychologist from BAU-5, and a Computer Forensic Examiner from Houston. Juliana Rodriguez, the BAU-3 agent assigned to lead the team, explained their agenda. She stood at the head of the conference table and addressed the group. With the suspect in custody, they expected to be in town for no longer than two days. After the press was notified they had made an arrest for the Butler killings, they would move the operation to the New Orleans field office. They had a warrant for the computer, and it would be taken to the lab in Houston where CFEs would attempt to extract all the information it held to identify the victims and crime scenes. Then she talked about strategy. "Jim Davis is a sexual sadist. He started killing when he was a teenager, and he's hidden behind a façade of respectability for decades. He never expected to be caught, and many of them are not caught. But thanks to some excellent teamwork, we've tied him to what may be his first victims, the Long family. When the DNA comes back from semen recovered from Catherine Long's body, and hair found along with the blood of the victims in the bathtub drain, we can nail him for that crime. Then he's going to be facing the needle in Texas. Our best strategy is to appeal to his narcissism. Since he's operated for so long, even with the films it will be very hard to tie him to all of his victims. He's been evading law enforcement and killing for most of his life. The films only cover the past two decades and there may be others during that time that he didn't document. Because he's a sociopath he won't be ashamed of his violent sexual proclivities—he'll be proud of his work. What we want to do is appeal to his ego and his craving for power. Our best chance of identifying the killings he's responsible for is to get him to talk, and how we're going to do this is to nail him to the Long killings conclusively, and convince him he's facing the death penalty. What we do is convince him that the only avenue of power left to him is to take full credit for outsmarting law enforcement while killing for decades. We want to take his power away and give it back to him in the form of notoriety. Nobody talks to him without first consulting with Dr. Randall Borg. Dr. Borg is a forensic psychologist with the Behavioral Analysis Unit. He has been interviewing serial killers for decades. His research has been instrumental in profiling and apprehending these killers all over the country."

Juliana sat down and a short, balding man with wire glasses and gray hair stood up and addressed the group. "What we're dealing with, which you'll see in the films is a sociopath who is devoid of conscience. He is completely lacking in compassion, and seeks stimulation through torturing his victims. He feeds off their fear and pain. Once this avenue of power is closed—being a free agent in society who outsmarts law enforcement and does whatever he wants to do to the people he gains control over, his next avenue to power will lie in bragging about the victims he's killed, his cunning in killing and evading detection, and in the notoriety of his crimes. Then he'll start to talk, and hopefully what he reveals will help us to solve open cases and provide closure to victim's families.

"We need everybody in contact with him in law enforcement and the media to cooperate in our effort to focus this investigation on solving past murders. A Dallas team is on the way here to bring him back to face charges for killing the Long family. At that time, we expect NOPD to issue a press release. What I need you to do is to focus on any mistakes he made at the Butler crime scene which caused him to be the main suspect. From what I've read in the reports you sent, he didn't make any mistakes here that can be traced back to him, but you can emphasize the bungling of the staged crime scene through lack of gunshot residue on Amanda Butler's hand. The press release should be scripted and we want him to think that the public sees him as an incompetent bungler who was apprehended immediately for the Butler killings, then tied to the Long family murders. We need him to look and feel like a powerless individual who bungled crime scenes and left enough evidence in both the Long and Butler cases for law enforcement to apprehend and convict him. There must be no credit for the murder films on the computer and no mention that he's a suspect in other crimes. But it should be clear that, once convicted he'll face the death penalty for the Long killings in Texas and the Butler killings here. Once he realizes he's facing death in two jurisdictions, he'll want to take credit for the other crimes. Serial killers have gained notoriety and a certain respect through media coverage in past decades. We need access to that kind of power to be denied him unless he volunteers information. We want him to feel that he'll be facing death for the two crimes which he botched, and that he will die a nonentity who won't get credit for all the crimes he got away with. Hopefully this will lead him to talk, but it may take some time.

"We are going to view the videos he made of torturing and killing his victims. Anybody who doesn't want to watch can leave now. As homicide detectives you've seen a lot. Viewing these films may help you to apprehend other killers. Thank you for the excellent work you've done so far. Any questions?"

Mace spoke up first. "How do we control information that may have leaked about the computer?"

"You lie. You say that the videos were fakes, not actual snuff films."

"What about the cops who heard about them already?"

"The NOPD has been under scrutiny by the Department of Justice for decades. They signed a Consent Decree a few years ago, and your officers are still in the hot seat. We'll turn up the heat a few notches if anything leaks to the press, and anybody found talking will be under federal scrutiny. You have my word on that, so you may as well get the word out to anybody who may know about the films. You can say the CFE examined the videos and found that they're hard porn. He was addicted to violent pornography, which led him to try to act out his fantasies, but he bungled the crimes and was caught."

Camille spoke next. "Why do you want us to view the videos?"

"There have been serious problems in Orleans Parish, including crimes against children and trafficking, and we've checked your backgrounds. We know you're some of the best homicide detectives in this area. We are hoping you'll spearhead future investigations and we have more training available for you both here and at Quantico if you agree to participate. We have a whole class of murderers who kill for sport. And trafficking's a big problem in New Orleans, especially around sports events and Mardi Gras. Some of the victims are children and teenagers, some are illegal immigrants. Many of the victims, especially small children, die as a direct result of being trafficked. We've found that training local law enforcement vastly improves the odds of catching these killers.

"We want you to recognize serial killings and possible serials when you investigate the crime scenes. It's complicated, but the best way to begin to understand what we're talking about is to see the evidence firsthand and these videos, though disturbing, can help you understand what kind of victims these killers select, and what to look for at crime scenes. Now, if there are no more questions, we're going to take a break and you should get something to eat now. After the break we'll watch the videos."

58

The kids were tired and hungry when they came up from the pool and everybody wanted pizza. Sylvie had left Brittney a hundred for dinner and whatever else came up. They called Dominos and ordered two large pepperonis and a six pack of Barq's, with cinnamon bread sticks for dessert. The girls clicked on the TV and ordered Walking With Dinosaurs and The Nutjob. Brittney was lying on one of the beds resting. She had nursed the same beer for two hours and was feeling a lot better. Sylvie had brought them a laptop and a set of headphones, and she'd told the girls their brother needed a break, so they got to watch movies while Kevin chilled. He was playing video games at the desk in the sitting room. For once he got to be a kid instead of having to be the parent.

The family felt safe. They were beginning to relax into a lifestyle where things could be fun. The other people they saw at the hotel looked like the kinds of families on TV sitcoms. They dressed well and smiled a lot and looked excited to be here. Did they now belong to this group? The girls looked around with cautious hope. When Sylvie had left them the laptop she'd suggested that maybe they'd want to make a list of houses for rent, places with three bedrooms and a yard for pets! And their mother was watching TV with them, laughing at the movies like another kid, but also, they got the sense that she was the one in charge now, not Kevin. She'd be home all night! She wasn't getting ready for work and going in the bathroom to smoke dope and apply her makeup. She seemed calm and more relaxed than they could remember seeing her and really trying to taper off the beer, which helped the kids trust that things were really going to be better this time.

59

Junie and Fr. Greg met with two agents in the lobby of the FBI field office. The interview took less than two hours. The agents introduced themselves as Sabra Cardenas and Zachary Potts from the BAU. Cardenas was young, dark, with short cropped curly hair, no makeup, and she wore a tan suit and a light blue blouse. She did most of the talking. Potts was fortyish and pale with graying red hair and cool blue eyes. He wore a light gray suit, white shirt, lavender tie. He did not look like the kind of guy who would go by Zach. They assured Junie that her identity for the record would be CHS 1. CHS stood for Confidential Human Source. They went up an elevator and down a hall to an interview room with a table and chairs. Cardenas and Potts sat across the table from Junie and Fr. Greg.

Cardenas asked the questions, Potts took notes. She began by asking Junie about the night of the carjacking. No, Junie said, she was not a prostitute, just an angry woman who had been stalked by sexual predators much of the time she was growing up. Her motive was payback, and Andre wanted payback, too. Junie told the agents about Valerie LeBlanc's shooting, how the NOPD officers took off right before the car full of gangsters pulled up. Cardenas was easy to talk to. She asked a lot of questions about Jim Davis—how he looked, what he said, what he did before and during the carjacking. She acted like she cared about what had happened to Valerie LeBlanc, and about Junie growing up unprotected in poverty and chaos. She said she grew up in the poorest section of Baltimore, and that she had been angry, too, which was why she wanted a career in criminal justice. She told Junie that the best way to fight sexual predators is to work for the law, not against it. When Junie said that the cops were criminals too, Cardenas talked about the consent decree between the DOJ and the NOPD. She said they would be back in touch, and that a family member would need to go file a report at the Office of the Consent Decree Monitor. Andre would be the best person to do this, but if he was too shaky his grandmother could go. The two agents promised both Junie and Fr. Greg that a full investigation of the report would ensue. Cardenas ended by giving Junie her card. She told Junie to think about what she wanted from life, and to call her if she wanted help climbing out of the neighborhood and doing something productive. Cardenas said she'd had a mentor and would like an opportunity to pay that favor forward. The interview left Junie feeling like for once in her life she didn't have to handle a problem alone, and she also was thinking about Cardenas's offer.

Beverly and Junie were making spaghetti when Andre woke up. They had decided not to tell him about the interview yet. He seemed different, more like the old Andre before the Z persona, but deeper. Junie felt changed too, and she wasn't sure what it was, maybe the beginning of hope. Her contact with people like Beverly, Fr. Greg, and even the FBI agent who had interviewed her had helped her to see a way out of the degraded life she'd felt trapped in growing up, like a dim light at the end of a long dark tunnel.

The smell of red sauce with freshly made Italian sausage from the neighborhood grocery and onions and garlic and herbs from the garden permeated the house. "You teachin' her how to cook, Maman?" Andre was smiling as he took a glass from the cupboard to fix himself a Dr. Pepper.

"We're teaching each other. This girl chops vegetables faster than a sous chef. How you feeling?"

"Better. Is Junie going to stay with us for a while?"

"She's welcome to, if she wants. I like having another woman in the house."

Junie said, "I love it here, Mama. But I'm worried about my family. I'm the one who always takes care of things 'cause my Mom's too sick."

"You've had a heavy load to carry for somebody so young," Beverly said. "Tell me about your brother."

"I'm gonna be watching TV," Andre said. "I'll let ya'll talk. Don't get so busy talking you forget about the food. I'm starved." He filled his glass with ice and took a soda from the fridge.

"Since when did we ever forget about food around here?" Beverly said. "I'll let you know when it's time to set the table."

"Sure, Maman."

"Go on out of here and let us talk." Beverly waved the spoon she'd been stirring the sauce with in the direction of the door.

"Yes, Ma'am." Andre took his drink, went in the front room, and they heard the TV turn on to a soccer game.

"Now where were we?" Beverly asked. "Here, baby, taste this sauce and tell me if it's got enough salt."

"I don't get to eat this good at home," Junie said, blowing on the spoon.

"Tell me about your family, girl."

"My brother Michael's eight. If I'm not there to whup his butt he be all over the place. He's, what you call it? Learning impaired. He's moving all the time, don't want to sit still, can't focus on his schoolwork. He already hangin' with gang members, doing stuff for them for pocket change."

Beverly noticed how, when talking about her family and home, Junie reverted automatically to street talk, but if she didn't have to think about them, she spoke better. "Listen, honey, this all sounds like it's too big for a young person to handle. How about if you let me help out?"

"What you gonna do for my family? Huh?" Junie's eyes flashed with anger. "My mama's all the time loaded, bringing bad people around. I caught one of them looking at my brother like he wanted to take him apart. And Mikey be playing him, asking for money when mama's too loaded to know what's going on. It's just a matter of time 'fore he be in the sex trade or a gang. He's already mixed up with dealers, running to the store and playing lookout for them. He's headed for big trouble. I can't protect him. How's he gonna listen to you?"

"We've got to keep him away from the neighborhood. We've got to get your mother some help."

"My momma don't want no help. She's too far gone for help. I think she'd sell my brother for dope if he'd do it."

"Where there's life there's hope. Let me talk to Fr. Greg and see if we can't get Michael into one of our schools. Maybe we can get your mother in a program. I'm willing to try but I need you to help me."

"I've been doing what I can for them all my life. I'd do anything to have some help. Just don't expect them to be too happy about it."

"You never know. Have they ever had a chance at something better?"

"No, but they be set in their ways. They're both running with some bad people."

"We're going to do what we can. But I'm going to ask you for a favor."

"What?"

"I want you to stay here with Andre and me for now. That mess is too much for a young lady like you. Besides, if they don't have you around to take care of things, maybe they'll want to do something for themselves. I've got a feeling they might not have any choice."

"I'd like to stay here. Thank you, Mama." Junie was beginning to see a new life for herself, one where she could relax, work a decent job, come home to relative peace and quiet instead of having to babysit lunatics in a nuthouse. "I think I should go check on them tomorrow. You want to come?"

"Can we do it tomorrow evening? I work in the morning."

"Sure. But there's no telling what they'll be up to by then."

"Don't you worry. It ain't none of it I haven't seen before. We are strong women and we've got God on our side. We'll go over there and set them on their toes. I raised two kids, and I had to live in the welfare projects myself when I was starting out. I buried my daughter, and she was my good girl. My son's in Angola for slinging dope. And I did all I could to help him, so I don't have to worry about that. But he chose the life he's living, and what I want to do is give your family a choice, too. That's all a person can do. If they want to take it, that's fine. But God gave us free will, and if they choose the hard life, that doesn't mean you've got to go there with them. You hear?"

"Yes ma'am. I feel like my family never had a choice. They've just been surrounded by badness all their life. And I can't do much about it by myself."

"Well, you're not by yourself anymore. You got that? We're a team now."

Junie nodded, too overwhelmed to say anything else.

60

CFE Anna Cho would operate the videos. She was a small woman with short, glossy black hair and a serious, almost grim demeanor. Her attitude was comforting because it was respectful of the victims. Camille wondered if she would lighten up in different circumstances. There were times Camille wanted to punch crime scene cops for their cavalier attitudes and the irreverent jokes they cracked, but she understood they were only trying to downplay the horror. Though Mason was seated next to her, she felt totally alone, like she'd felt during her worst times in the years since her sister's death.

She looked around the table at the others—nobody had eaten much of the deli food Andy had catered. Besides Rodriguez, Borg and Cho, there was another agent from BAU-3, Reginald Carter, and two agents from BAU-4, Sabra Cardenas and Zachary Potts. Nobody looked like they wanted to be there.

Juliana spoke to the group. "We're going to watch the first video. Then we'll talk. Andy, would you dim the lights?"

Andy used a remote to dim the chandelier lights. Cho hit the first link and a video came up. It was the first one, with the woman gagged and chained next to a concrete block wall. She clicked on the arrow and the film started. They watched as the man in the leather suit and the obscene Reagan mask

270

poured gasoline all over her and set her on fire. The video lasted under three minutes, ending when the woman stopped thrashing about in the flames. Camille felt dirty watching it.

Rodriguez stood and addressed the group. "This looks like an abandoned warehouse or factory of some kind. We have so many of these around the country it would be very hard to tell what state it's in, much less which location. We can do a database search through missing persons for a photograph of the victim. Our best chance of locating this victim is for him to talk about the murder—where he abducted her, where he dumped her body. Alright, next film."

The victims were girls and women. There seemed to be no consistent type preference such as ethnicity or hair color, except that some of the women resembled Bernice Davis in her younger pictures. Most likely the victims were chosen because of accessibility—these people had been easy to grab. The ones who conformed to stereotype were probably the hardest to capture—he may have taken risks to capture these victims, so that might be a good place to start checking the records. The fact that most of the vics didn't conform to this preference showed that opportunity was a big factor in his choices. The similarity with all of the victims was that there was always some type of burning—with cigarettes, electrical gadgets, blowtorches—it seemed like he wanted to try different methods and see what the victim's pain level would be, how he could extract the most pain before killing. One girl was burned repeatedly with an iron. Another woman had markings of what looked like acid dripped all over her body. Another, a child, was put in a tub of water and electrocuted with a plugged-in hairdryer. Most of the videos lasted less than five minutes. They were taken to record the deaths, not the entire time the victims were held, tortured and raped, which looked like it had gone on for hours and in some cases maybe days. The filming of their deaths was a way to prolong and enjoy their suffering forever. For all the films he wore leather bondage getups that could be unfastened at the crotch to expose his genitalia, which was clearly outlined through the leather so that it was obvious he was sexually aroused. The first film was the only one where he wore a caricature mask. He wore a bondage hood for the others, the kind that covered the entire head and zipped up the back with holes for the eyes, mouth and ears. All the videos but two were taken indoors, mostly in what appeared to be motel rooms of the kind that you can rent by the hour, day or week. The two that were outdoors were the worst.

One of the outdoor videos took place in what appeared to be a clearing in the woods. A young girl with dark hair was chained to an antique portable cast iron hitching post. The chain was attached to a leather collar with a metal ring through it, the collar buckled around her neck so tight she was almost choking. She was naked, gagged with what looked like her own underpants, stuffed into her mouth then held fast with duct tape wound around her head. He had used steel handcuffs to secure her hands behind her back. He entered the picture wearing the bondage getup and carrying a blowtorch. He faced the camera as he turned the torch on, then turned and chased her around the post, burning her in stages, standing over her when she finally collapsed to finish her off. This film was the longest, at twenty-seven minutes. The other outdoor video was taken at night, in the desert. A little girl who looked to be under four years old was stuffed into a wire cage like the kind you'd put a medium sized dog in. The location could have been New Mexico or Arizona from the sandy ground, the brush, the dark outlines of large cacti and what appeared to be rock formations in the far distance. The cage was set next to a large campfire. She looked Hispanic, with big brown scared eyes and dark tangled hair. Her fingers were clutching the wires of the cage and her face was contorted with terror. She was the only victim who was not gagged. She was crying and calling for her mommy in Spanish. He came into the picture wearing the bondage outfit, carrying an armload of kindling which he threw on the fire. Next, he picked the cage up by its wire handle and set it on the flames. Then he took a plastic bottle of charcoal lighter, unscrewed the cap, stood back and tossed it in. He unfastened the front of his leather outfit, took out his penis, and masturbated while the girl burned. Her screams were the worst part. They lasted over a minute.

Nobody said anything for a while. Potts was crying.

Andy spoke up first. "I'm having a drink. Anybody else?" Several people nodded and she told them there's an open bar in her office.

Rodriguez said, "Let's break for twenty minutes then we'll meet back here for another briefing. After that I want you all to go get some rest." Like anybody would be able to sleep.

61

Thunder boomed, rain poured down like somebody turned on a giant faucet and lightning lit up the bedroom like a strobe. Camille swigged from a fifth of Dewars, replaced it on the bedside table and drank from a steel water bottle. Then she lit a cigarette and began to pace the floor while Mace watched her in the flashing light. She finished the smoke, lit another one, sat on the bed and started to cry in loud, angry moans. "I hate those bastards!" She sounded like she was choking on her frustration and rage. "How many are there? How many out there right now?"

"We didn't make this world. We can spend our whole lives fighting and it won't ever be over. But somebody has to go after these monsters and make them pay for what they do." What Mason was thinking but would never say was that the suffering of the victims in the films, horrific though it was, was over. But for the people who went after these killers, those who saw the crime scenes and talked to the relatives, it would never be over. There was a hellish knowledge that was with you every day of your life. It was never over for the families either. He knew Camille was thinking about her sister. So, he just sipped his beer and let her rage and waited for her to burn herself out, like a child who was finally numbed by an overload of anger and grief. Eventually she collapsed on the bed in her clothes and let him put his arm around her and hold her.

Monday

62

Heavy rain pounding on the skylight over the bed woke Sylvie up. She lay there enjoying the coziness of the storm and thinking about the transformation her life had taken in the past four days. She would miss this place, even with the aggravation of the street singer. There was a loud boom and the room flashed with electric light. She got out of bed to go smoke out the bathroom window and watch the storm.

Water poured out of the stone gutters and splashed on the paving stones below and banana leaves rustled in the wind, their dancing shapes outlined in the occasional flashes of light. She would miss this view out of the bathroom window. She wondered if the killer would be let out of jail after his arraignment today. She needed to talk to somebody. Andy would know what's going on, but it was two in the morning and she couldn't talk to her yet. She put out the smoke and went to the medicine cabinet, took a couple of Benadryl out and went in the kitchen for a Heineken to help them along. She'd set her alarm for seven so there were a few hours left to sleep.

63

Of all the spooky people on the streets of the Quarter, there was nobody scarier than a rogue cop and Garvey was the worst. Lionel had never seen him in street clothes but he recognized him right off, and the way he was hanging around, all dressed in black like he was going to do something in the dark and didn't want to be seen was creepy. Lionel knew Garvey was up to evil and he was casing out the building where Trey and Sylvie lived. Lionel had seen him coming round the corner from Royal, so he picked up his tip bucket and beat feet for the square, then he went up Pirates Alley and cut back through the little alley behind the Cabildo where he'd talked with the cops last night. He stood in the shadowy alley and watched. He saw him cross the street and check the mailboxes on the building, but there were no names on the boxes so he gave up and walked off towards Bourbon.

Lionel thought about calling Trey, but he couldn't be sure it was connected. Only that cop was into everything—making folks give him a cut of their money to stay out of jail, making the strippers give up the pussy to stay out of jail, shaking everybody down for whatever he could get. He was the worst thug out here. Maybe he heard about the money that Sylvie came into and he was sniffing around for his cut. It was like the Quarter was his territory and he wanted everybody on the street to give him a cut just to be here. He was worse than any gang member, and Lionel knew for a fact that at least one of the homeless on the Square never made it to the jailhouse after Garvey put him in the car. The dude was scary. When you looked in his eyes you saw the devil. Come to think of it, he had the same look that square psycho had, like there was a meanness about him that wanted an excuse or just an opportunity to cause pain, like he got off on it the same as sex.

Lionel liked to work the occasional rain storm because the people who were out in the weather were mostly drunk and generous with the tips like they felt sorry for him. Plus, he wanted to see what was going on around here. He was getting addicted to this drama and now with this scary cop coming around he felt vindicated. The money he'd made wasn't that great, but with the hundred dollars Trey had given him earlier and what he had left from yesterday and the day before, he had enough to make the down payment on a throwaway gun, along with a little something to smoke and a bottle. The way things were going, he didn't want to be around without something to protect himself with, especially if that psycho dude got out of jail in the morning. The more Lionel thought about it, the more things made sense— that white bitch got control of a whole lot of money and that's what all this is about. Let somebody from the street come into money and everybody starts circling around like sharks when there's blood in the water.

He dialed K's number as he headed back up towards Esplanade. "Hey, it's me," he said into the phone.

"What you want?"

"I'm coming by now. You'll be there?"

"Yeah."

"You got it?"

"Yeah."

Lionel hung up the phone. He'd ordered the gun from K-boy the other night, soon as that bitch made him get in his car. Now he was going to pick it up, along with his smoke. K was letting him pay half now, the rest when he had it. He didn't like carrying a piece with his record. But there was no way around it. He was damned if he was going to let some crazy piece of shit cracker blow out his light without even putting up a fight. Let that creepy motherfucker get out of jail and come messing with him. He'll wish he'd stayed in Parish Prison.

There was nobody out and the lights of the bars, restaurants, and souvenir shops were reflected off the wet pavement. A lone cyclist wearing a hooded slicker rode by making a delivery for one of the all-night grocery-delis. Lionel thought about maybe getting a job like that but no, he liked to be his own man and keep his own hours. At least that's what he told himself, but the truth was one he didn't allow himself to dwell on if he could avoid it. He was a meth addict and an alcoholic and he didn't think he could keep it together for a regular job and a regular life. Besides, how many ex-cons got hired for regular gigs? Sometimes he wished for a different life, one with a place of his own and a woman and maybe a cat. But those things were out of reach for somebody like him. He almost had himself convinced that what he had was better anyway but at times he couldn't keep up the self-deception. It was a vicious circle—the drugs helped him deal with the loneliness, but they kept him from having more than what he had, a hand-to-mouth existence where there was nowhere but inside of a pipe and a bottle of booze to come in out of the weather.

64

Jim Davis had enough money in the bank to secure the services of Avery Hekler and, equally important, he was white. The fact that Hekler had offered to represent him pro bono was lagniappe—a little something extra for free. He was led into the courtroom on a chain with nine other prisoners, all dressed in orange jumpsuits that had OPP stenciled on the back in block letters. Hekler had requested that he be allowed to appear in regular clothes but that request was denied. Along with the jumpsuit, he was sporting a black eye, a fat lip, and a couple of chipped teeth. After his beating he was put in isolation for his own protection. The guards took their time stopping it, and when they finally stepped in, they were sniggering. They threw him in a cell by himself. The cell was freezing cold. They ignored his requests for a blanket, for toilet paper, for water. Somebody hawked a lugey in his oatmeal; his coffee was salted; his grits were served without cheese He had not been allowed to shave so when he entered the courtroom on the chain he looked like a bum and he stank.

Hekler met with him Sunday evening and promised that not only would he be released come Monday, they would file a lawsuit against the sheriff's office for reckless endangerment, wrongful arrest, civil rights violations, torture and damages. Hekler bridled every time the judge called another prisoner to the bench, leaving his client to wait until last.

Judge Warren Seaburg was known for his biting sarcasm and his innate fairness—he wanted to release prisoners whenever possible because the system in Louisiana was overcrowded and broken, but Jim Davis was one prisoner he was reluctant to let back out on the street. He was staring at the arrest report, and then he looked up at Davis. "Mr. Davis, or is it Mr. Smith or Mr. Legitt? Or maybe it's Mr. Lewis. Which one is it today?"

Hekler spoke up, bristling with indignation. "Your honor, my client's name is Jim Davis."

"I know that. But it seems to me that he's been operating under a few aliases here. Now shut up, Hekler. If you say anything else until I'm done talking, I'll hold you in contempt. For once you are going to spare me the theatrics while I say what needs to be said about all this. We have before us a criminal of the worst kind, a sadist who preys on helpless women and children. And I'm going to have to turn him loose on society because the arresting officer violated his Fourth Amendment rights against unlawful search and seizure and his Fifth Amendment rights by interrogating him in the back of a squad car without giving him a Miranda warning. Where is the arresting officer?"

Garvey stood up, his eyes sullen. "Your honor…"

Seaburg glared at him for a long moment, causing him to swallow hard. "Fred Garvey, is it?"

"Yes, your honor."

"How long have you been with the New Orleans Police Department?"

"Twelve years."

"Twelve years on the police force and you don't know how to make an arrest? Haven't you heard of the United States Constitution? The Bill of Rights?"

"Yes, your honor."

"So, you know that since you violated the rights of the accused, he's going to walk out of this court today, no matter what he's done?"

"Yes, sir."

"Get out of my court, Garvey. You're a disgrace to the city. I'm going to recommend that you be fired."

Garvey opened his mouth to speak and Judge Seaburg slammed his gavel down with a thunderous boom that made Garvey cringe, leaned forward, his eyes glowering, and spoke through his teeth, "Not one word or I'll hold you in contempt."

As Garvey left the court, some of the prisoners started to clap and hoot. Seaburg looked at them. "I don't know what you're clapping about. An officer like that is the criminal's best friend." He turned to Jim Davis, who was standing at the bench with a smug grin on his face. "You get out of here, too."

65

Davis left the courtroom smirking, with Hekler fuming at his side because he didn't get credit for demanding his client's release. The moment they stepped into the marble hallway Detective Clyde Betson stepped up, flanked by two burly Texas Rangers. Betson was a short graying man with a big belly, dressed in a beige suit with a black string tie, a white Stetson and tooled leather boots. "Jim Davis? You are under arrest for the murders of Scarlett Long, William Long, and Catherine Long." JD's smirk faded to deadpan as Betson began to read him his rights off a laminated card while the rangers spun him around and zip cuffed him.

Hekler's jaw dropped and he looked at his client, who shrugged his shoulders. "Don't say anything," Hekler said. He turned to Betson. "You from Texas?"

"Dallas, Texas. Here's the warrant. And here's the extradition order, but we don't need it. He's been released." Betson held out the papers for Hekler to see, but he would not let the lawyer touch them. "If you want to talk to your client you'll need to come to Dallas. We've been looking for this man for over four decades. And now we've got him and we've got a flight to catch." Betson turned to the Rangers and said, "Come on, boys." They each grabbed Davis by an arm and followed Betson down the hall to the elevators.

Hekler walked beside the group, speaking to Davis. "Look, I don't do pro bono for out of state cases. Call me when you get there. Don't talk to anybody but me."

"How much?" Davis asked.

"Hundred K to start. In a capital case that's nothing."

"I'll think about it."

Tyler had followed them out of the courtroom and was filming the arrest with his phone. Camille had given him the heads-up that morning. He knew she was holding something back. He did not believe her that the videos were fakes, and she told him he could not print Sylvie Compton's name. He could write that the money went to an anonymous trust to benefit kids. She told him Davis had used Amanda Butler to get to Bernice, that he'd forced her to comply by holding her son hostage and torturing the child, and that he bungled the staged crime scene so that they knew a third party committed the murders. She gave Tyler most of the details, including a copy of the CD Bernice had made for police. Tyler wanted to know more about the trust fund, but Andy said that if he printed a story about Sylvie Compton she'd be swamped with requests for help, so she needed to remain anonymous.

Even with limited information it was a good story. Tyler was eager to take it and run, at least figuratively—if he tried to actually run, he'd trip over his shoelaces, which were coming untied. And his pants might come all the way down, and from the look of it he wasn't wearing underwear. Before she left him that morning, Camille told him he would look more ghetto with boxers. But he didn't have time to change. He was headed to Jim Davis's apartment over on Chestnut next. They'd got the warrant an hour ago, and it was being taken apart by CSI. Mace and Charley were there, along with BAU agents Carter, Cardenas and Potts. Agents Rodriguez and Borg were going to the press conference, which would be held at NOPD headquarters on Broad. No other reporters knew about the Chestnut Street crime scene yet. They could have the canned press release; he had the exclusive where the action was going down.

66

They found shoe covers, a hair cover, and latex gloves in the kitchen trash. The arrogant shit hadn't even bothered to dispose of this evidence in a second location. They would send these to the lab for analysis, but the most damning evidence was in a lock box on a low shelf in the bedroom closet. The box contained a freezer bag with snapshots of Adrian Butler, hogtied in the same way Camille had found his body. His golden-brown eyes were swollen from crying, his face wet and streaked with tears. One picture showed him screaming. Other pictures were close ups of the burns on his legs and feet.

Mace went to the front room, stood at the picture window and looked down on the old-fashioned neighborhood. The slob reporter was on the sidewalk in front talking to neighbors who had gathered at the crime scene. God, he wished he could scrub his mind. It was hard to think. He had never had to confront such evil. Camille could not come here today after viewing the videos last night. She'd said she had paperwork and other cases to get back to, but asked him to call her if they found proof linking Davis to his mother's death. He thought about a likely scenario. Jim tortured the boy, recorded the torture with Polaroids, then gave the pictures to Adrian's mother Amanda and forced her to go show

them to his mother. He hadn't counted on the pictures killing Bernice; he had wanted to extort money from her in
exchange for the boy's release. It was a crazy, desperate
scheme, and if Bernice had capitulated and given in to his
demands, he would have had to kill everybody anyway in
order to get away. But how could he be sure Amanda would
not go to the police instead of going to Bernice's room at the
motel? He must have used some kind of surveillance gadget
to track her actions when she left for the motel. Mace had
noticed the phone was missing from the evidence on the
table at last night's meeting with BAU. He went back to the
bedroom and asked Burell if he had a minute. Burell gave
a nod and followed him to the front room. "Where's the
phone?" Mace asked.

"Which one?"

"The one Garvey turned in."

"In my car."

Mace relaxed a little. Central Evidence and Property
was like a black hole that sucked in matter and it was gone
forever. Let a perp find out they put damning evidence in
CEP and all it would take would be a little grease to make it
vanish.

Burell lifted a finger to his lips to signal silence. He took
out a pad of paper, wrote that he had not gone through the
phone yet.

Mace took the paper, wrote that he was telling Hebert to
get a warrant for the phone. Would he hold it until she got
there?

Burell gave a curt nod, ripped the paper off the pad and
pocketed it, glancing around first to make sure they weren't
being watched.

Burell walked back to the bedroom while Mace texted Camille. She was working out of the Detective Bureau in Harvey. She had begged off that morning with the excuse that she needed to catch up on paperwork, but they had a deal that he would call her if they found anything relevant to her case. Mace advised her to get a warrant for the phone. It might contain a surveillance video of Amanda going to the motel, and what had happened in Bernice Davis's room. He advised her to look at the motel video again to see if Amanda was wearing some kind of body cam.

Camille texted she'd call when she had the warrant.

With the pictures and probable trace evidence from the body coverings Davis wore for forensic countermeasures, they had enough to charge him with the Butler murders, and possibly with his mother's death if they could recover video from the phone. But it had been decided to let Texas have him first—capital cases were expensive. Texas was eager to foot the bill, but in the unlikely outcome of a Texas jury acquitting him or giving him a lesser punishment than the needle, he could come back here to face trial. Hopefully a capital conviction would get him talking about the rest.

Cardenas came into the front room and told Mace that Cho called and said somebody plugged a USB into the computer at 4:38 pm Saturday. Since this was after CHS 1 had surrendered the computer to the priest, it remained to establish who had done this, and why they did it. They needed to confirm the timeline when Garvey had the computer in his possession before he turned it in on Broad. They could watch the surveillance feed of the Eighth District lobby, but Cardenas wanted to talk to the priest in person. She was headed out to the Ninth Ward and asked Mace to ride with. A picture of

Garvey came to mind. He looked like Mr. Clean with his blonde hair, regular features and muscle man build. He was smug, used to getting away with everything; making a copy of the murder films for personal use would be just like him. They'd need a warrant to search his apartment and truck, but that would be easy with the trouble he was already in.

Mace was relieved to get away from this crime scene. It was almost too much for him. He had never before dealt with a killer who tortured preschool kids. He had never had to see films and pictures of torture. The crime scenes he had dealt with during his career were bad, but this was overwhelming and going to talk to a priest sounded good right then.

67

Cardenas insisted that they surprise Fr. Greg with the visit. She wanted to gauge his reaction when she told him about the USB. The church was on Saint Claude, between Mazant and France, a few blocks from the industrial canal. The neighborhood was poor and most of the buildings were old and had not been maintained. There weren't many people out—a few people hanging at a corner grocery, some people who couldn't afford AC wilting on their porches in the late afternoon heat. This was the strangest church Mace, who was Catholic, had ever seen, but he liked the concept. The building had been a family-owned restaurant in the days before Katrina, old clapboard and brick, the kind of business with a screened porch on the top floor where the owners lived. The glass door was so clean you wouldn't know it was there if not for the steel handle which dissected it on the inside. There were signs taped on the big picture windows like the kind advertising plate specials, only these advertised church events—bingo, bible study, a monthly pot luck dinner and youth dance, homeless sleepover and a meal on Thursdays. The door was unlocked but there was nobody downstairs. Inside it was ten degrees hotter, with ceiling fans pushing the heavy air around but doing nothing to dispel the muggy heat. The old tile floor was shiny with wax, there were metal folding chairs leaning up along one wall and long folding tables leaning against another, and an old wooden podium was pushed into a corner. A counter with round vinyl and steel stools ran along the left side of the room and behind it was a grill, sinks, coffeemakers and swinging galley doors with porthole windows leading to the kitchen. In the right-hand corner, an open doorway with stairs beyond had a sign posted next to it which read Office Upstairs.

At the top of the narrow stairway there was a short hall with two doors, the right door said Office. Cardenas rang the buzzer and after a moment they heard footsteps, the door on the left opened and Fr. Greg Lee stood there, dressed in khaki pants and an old blue golf shirt. "Detective Delaroux, good to see you," he said. "Come in, please." He stood aside and they entered his living room, which was blessedly cool, with a window AC humming and dripping water into a foil pan on the hardwood floor. "I'm Greg Lee." He held out his hand to Cardenas.

"Sabra Cardenas" she said, taking his hand. "I'm with the BAU."

"Yes. I thought you'd be law enforcement. Would you like something to drink? I was just having a Barq's, but I have beer and water if you don't care for root beer."

"Thanks, water sounds good."

Fr. Greg turned to Mace. "What can I get you?"

"I'll have a Barq's, thanks."

"Please sit down, I'll be right back." As the priest left the room Cardenas looked around—despite the worn furnishings the room had a pleasant, restful ambience. She sat in a cushioned rocking chair and Mace sat on the sofa.

"You can see why I don't think he's the one who copied

the videos," Mace whispered. "He told me he didn't even open the computer. He just boxed up the evidence and brought it to the station."

"Okay, but some people can fool you. Bundy was so good at compartmentalizing that people who knew him wouldn't believe he'd killed anybody, even years after he was caught."

"Yeah, but when you got two possibilities and one of them's a dirty cop and the other's a priest who runs an operation like this, I'm gonna check out the cop first." They heard Fr. Greg's footsteps approaching. "Anyway, Garvey's history; he was told to resign earlier today," Mace said.

Fr. Greg was carrying two glass mugs beaded with moisture. He handed out the drinks, then sat down in an easy chair where his own mug of root beer waited on a side table. "How's the investigation coming along?" he asked.

Cardenas gave him the update on Davis's release from custody and arrest by Dallas authorities. She told him about the evidence they found at the Garden District apartment. "We've got enough to tie him to the Butler murders and get a conviction."

"That's good to hear," Fr. Greg said. "What can I help you with today?"

"We need to know what exactly happened when you turned in the box of evidence on Royal," Cardenas said. "What time you turned it in, who else was there, what Garvey said to you."

"A parishioner had called me that morning and asked for help with her grandson. This was my priority that day, to make sure that young man was okay. I didn't have time to take the box in until later, around two. As far as I could tell Officer Garvey was the only person there, and he wasn't very friendly. I don't think he has much use for clergy. He didn't like the fact that I couldn't tell him who gave me the stuff. I gave him the box and got out fast. The way he acted I had the impression that he wanted to hold me for questioning."

"Our computer forensics expert is going over the computer. She told us somebody plugged in a USB flash drive yesterday. We think whoever did that copied the films on it." Cardenas watched the priest. His face showed surprise and concern, but there was nothing to lead her to think he was hiding something.

"What time did this happen?" Fr. Lee asked.

"About 4:30 that afternoon."

"Did the police make a copy?"

Mace spoke up. He told the priest what Garvey did wrong and how the suspect was released at the arraignment. He said they were looking for probable cause to search Garvey's house and car for the USB. He said that copying files from a computer that doesn't belong to you is illegal, and if he copied the videos there's something wrong with him, because no sane person would want to view such horrible images, much less own copies of them. "How is the grandson doing? Do you think he'll be able to talk to us about this?"

"I don't know. He was a good kid before his mother got killed. You can understand why her death might have him a little confused, can't you? She was playing by the rules, and she taught him to play by the rules. His career goal was to be a police officer. How many people do you get who agree to testify against gang members?" Fr. Greg took their silence as his answer. "It will help him a lot if you investigate his mother's death. Is somebody looking into that?"

"We made a report, but it's up to the DOJ to follow

through," Cardenas answered. "It will help if he can go in to the Office of the Consent Decree Monitor and file a complaint. They'll want to know details so he will have to be prepared to talk about it. Is he going to do that?"

"I don't know. Maybe. He's still shaky after seeing whatever was on that computer. He's sorting things out right now, but I don't think he'll be a problem in the future. If anything, I think seeing those images helped him. Kind of like that old movie they made into a TV show, Scared Straight. It will help if there's some kind of justice for his mother, especially if the police who sold her out are held accountable."

Cardenas spoke. "We want to find out what happened too. There've been problems with NOPD over the years. We suspect some officers operate like a criminal gang, only worse because they hide behind their badges. It won't be the first time we've caught NOPD officers involved in this activity. We've been trying to weed out the bad cops, but we need citizens who are willing to file complaints. And that's hard for people to do because they don't trust us. They're afraid of retaliation, and with good reason. Aside from putting them into witness protection there isn't much we can do. Body cams won't help with some of it. We're not just dealing with police violating people's rights, we're talking about organized crime and many of the deals go down when the officers involved are off duty."

"Garvey's been an ongoing problem," Mace added. "He was told to resign today, and now if he copied the files, he'll face criminal charges. Maybe we can get him to talk about other cops in exchange for leniency. But if he copied the videos, he may be sicker than I thought."

"Well, there did seem to be something wrong with him. I

felt a need to get away from him quick. Please let me know if there's anything else I can do."

"You can talk to the young man involved in this about filing a report on what happened the night his mother was killed," Cardenas said.

Mace added, "Tell him that maybe he needs to go back to wanting to be a cop. We need good people on the force. Giving up over what happened to his mother is like letting the bad guys win. I'll help him, if he's serious about it."

"I'm not going to talk him in to doing something that will harm him, but I'll keep your offer in mind," Fr. Greg said. "Is there anything else I can do for you today?"

"No, but we may be back in touch," Cardenas said.

"I would definitely like to stay in touch," Mace said. He took out a card and gave it to the priest. "Give this to your young friend, will you? Tell him to call if he wants to talk."

"Will do."

68

After Mace called, Camille filled out an electronic affidavit for a search warrant on any and all phones Jim Davis owned. It was late afternoon and she felt sapped by the case—it had only been five days, but viewing the videos last night and then getting drunk had used her up. She did not want to see what was on the phone, but she owed it to Bernice Davis and to the Butlers. Especially Amanda Butler, who needed to be cleared of wrongdoing though it was against Camille's personal code to think like this about somebody directly involved in a murder, at least until she had all the evidence. Still people's houses can tell stories, and the house Amanda had lived in with her son had already cleared her in Camille's mind. Camille wanted very much to have evidence that would exonerate Amanda Butler beyond a doubt. She might have Tyler write up a piece about her for the Picayune. She was tired of seeing serial killers get all the media attention, as if they subsumed their victims' lives into their own monstrous beings. Camille wanted Amanda Butler cleared at the same time the story came out in the news. Once most people decide you're guilty there's not much that will change their minds, and for Amanda Butler's rep to be stolen along with her life was not going to happen if she could stop it.

She emailed the electronic affidavit and faxed the hard-copy, then called to expedite things. Shantelle Williams was the go-to judge and it was almost five so if Camille couldn't get her now, she'd have to call her at home. Judge Williams's rule was if you called her at home, it had better be good. Williams did not need convincing. She wasn't given to expressing personal opinions, but made an exception with this one. "You nail that fucker's dick to the floor or I'll want to know why not," she barked. Camille knew her badge would be on the line if she made a mistake that allowed this perp to skate on anything else.

Camille printed the warrant, grabbed her purse and headed out. She needed to go to NOPD headquarters to get the phone. She was hoping by the time she got there they would have any other phones recovered from the apartment on Chestnut. She called Mace, and he told her they didn't find any phones at the apartment. They had the one Davis had on him when he was arrested, and the one that was in the box the priest turned in. What she was looking for would likely be in the one from the box. He told her to meet him at the gay bar down the street from South Broad headquarters. Camille decided that if she found the surveillance footage in the first phone, she did not want to see anything else. She would close her case; let the feds and NOPD deal with the rest. Enough was enough.

69

Sylvie thought about if there was any reason at all that she'd have to go back out tonight and couldn't think of a thing. The day had been a long one. She'd woken early with a sense of dread that she figured was connected with the possibility of Jim Davis walking out of jail after his arraignment. Andy told her he'd been watching her place, and this scared her in a way she had never felt in her life, not even when she had to run away from the last foster home. She feared that he would target Brittney and the kids. She felt better when Andy told her Davis was still in custody and headed for Texas. Still the feeling of dread lingered throughout the afternoon, as she worked her way down a list of priorities with the Peters family. She'd spent time on the computer that morning researching housing and she had checked on AA meetings around town. She picked up Brittney and the kids and they had gone shopping for clothes, a task made easier when she assured the kids that this would not be their last trip, but they needed to look good when they went house hunting. Afterwards, they ate at College Inn in Mid City, and they went to the grocery and got drinks and snacks for the mini-fridge.

Persuading Brittney to check out an AA meeting had not been hard. Sylvie was armed with facts she'd researched online, though it was hard to find them because the ads for pricy rehabs outnumbered medical links by about twenty to one. AA was a not-for-profit organization which had a good success rate for people serious about quitting. It would be a good place to start. Brittney looked like a different person that morning, closer to her age, thirty-one, than a tired and played out forty. She acted different too, smiled more, and didn't seem as guarded. She did not want any more beer, and she seemed willing to do whatever she had to do to be okay. It was the hope of something better, Sylvie felt sure, that made her so eager to face life without being sedated.

Sylvie offered to go with her to the meeting that night, held in an uptown church, but Brittney said she would be fine on her own. By the end of the afternoon Sylvie was relieved to go home and rest. She had given Trey a much-needed day off, and he agreed to watch the kids that night while Brittney went to the meeting, then drive the family out for a treat after.

Sylvie decided that, since she had no more plans to go out, it was pajama time. She changed into boxers and a big t-shirt, grabbed her smokes and bottled water and went out the window onto the roof. The heat and humidity were like breathing through a damp veil, but this was a small inconvenience compared to the loveliness of the evening viewed from her perch four stories above a street on which history lingered like a palpable presence. The sun was setting, the charcoal clouds awash with orange, pink and gold. She could hear the faint sound of a Dixieland band playing across the square, and the loud, lonely voice of the street singer below—"Sometimes I'm up, sometimes I'm down, coming for to carry me home, but still my soul feels heaven bound, coming for to carry me home...Swing low, sweet chariot, coming for to carry me home...

70

Camille looked around the bar where she was meeting Mace. This was the first time she'd been in the place, one of a handful of new businesses on Tulane Avenue. The establishment was a well-done oasis in the bleak landscape surrounding the jail, courthouse, NOPD complex—you could duck inside and escape, have a couple of drinks. A long bar ran the length of the room, with tables against the opposite wall and a red curtained stage in back for shows. Framed photos of burlesque performers hung on the lavender walls, and dim lights cast a pink glow on a couple of guys seated at the far end of the bar, the only customers here on Monday evening. She took a stool midway down and ordered an Abita, no mug, from the barman who'd got up from his stool and placed a napkin in front of her. She saw his eyes go beyond her, turned to see Mace at the door, saw the relief and exhaustion in Mace's eyes as they found hers. The look on his face when he walked in the door let her know she had done good to stay in Harvey catching up on paperwork. The man took Mace's order, an Abita with a shot of Johnny Walker Black.

When the guy left to get the beer, Mace told her Burell would be by soon with the phone. He was up the street doing paperwork after spending the afternoon at Davis's apartment with CSI and the feds. Camille could tell Mace was played out, that he'd seen enough for one day. He agreed to stay with her while she went through the phone. She had called Tyler and told him to standby for another story. Once she cleared Amanda Butler of wrongdoing, she wanted him to do a profile of her life, focusing on her dedication as a mother and achievements as a student and how profound a loss her death was to the community. Amanda's death had struck a deep chord in Camille.

They met Burell on the street in front of the bar. Camille gave him a copy of the warrant and he gave her the iPhone, then she and Mace went to her car to go through it. The surveillance video was hidden in a file labeled B.

As the video started it showed the interior of a Honda Civic, likely Jim Davis's. It was obvious that she was driving, the film showed the steering wheel and part of the window as she drove across town from her house in Mid-City to the Motel on Airline Drive. She parked in back by Bernice's room. Amanda took the body cam off before she exited the car. She clipped it back onto the front of her shirt after she entered the motel room. The film showed the bathroom door getting closer, then a knock; the door opened and Bernice was standing in the bathtub her eyes glaring, holding the shower curtain in front to shield her naked body.

"Amanda, what on earth are you doing in my room?"

"Your son made me come here. He has my little boy. He's hurting him. He told me to show you these."

As Amanda spoke, Bernice's eyes focused on something Amanda was doing. The camera showed Amanda's arm stretch out toward Bernice, her hand shaking violently as she held out what looked like a bunch of photo prints. Bernice's expression went from anger to wide open horror. She gasped as if she couldn't get air, swayed, staggered then fell back into the tub, taking the curtains with her.

After a moment Amanda spoke, her voice panicky. "Please don't hurt him, I'll look." The camera showed her bending down to check Bernice's vitals. "No pulse," she whispered. Now Amanda began to sob but kept moving, following directions, presumably from whoever was monitoring the live feed. She exited into the main room, approached the laptop and unplugged the cord. "I don't see any gun." After a pause she went to the bedside table and opened a drawer. There was an old .38 revolver, nothing else. It was the same gun that was found at Amanda's and Adrian's death scene. She took the gun out, then whispered, "Wait, there's somebody knocking." She went back in the bathroom and closed the door, waited until the knocking stopped. After a couple of minutes, she spoke to the invisible presence again. "What if there's traffic?" A short pause. "Okay okay, twenty minutes." She found a plastic trash bag in the kitchenette and put Bernice's gun and her laptop in it, took the chain off the front door and exited the glass door at the back, locking it on the way out. Then she went out to the back lot, got into a gray Civic and left. She did not turn the camera off until she pulled into a parking lot in a Mid City church around the corner from her house, seventeen minutes later.

Camille was relieved to have confirmation of Amanda's innocence, but she was also sad. As she went through the phone she found a Security Surveillance app, and told Mace he might want to check it out, but she was finished.

71

The meeting was held in the hall of a big church on Jackson Avenue, not far from the apartment on Chestnut and Second. It was closed; only alcoholics were welcome. Brittney helped herself to a cup of coffee and took a seat in back on one of the folding chairs that filled the big room in rows. She wished she could be invisible because she was scared—this was her first AA meeting. Finally, a man stepped up to the podium and spoke into the mike. "Welcome to the Keep It Simple Monday night meeting of Alcoholics Anonymous. My name is Ben and I'm an alcoholic."

The people answered in unison, "Hi Ben!" The sound made Brittney jump in her skin and she wanted to bolt. She thought about her kids, and kept her seat. She tried to calm her fear by tuning out the readings, decided maybe she should have taken Sylvie up on her offer to come with. But it was too late now. Her attention shifted and she began watching the other people, some of whom she could see weren't paying any more attention than she was. A few people were busy with their phones and two women were whispering and giggling a few rows up, a shaggy man who looked like he might live under the bridge was standing at the refreshment table, eating cookies one after another. Brittney related to these people; it was the majority of the people in the room who looked like they were fine with being there that scared her. She decided she'd rather be in the club, an environment she understood, where it was all about money and sex, in other words, real.

Ben announced they had a speaker and a woman who looked like she could be in films walked up to the podium. Everybody in the room was clapping. The woman was tall and thin, with a long dark braid which hung down her back, sparkling dark eyes, and beautiful features. She wore a simple white cotton dress. She introduced herself as Crystal, an alcoholic. She spoke about being raised in homes in Shreveport; not ever knowing who her parents were; running away at fifteen; working truck stops across the South; giving blowjobs for a bottle of cheap vodka or a couple of rocks; going in-and-out of jail; and doing a three-year stint in San Gabriel.

Brittney got up to go to the bathroom. The coffee she drank had gone straight through her. When she stepped into the hallway, she saw a tall, muscular man, leaning against the wall opposite the door. He wore black jeans and a tight-fitting black T-shirt with a dark green baseball cap tilted low on his face so the brim hid his features. He looked up and she saw it was the cop who made her give him blowjobs in his squad car. Though it was past dark he was wearing aviator sunglasses. He flashed a wolfish grin and Brittney knew instinctively that he was after more than a blowjob this time. As she opened her mouth to scream, he stepped forward quick, then he was beside her and he'd clamped a hand over her mouth and was whispering in her ear, "No noise or I'll do your kids. Come on babe, you'll like it this time." His breath stank horribly and she averted her face, overwhelmed with nausea and fear. He grabbed her arm above the elbow in a bruising grip and began steering her down the hallway towards the street door in long strides so that she had to move fast to keep pace. When they reached the door, she looked back and saw a woman emerge from the meeting. The woman opened her mouth to speak and Britt nodded her head no, just a slight signal and then she turned and allowed him to take her through the door out into the night.

He drove a black big wheel truck with tinted windows. She started to cry, the tears coming fast as he told her to climb up, still holding her arm in a tight grip that felt like having a vice clamped down on it. He took a set of steel cuffs out of the glove box and snapped one on her left wrist tightening it so it hurt, then belted her in and fastened the other one to the shoulder strap. When she sobbed out loud, he laughed, slammed the door and went around to the other side, looking up and down the street to see if anybody was watching, but there was nobody. She hated that he could see her fear. After he shut the door, she wiped her cheeks with her free hand.

He climbed into the driver's seat and asked, "What happened to you?" The deep rumble of the truck starting made Brittney feel like she was inside the belly of a monster. She didn't answer so he continued with, "I thought we had a date the other night." He glanced sideways and gave her a twisted grin. She remained silent so he continued, "I've been watching you and that other whore lives in the Quarter. We're going to pay her a visit. I need you to help me get in then I'll let you go, if you're good. By the way, those daughters of yours are sexy. You better do what I say tonight, you understand?" When Brittney didn't say anything, he slammed on the brakes and said, "I asked you a question, cunt. Do you understand?"

She nodded.

His hand shot out a slapped her hard, fast as a rattlesnake strike. She'd been hit before, but never with such force. "Answer me cunt."

"I understand" she said, her voice cracking into a plea that made her hate herself. Her main hope was to keep him away from her kids. Whatever he wanted to do, she prayed it would be over fast for both her and Sylvie.

72

Lionel was about to go get another pint when he saw the bad cop turn onto Saint Peter from Chartres with that stripper who'd been with Trey and Sylvie at the restaurant. He was dressed in black like the night before and he had a fanny pack slung over one shoulder. She looked different tonight, sober and dressed like a soccer mom in shorts and a cotton tank. Still, her eyes were red and swollen like she'd been crying, and he could see by her stony expression that this was not a walk she was taking willingly. He held her hand in a grip that looked too tight to be friendly. Lionel started singing as if there was nothing wrong. He watched them walk up to the gate of the building where Sylvie and Trey stayed, saw the cop glance around quick as he took out a card, then he picked the lock of the gate, all the while holding Brittney with his other hand. They entered the gate and he slammed it closed after them. Lionel watched them go in and speed dialed Trey as he crossed the street. This was the first time he'd had to call, and Trey answered fast.

"What's happening?"

"Something ain't right." Lionel was holding the phone with one hand and using his ID to pick the lock with the other. "There's this bad cop, the guy's a psycho. He just went in the gate to your place with that stripper you and Sylvie been hanging out with." Lionel entered the gate, and as he walked through the brick passage that led to the stairs, he heard the door at the top close. "They went in Sylvie's place just now. The cop didn't ring the buzzer on the gate, he picked the lock."

"Can you go up? I'm on my way but I'm uptown with the kids. It'll take me a minute to get there." As Trey spoke, Lionel could hear a horn honking and somebody started yelling in the background. He heard Trey yell "What the...!" It sounded like he'd dropped the phone, and the girls screamed. After a moment, Trey picked up the phone and said, "I'll be there as soon as I can but right now it's on you." Then the phone went dead.

Lionel pocketed the phone. He felt overwhelmed by fear, by wanting to turn around and go, and keep on going. He was already back out the gate and headed to Rouse's. He went in the grocery which was thankfully almost empty, and bought a roll of duct tape. He needed a way onto the roof.

73

Trey was headed up Magazine with the kids while he was talking to Lionel, and they were almost to Jackson Avenue when the Caravan started wobbling and listing to the driver's side in front, like it was lame. The wobbling was becoming more violent as they rolled to the side. He made it to the Shell station on the corner and, as he began to turn in, the front left side of the Caravan dropped, like the wheel fell off. That's what the honking was—the driver behind him was trying to warn him.

The girls screamed and Kevin turned around in the seat to calm them while Trey got out to look at the damage. The front left end of the Caravan was down on the concrete, and the vehicle was half-in the drive, the wheel lying on its side a few feet up on Magazine.

The AA meeting was only a couple blocks up Jackson but he didn't need to go there anymore; he needed to get back to Sylvie's place, fast.

74

Sylvie was cozied up in bed reading "Out of the Easy," a crime novel set in a mid-century French Quarter whorehouse, when somebody knocked. The vague dread she'd felt all day kicked in. She found her robe, grabbed her pepper spray, held it on ready as she crossed to the door and spoke loud, "Who is it?"

"It's me. Brittney."

Sylvie dropped the pepper spray into her pocket, unlocked the deadbolt and opened the door. A tall blonde man with features so regular he looked like a plastic doll stood behind Brittney, glaring at Sylvie with sick, evil eyes over the top of her head. He was holding Britt's left arm in a tight grip with one leather-gloved hand, and the other gloved hand held a gun to her temple. He kicked the door open wider and shoved her into the room. Just then Sylvie's cell rang. "Answer that and I'll shoot you both," the man said, grinning, his voice coming out in a whisper of breath that smelt like something had crawled into his mouth and died there a long time ago.

"Shut the door and lock it," he commanded. Sylvie turned her head to the side as he spoke, trying to avoid the foul odor, which lingered in the air around him like a miasma of decay. After she shut and locked the door, he gestured with the gun for her to walk into the bedroom. He followed behind, then told her to stop when she was in front of the wall closet where her clothes hung. "Move the clothes to the side of the rack," he said.

He was wearing a fanny pack on his shoulder. He shrugged the pack down onto his arm, still holding the gun on Brittney, and told Sylvie to reach in and get the handcuffs out. When she hesitated, he smacked Brittney in the head with the gun so hard that her body sagged toward the ground. "Now, bitch."

Sylvie reached into the pack for the handcuffs, and she felt the smooth hard shape of a big roll of duct tape. She heard him cock the gun so she pulled the cuffs out fast. He grabbed the cuffs, slammed the gun into her head and knocked her down. "Kneel, hands on your head."

As she knelt and placed her hands on her head, she felt blood trickling down the side of her face from where he'd hit her.

He pulled Brittney over to the closet, told her to grab the rack with both hands, then cuffed her to it. He moved fast, keeping control of both women with the gun while he used one hand to cuff Brittney. He riffled through the hanging clothes and pulled down a filmy scarf, ripping it off the hanger and bunching it up in one swift movement. "Open your mouth," he said, looking at Brittney with crazed eyes that were devoid of mercy. He stuffed the rag in her mouth, then threw the roll of duct tape at Sylvie so it bounced off her head. "Tape her mouth," he ordered.

As Sylvie got up and obeyed him, he reached around from behind and grabbed her by the breast hard, pressing into her and whispering into her ear in a cloud of funk. "Now we're gonna party, me and you." When she finished winding the tape around Brittney's mouth and the back of her head, he pulled a knife out of his pocket and sliced the tape. Then he grabbed the tape, told Sylvie to drop her drawers, take her panties off, and put them in her mouth.

Sylvie began moving slow, aware that Trey would be on his way by now, and praying that he got here soon. She willed herself to stay calm and think. She noticed that Lionel had stopped singing a while ago, hoped that he'd seen something and decided to come investigate. After she balled up her panties and stuck them into her mouth, he wound the tape around her head to secure the gag in her mouth the same way she'd taped Brittney, only tighter. He grabbed her by the shoulder, jerked her around, and then he taped her wrists behind her back. Then he grabbed her by the hair and slung her onto the bed, holding the gun on her as he began to unbuckle his pants.

75

Lionel went back in the gate of Sylvie's building, went out to the courtyard, and looked around at the tall brick buildings that surrounded it. Two sides had galleries on the upper floors, the one where Sylvie and Trey stayed didn't, and the other wall was the building that faced the alley in back of the Cabildo. He crossed over to the slave quarters, went up three flights of stairs, and out onto the top gallery. He looked across the courtyard to Sylvie and Trey's side and saw two windows close together, right below the roof. That's Sylvie's place, he thought. There's the way in, but first I got to get over there. If he stood on the rail, he might be able to hoist himself up onto the roof. But he would need a handhold. He decided to play it safe and stick to what he knew. He looked in a window of one of the old slave quarters, and saw the space was filled with boxes and shapes covered in grimy tarps. He taped the glass, took the gun out of his pocket and tapped it, unlocked the window but it was painted shut so he pulled out the broken glass, taped around the windowsill to protect his body and crawled in.

The room was small and dusty. It hadn't been used for anything but storage in years. It was filled with bulky shapes under grimed tarps, and dust motes danced in the light coming in from the galley. Lionel tied his kerchief over his face to keep from breathing in dust then sneezing when he had to stay quiet. There was a high window in the back wall. He went through the small two-room space and found a couple of old crates. He stacked them and climbed up. The window was painted shut. He taped the glass, broke it, taped the edges then hoisted himself up. He turned his body around so he was sitting on the windowsill with his legs hanging into the room and the rooftop at eye level. Slowly, he wiggled his body out and up onto the roof. He lay there for a moment; he was out of breath and his muscles were aching. A picture came to his mind of the evil cop alone with the two women, and he got up.

He climbed up the steep incline to the ridge and hunkered low so nobody looking out a window could spot him. The buildings surrounding the courtyard were connected, and he made his way around as fast as he could with only moonlight and the lights from below to see by. When he got to Sylvie's area and saw the skylight, he crept down the steep incline and looked in. What he saw froze him.

The skylight was directly over Sylvie's bed. She was lying on the mattress with her shirt pulled up around her neck and the cop was straddling her, naked except for black leather gloves. There was a gag stuffed into her mouth and secured with duct tape, which was wound around her head tight. Her eyes were squeezed shut, and tears ran down her swollen face, making tracks in the blood smeared across one of her cheeks. It looked like he'd tied her hands behind her back, probably with the tape. The cop had a gun lying on the floor next to the mattress—a 9mm Beretta. Lionel could not see the other woman from the skylight view, and he hoped she was still alive.

As Lionel watched, the cop lit a cigarette and held it against her cheek. Just then Sylvie opened her eyes and looked straight up at Lionel, her pained eyes pleading for help. He put a finger over his lips, signaling silence. The cop lowered the cigarette to her left breast. As he ground it out on her breast, her eyes squeezed shut in pain and shock; she was thrashing around underneath him. Then, he lowered himself until he was prone on top of her, and he began trying to force her legs apart with a knee. Lionel took out his gun and rapped loud on the skylight, trying to distract the cop before he could force himself inside Sylvie. Then he took out his phone and called Burell.

76

Monday nights were slow at Jimmy's Corner, which was great as far as Camille was concerned. She was relieved to have closed the book on the worst case she'd ever worked. Mace came out of the john, and took a seat across from her at the table.

"You like red beans and rice?"

"If they're cooked right, I love them."

"Trust me, these are the best. And they only have 'em on Mondays. I'll go order us some." He got up, went to the bar to place their order, then Camille saw him answer his cell, and she felt a pang of apprehension. He turned to look at her, put his hand over the speaker and said "I'll be right back." By the look on his face, she knew it wasn't good. He walked out the front door and she took a long pull from her Bud, then found her smokes in her purse and lit up.

Mace came tearing back in the door, crossing the bar in a half run that made the old timers turn on their stools and stare. "Come on, we gotta go. I'll explain in the car." He reached for her hand like he wanted to drag her out of the barroom double time. She managed to grab her beer and her purse as he grasped her arm, pulled her up and out of her seat, and headed for the door.

As soon as they were out on the street he started talking. "We gotta be in the Quarter, like now."

"What happened?"

"Sylvie Compton."

"She isn't dead, is she?"

Mace let go of her, unlocked the car, and got in. "She might be by the time we get there. It's fucking Garvey. He's up in her apartment; got her and another woman hostage. Lionel called Burell and said he's hurting her. Burell didn't know the details. He's on his way, too." He had the car started by the time she got in, and soon they were racing down Banks Street towards downtown.

77

As Garvey tried to get her legs apart, Sylvie's pain and fear evaporated, replaced by pure outrage and a fury so terrible she felt she could kill him, even with her hands tied behind her back. In her mind, this evil monster was one with the creature who took her mother. Just as he lowered himself so his smirking, lust filled face was right above hers, a loud rapping noise came from overhead. Seizing the distraction and momentary confusion on his face, she head butted him; there was an audible crack and blood gushed from his nose which was now sideways. He grabbed his face and shrank away from her and she brought her right knee up hard, getting him in between the legs. He howled like a demon, doubled up in pain, and she scooted her legs out from underneath him as he was hunched over by the foot of the bed holding his genitals. She kicked him in the head, and then kicked him again in the chest so that he went backwards onto the floor.

There was a loud crash behind the sheet Sylvie had nailed up over the window. Lionel reached in, ripped the sheet off the window and used it to shield his hand as he punched the broken glass out of the way. Sylvie rolled off the side of the bed to escape the broken shards, while Garvey looked up surprised from the floor at the foot of the bed, just as Lionel aimed his gun at him and pulled the trigger. Garvey's face changed from horror to relief as the gun clicked. Lionel looked down at the malfunctioning gun, decided to pistol whip Garvey, and crawled in the window.

Sylvie realized she'd rolled onto the floor on top of Garvey's gun. His blood covered her face and eyes so she was half blind. She quickly wiped her face on the side of the bed, groped for the gun, until she was holding it in her right hand with her finger on the trigger. By this time, Lionel had reached Garvey and they were struggling at the foot of the bed. Garvey got the gun away from Lionel, bashed him repeatedly with it and, as Lionel crumpled to the floor, Garvey kicked him a couple of times and threw the gun out into the front room. Then he turned towards the side of the bed where he'd left his gun. As he started to bend down over her, Sylvie twisted to the side and brought the gun around fast, ignoring the pain as the muscles in her left shoulder tore. By the time he saw what she was doing it was too late. The first shot hit him in the stomach. His face froze into a look of stunned surprise, blood burbled out from the hole in his gut and she depressed the trigger again, hitting him in the side just below the ribs. His body jerked spasmodically, and blood gushed from his mouth. As he pitched forward, she rolled to the right to get out of the way. He landed on his stomach and lay there, convulsing, his bloody face turned towards her, eyes wide open and shocked, mouth working like a fish on the deck of a boat. She scooted away from him, struggled to her feet, and stood over him shaking. Then she twisted her body to the left and brought her hands back around the right side of her torso, steadied the gun against her hip and took slow aim, and sent him to hell with a head shot.

Epilogue

New Orleans, September 2017

Maybe meeting at Café Du Monde for a late brunch wasn't such a good idea in September, Camille thought. The temperature was already above eighty and humidity had stayed near 100% for weeks. Andy looked like she was wilting in the heat as she trudged through Jackson Square, past the few sidewalk artists and tarot readers who were already set up, and a scattered mix of locals and tourists. She'd walked in from her law office, a few blocks away on St. Charles Avenue. Camille picked a corner table outside, under the striped awning of the famous café, which wasn't too crowded at eleven Tuesday morning in the off-season. Andy walked past the line of horse-drawn buggies parked at the curb and crossed Decatur. Camille stood up, and waved her over as she approached the café.

Andy removed her wide-brimmed straw hat as she sat, fanning herself with it briefly before setting it next to her on a vinyl and chrome chair. "Great idea to meet here. I haven't had coffee and beignets for ages," Andy said.

"That's kind of you to say, but you look like maybe you could have done without the walk in the heat."

"No, I really need to exercise more. Gyms bore me and I

don't have much time. Hopefully, I just sweated off some of the weight I've been gaining lately."

"You don't look any heavier than the last time we saw each other."

"I'm in a loose sundress. But I didn't come here to discuss my health issues. How've you been?"

"Okay I guess. Truthfully, I'm still having nightmares from the case involving your client, Sylvie Compton. Watching those films Jim Davis had on his computer and all. And then to find out an NOPD officer was operating as a serial-predator here in the Quarter. I mean, we all know there's some bad apples in the NOPD. But that doesn't make learning the details any easier to stomach. I guess I just want to know they're all okay. I mean Sylvie, Brittney, and the kids. I figured you'd be able to tell me how they're doing."

Just then a waitress arrived with a tray, set down two glasses of ice water, some napkins and cutlery, and asked what they were having. They both ordered beignets, café au lait and fresh-squeezed orange juice. After she left Andy said, "You know, Jim Davis's mother, Bernice Davis, was the first pro-bono client I ever had. I mainly deal with Trusts and Estates and my clients aren't the most generous group as a whole, though there are a few notable exceptions; they mostly use charitable contributions as tax shelters. Having said all that, this has been the most difficult case I've ever represented, and the scariest."

"Same here," Camille said. "And investigating homicides is my job."

"But considering how things are turning out, representing Bernice and managing the trust for Sylvie has been the most rewarding work I've ever done. Seriously, I'm very happy to be involved."

Camille looked hugely relieved. "So, tell me how they're doing," she said.

"Aside from being traumatized, great! They've rented a big house together near City Park in Bayou St. John. Brittney's been staying sober and the kids are back in school. Brittney's taking classes at Delgado to get her G.E.D. After she gets that out of the way, she'll be enrolling in their nursing program."

"That's wonderful news. Is Sylvie facing any charges for shooting Garvey?"

"Are you kidding?" The NOPD is hoping to avoid being sued. I mean, I got Trey to investigate and he came up with six strippers who are willing to testify that Garvey extorted sex from them regularly. And that's just the tip of the iceberg. I talked to the A.D.A. about it, and they've agreed to not file charges against Sylvie for that last headshot, which was avoidable, and for the unregistered handgun they found in the front room. Sylvie told the cops it was hers, but I strongly suspect it was the street performer Lionel's. She gave Lionel the apartment on St. Peter, rent paid for six months as a thank you for being the hero who helped her survive Garvey."

The waitress came back with a big tray, set them up with their food and drinks and left. While Camille took a bite of her beignet, Andy kept talking.

"The D.A.'s office had Sylvie and Brittney sign an agreement not to file a lawsuit in exchange for immunity from charges, which they were both happy to do—they just want to move on. But the city still has the other women Garvey attacked to worry about. True, there's no evidence but their collective word, but there's six of them so far."

"So far? How many do you think they'll be able to dredge up with a class action?" Camille asked.

"Who knows? Trey stopped when he found enough women to back Brittney's story. And he didn't even talk to the streetwalkers. I'm betting there's been dozens, maybe hundreds over the years."

"It's sickening, but I'll bet you're right. Garvey wasn't operating in a vacuum."

"If they team up and get a good lawyer, now that they know about each other, they could even file a class action against the city and the NOPD. I don't think Garvey's the only dirty cop in the quarter. But aside from being subpoenaed to testify in a lawsuit, I believe Brittney and Sylvie can put this behind them.

"Of course, they're still traumatized. There's a garage apartment included in the property they're renting, and they persuaded Trey to move in up there in exchange for free rent. Having a trained bodyguard on the premises helps them feel more secure and he's teaching them some self-defense techniques."

"I have the same deal with my rental in Metairie," Camille said. "The elderly woman who owns the property rents me the back house for cheap because I'm a cop. Listen, I really appreciate you meeting with me and letting me know how everybody's doing. I hope we can stay in touch. Let me know if there's anything I can do to help out. I mean, this has been a horrific experience for all of us so I just want a good result, right?"

"I totally get that. And thanks for the offer. I will definitely keep it in mind. I hope we can get together once in a while, you know, just say hi, have a couple of drinks or lunch. I have my hands full with my law practice and my kids so I don't have much time and zero women friends to socialize with."

"Yeah, me either. I mean, my job can be depressing and time consuming, especially if there's a really bad case. I've been seeing that detective, Mace Delaroux, but I don't have any women friends."

"Well, I guess I'd better be getting back to work," Andy said. She took her last bite of beignet, downed her juice and took her purse off the chair and opened it to get out some money to pay for the food.

"Please, let me treat," Camille said. "I mean, I invited you here."

"Okay, thanks. But I'll leave the tip, okay?"

"Deal."

Andy put a few bills on the table and stood up, gathering her purse and the hat, which she slapped back onto her head. "I guess that coffee went right through me. I'm going to use their bathroom first."

"Okay, thanks for coming, Andy. We'll stay in touch."

Just then, they both heard a street performer start up singing a cappella in the distance—it sounded like it was coming from the street on the other side of the square.

> *"Swing low, sweet chariot*
> *Coming for to carry me home*
> *Swi-ing low, sweet chariot*
> *Coming for to carry me home.*
>
> *"I looked over Jordan and what did I see*
> *Coming for to carry me home*
> *A band of angels coming after me..."*

Acknowledgments

Nobody writes alone. The people who helped me by reading and offering suggestions, encouragement and, in some cases, professional expertise: Alan Brent; Casey; Rev. Dr. Duane Day; Mary DeGuelle, SFS; Kitty Kashar; Laura Mershon; Deanna Richeson; Veronica Robinson; Layne Saltern; Mick Schott; Win Shields; Celia Sinclair. I owe a special debt of gratitude to my dear friend, Christine Wiltz.